THE
COLTONS
COMANCHE'S CHILD

Welcome to Black Arrow, Oklahoma—
the birthplace of a proud, passionate clan
of men and women who would risk everything
for love, family and honor.

Bram Colton:
This sexy but serious town sheriff has wanted blond beauty Jenna Elliot for years, but will he let his Comanche pride destroy his chance for true love?

Jenna Elliot:
She had loved Bram Colton since she could remember, but he was as prejudiced as her father. She knew she could prove their love was color-blind…if hardheaded Bram would just give her the chance.

Gloria Whitebear:
Will the secret past of the Oklahoma Coltons' matriarch come back to haunt her grandchildren?

Willow Colton:
Bram's younger sister hasn't seemed the same since she returned from vacation. But her secret will soon be hard to hide.…

Dear Reader,

This August, I am delighted to give you six winning reasons to pick up a Silhouette Special Edition book.

For starters, Lindsay McKenna, whose action-packed and emotionally gritty romances have entertained readers for years, moves us with her exciting cross-line series MORGAN'S MERCENARIES: ULTIMATE RESCUE. The first book, *The Heart Beneath,* tells of love against unimaginable odds. With a background as a firefighter in the late 1980s, Lindsay elaborates, "This story is about love, even when buried beneath the rubble of a hotel, or deep within a human being who has been terribly wounded by others, that it will not only survive, but emerge and be victorious."

No stranger to dynamic storytelling, Laurie Paige kicks off a new MONTANA MAVERICKS spin-off with *Her Montana Man,* in which a beautiful forensics examiner must gather evidence in a murder case, but also has to face the town's mayor, a man she'd loved and lost years ago. Don't miss the second book in THE COLTON'S: COMANCHE BLOOD series—Jackie Merritt's *The Coyote's Cry,* a stunning tale of forbidden love between a Native American sheriff and the town's "golden girl."

Christine Rimmer delivers the first romance in her captivating new miniseries THE SONS OF CAITLIN BRAVO. In *His Executive Sweetheart,* a secretary pines for a Bravo bachelor who just happens to be her boss! And in Lucy Gordon's *Princess Dottie,* a waitress-turned-princess is a dashing prince's only chance at keeping his kingdom—and finding true love.... Debut author Karen Sandler warms readers with *The Boss's Baby Bargain,* in which a controlling CEO strikes a marriage bargain with his financially strapped assistant, but their smoldering attraction leads to an unexpected pregnancy!

This month's selections are stellar romances that will put a smile on your face and a song in your heart! Happy reading.

Sincerely,

Karen Taylor Richman
Senior Editor

Please address questions and book requests to:
Silhouette Reader Service
U.S.: 3010 Walden Ave., P.O. Box 1325, Buffalo, NY 14269
Canadian: P.O. Box 609, Fort Erie, Ont. L2A 5X3

Jackie Merritt

THE COYOTE'S CRY

Silhouette®

SPECIAL EDITION™

Published by Silhouette Books

America's Publisher of Contemporary Romance

Special thanks and acknowledgment are given
to Jackie Merritt for her contribution to
THE COLTONS: COMANCHE BLOOD series.

 SILHOUETTE BOOKS

ISBN 0-373-24484-3

THE COYOTE'S CRY

Books by Jackie Merritt

Silhouette Special Edition

A Man and a Million #988
*Montana Passion #1051
*Montana Lovers #1065
Letter to a Lonesome
  Cowboy #1154
†For the Love of Sam #1180
†The Secret Daughter #1218
The Kincaid Bride #1321
The Cattleman and the
  Virgin Heiress #1393
Marked for Marriage #1447
The Coyote's Cry #1484

Silhouette Books

Montana Mavericks

The Widow and the Rodeo Man
The Rancher Takes a Wife

The Fortunes of Texas

A Willing Wife
Hired Bride

World's Most Eligible Bachelors

Big Sky Billionaire

Summer Sizzlers Collection 1994
"Stranded"

Harlequin Historicals

Wyoming Territory

*Made in Montana
†The Benning Legacy
‡Saxon Brothers

Silhouette Desire

Big Sky Country #466
Heartbreak Hotel #551
Babe in the Woods #566
Maggie's Man #587
Ramblin' Man #605
Maverick Heart #622
Sweet on Jessie #642
Mustang Valley #664
The Lady and the
  Lumberjack #683
Boss Lady #705
Shipwrecked! #721
Black Creek Ranch #740
A Man Like Michael #757
Tennessee Waltz #774
Montana Sky #790
Imitation Love #813
‡Wrangler's Lady #841
‡Mystery Lady #849
‡Persistent Lady #854
Nevada Drifter #866
Accidental Bride #914
Hesitant Husband #935
Rebel Love #965
Assignment: Marriage #980
*Montana Fever #1014
*Montana Christmas #1039
Wind River Ranch #1085
†A Montana Man #1159
Tough To Tame #1297
The Bachelor Takes a Wife #1444

JACKIE MERRITT

is still writing, just not with the speed and constancy of years past. She and hubby are living in southern Nevada again, falling back on old habits of loving the long, warm or slightly cool winters and trying almost desperately to head north for the months of July and August, when the fiery sun bakes people and cacti alike.

THE COLTONS: COMANCHE BLOOD

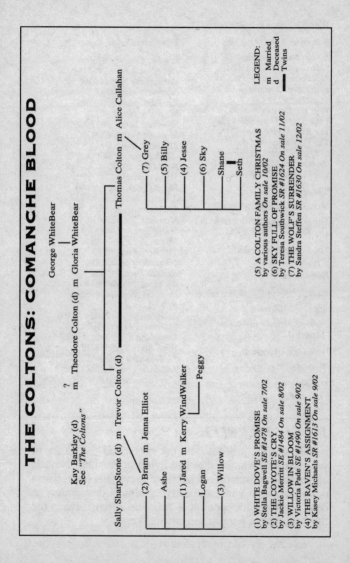

George WhiteBear

?
m Theodore Colton (d) m Gloria WhiteBear

Kay Barkley (d)
See "The Coltons"

Sally SharpStone (d) m Trevor Colton (d)

Thomas Colton m Alice Callahan

(2) Bram m Jenna Elliot

Ashe

(1) Jared m Kerry WindWalker

Logan

Peggy

(3) Willow

(7) Grey

(5) Billy

(4) Jesse

(6) Sky

Shane

Seth

(1) WHITE DOVE'S PROMISE
by Stella Bagwell SE #1478 On sale 7/02

(2) THE COYOTE'S CRY
by Jackie Merritt SE #1484 On sale 8/02

(3) WILLOW IN BLOOM
by Victoria Pade SE #1490 On sale 9/02

(4) THE RAVEN'S ASSIGNMENT
by Kasey Michaels SR #1613 On sale 9/02

(5) A COLTON FAMILY CHRISTMAS
by various authors On sale 10/02

(6) SKY FULL OF PROMISE
by Teresa Southwick SR #1624 On sale 11/02

(7) THE WOLF'S SURRENDER
by Sandra Steffen SR #1630 On sale 12/02

LEGEND:
m Married
d Deceased
— Twins

Prologue

A June article from the *Black Arrow Daily Chronicle:*

Yesterday, Comanche County Sheriff Bram Colton brought the newspaper up-to-date on several ongoing investigations, primarily the courthouse fire and the burglary of the *Chronicle*'s office.

The courthouse fire was unquestionably arson, the sheriff reported, a sad fact confirmed by State Investigator Harold Bolling. Apparently Mr. Bolling provided evidence that proved the fire was started with candles and gasoline. Mr. Bolling has returned to Oklahoma City and has given his permission for the insurance company investigator to examine the damage for his own purposes—namely, to approve or deny the claim filed by the county for funds to restore the historic old courthouse to its former glory. Arson is covered by the insurance policy, according to the county officials in charge of the claim, so they're quite certain of eventual approval and anticipate little delay in getting repairs started. There have been no arrests, however, and Sheriff Colton admits that while the case is of high priority, he does not have a suspect.

When asked about the unusual coincidence of his brother and friend reporting the fire, the sheriff replied that the residents of Comanche County are fortunate that Jared Colton and Kerry WindWalker spotted the flames and phoned the fire department when they did.

Perhaps relevant to the mysterious crime is Sharon Fisher's report of a stranger requesting privacy to research birth records the same day as the fire. "He's not a man who would stand out in a crowd," Fisher said. "Brown hair and eyes, not at all memorable in looks, but I got the impression of nervous tension from him, as though he had something to hide." Sharon has worked in records at the courthouse for five years.

When Sheriff Colton was told of Sharon's comments, he allowed that she may have seen the arsonist, but since the man's identity is unknown, and he hasn't reappeared, he could simply have been someone passing through town researching his family tree. "No crime in that," Sheriff Colton said. "We shouldn't lay blame or accusations on anyone without strong evidence."

As for the newspaper office break-in, there seems to be no logical purpose, as nothing was taken. Was the perpetrator researching his family tree in there as well, Sheriff?

Chapter One

Driving his patrol car, Sheriff Bram Colton preceded the ambulance from the accident site into town. He'd been in his car when the radio dispatcher reported the one-car rollover about three miles west of Black Arrow, Oklahoma. Grabbing his radio, Bram had told Marilu Connor that he was nearby and on his way to the site. The ambulance had arrived at almost the same time he had, and now the two official vehicles were on their way to the hospital.

Bram had his overhead lights flashing, but hadn't turned on his siren, as the ambulance was making enough noise to alert motorists and anyone else within earshot. In mere minutes they pulled up to the emergency entrance of the Black Arrow Hospital.

ER personnel took over, and Bram headed straight for the administration desk.

"Here's his driver's license," he told the clerk, who began filling out forms. "The paramedics said he wasn't badly injured, considering it was a rollover."

"Apparently he was wearing a seat belt," the middle-age woman said.

"Appears so. I'll be back later to talk to him."

"See ya, Bram," the clerk said absently, intent on her emergency admittance forms.

Two hours later Bram returned to the hospital and was told that the young man had been installed in a room on the second floor. Bram walked past the elevator, which he knew from experience was slow as molasses, and opted for the stairs. He took them two at a time, mostly out of habit, although there was no question about his feeling hurried and unusually anxious lately. He was busier than normal, what with the courthouse fire and that peculiar burglary of the newspaper office, added to the usual roster of domestic disputes and petty crimes common to the town and county.

He easily located the accident victim's room. But when he walked in, he suddenly became a tongue-tied school-boy. Nurse Jenna Elliot was in the room, the beautiful young woman that Bram had secretly had his eye on for a very long time.

Jenna saw Bram's tall, dark form enter the room, and her pulse rate quickened. "Hello, Bram," she said, managing to sound like her usual self in spite of the explosion of adrenaline rushing through her system. That was what he did to her—what he *always* did to her—and not once had he ever smiled directly at her. She'd seen him smile at his sister, Willow, who was a good friend of Jenna's. Smile at *his* friends, and even at total strangers. But he would not smile at her, and she knew why. It was because of his Comanche blood, and because her father, Carl Elliot was a snob. Jenna had always wished Bram wouldn't lump her and her dad in the same category of ignorant intolerance, but she didn't know how to change his mind. The whole thing was frustrating and worrisome and just plain dumb; the other Coltons—and they were plentiful in and around Black Arrow—didn't snub her as Bram did. He had no right to assault her senses so powerfully and then treat her so coldly, no right at all.

"Jenna," Bram said stiffly. "Sorry for the interruption. I'll come back later."

Before Jenna could tell him to stay, that her patient was only slightly sedated and quite capable of talking to him, Bram was gone. She glared at the door he'd whisked through, then shook her head in abject disgust and shoved Bram Colton to the back of her mind, something she was well-practiced at doing.

Bram's teeth were clenched as he walked up to the nurse's station. Running into Jenna always set his hair on end. "How long are you planning to keep James Westley in the hospital?" he asked the nurse on duty.

"Just overnight. He'll be released in the morning."

"What time is the shift change around here today?"

"At six. Same as always."

"Thanks." Bram left. He would come back later in the evening to talk to James Westley and get the information he needed for an accident report.

Jenna was relieved that her dad wasn't home for dinner that evening; she was always relieved when he wasn't there to harangue her for becoming a nurse. "It's such a common profession! Nursing is beneath you, Jenna," she'd heard him say a hundred times. "Disgusting, considering some of the things you have to do to strangers, no matter who. You should have finished college and gotten your degree in art history, as you set out to do."

Jenna's relief at her dad's absence was shortlived. Because she was such a softie when it came to hurting anyone, or even *thinking* about hurting someone—especially

her father, whom she loved in spite of his horrid, undeserved sense of superiority—she next felt a wave of guilt.

After all, she was living under her dad's roof. Not by
choice, God knew, but because Carl Elliot had acted almost mortally wounded when his only child had returned
to Black Arrow as a full-fledged registered nurse and announced that it was time she got a place of her own.
Jenna's mother had died several years before, which had
left Carl rattling around alone in the large and quite elegant
home he'd had constructed in what he considered the best
part of town. Losing her mother had been hard on Jenna,
and it was during her mom's illness that Jenna had become
profoundly focused on the nursing profession. She wished
her father possessed just a fraction of the compassion for
mankind with which her mother had been blessed.

But he didn't. Jenna could argue against prejudice and
bigotry until she was blue in the face, and nothing she said
ever made a dent in Carl Elliot's supreme confidence that
the color of his skin—and that of his ancestors—made him
superior to anyone who wasn't as white as the driven
snow. Actually, Jenna had given up on trying to change
her father's infuriating intolerance. It cut her deeply that
he'd made so much money from those residents of Black
Arrow with Comanche blood, yet still looked down on
them. As a youngster, she'd been forbidden to play with
Indian children and had been sent to a private, all-white
school. All the same, she'd had Indian friends growing up.
Willow Colton would always be a friend, and Jenna would
give her eyeteeth if Bram would relax his guard and *become* a friend.

Martha Buskin was chief cook and bottle washer in the
Elliot household—had been for many years—and she had
roasted a chicken that afternoon. Jenna thanked her and
told her to go on home. Normally Martha's final chore of

the day was to tidy the kitchen after the evening meal, but whenever Jenna ate alone she let Martha leave early.

When the housekeeper had gone, Jenna ate some chicken and salad at the table in the kitchen. Then she went upstairs with a glass of her favorite wine and ran a bubble bath. Lighting scented candles placed around the tub, she switched off the bright bathroom lights, undressed and sank into the sudsy hot water. Sipping wine and feeling all the kinks of the day leave her body, she did what she'd known she would when she began this delightful ritual: relived and dissected those few moments in James Westley's hospital room when Bram Colton had come in.

She could see Bram in her mind's eye as clearly as if he were standing next to the tub…which she found herself wishing were true. She thought him to be the most physically attractive man she'd ever met or even seen. He made her spine tingle and her legs wobble, her heart beat faster and her mouth go dry. She loved his thick, lustrous black hair and black eyes. She loved the deep bronze tone of his skin and his perfect white teeth. The sight of his broad shoulders, flat, hard belly and long legs clad in his tan sheriff's uniform, with a big gun on his hip, almost caused her to go into respiratory failure. Was she in love with him? No, she couldn't say that. But lust? Oh, yes, she most definitely lusted after the county sheriff; after Willow's big brother. And if Bram ever decided to give her the time of day, she would give *him* a lot more than time. She'd give him…

''Oh, stop,'' she mumbled, finishing the last of her wine and hitting the small lever to drain the tub. Why did she torture herself over a man who was never going to do anything but look through her? Bram was every bit as stubborn as her dad. Her father would have a heart attack if his daughter took up with a Native American, or a ''breed,'' as he called those with even a drop of Indian blood, while Bram's stiff-necked pride would never permit him to get involved with Carl's daughter. She was in a no-win situation and she might as well forget that Bram Colton even existed.

That was easier said than done, but she hoped she would at least leave him behind when she went to Dallas for her week's vacation on Saturday. She was going to visit an old college friend, Loni Owens, and there was no doubt in Jenna's mind that she would have a good time. Loni was a bright, upbeat and extremely uninhibited gal when it came to fun, especially fun with guys. Jenna had hesitated in accepting Loni's invitation to spend her week off in Dallas because she knew Loni would have a dozen male friends lined up to meet her.

But what the heck? she'd finally concluded. She sure wasn't getting anywhere with the one man she would *love* to get somewhere with, so she might as well settle for second best.

She would be leaving very early on Saturday morning.

After obtaining the accident information that he needed and then leaving the hospital that evening, Bram stopped in to see his grandmother. He did that three or four times a week, and not just out of a sense of duty. He genuinely loved the elderly woman and thought her witty, wise and wonderful. Gloria was eighty years old, but since *her* father, Bram's great-grandfather, George WhiteBear, was still living at ninety-seven—at least that was the age George claimed to be—Bram was sure Gloria had many good years left. Occasionally he could get her talking about the old days and her youth, but not very often. "Live in the present, Bram," she usually told him. "Let the past stay in the past."

She always had something good to eat in her apartment above the Black Arrow Feed and Grain Store, a business that had supported the WhiteBear-Colton family for a good many years, and Bram enjoyed a cup of coffee and a slice of Gloria's delicious cinnamon-applesauce cake while they talked. She was very proud of his being sheriff, which she considered to be a very high position in the United States government. Bram let her think it, for anything that made her happy pleased him.

"Gran, Willow's been working in the store long enough to take over. Isn't it time you retired?" he said just before taking his leave.

"You've been trying to retire me for years, Bram," Gloria said briskly. "What do you want me to do, sit around up here in this apartment and watch soap operas and talk shows on TV?"

Bram had to laugh. "Forget I mentioned it, Gran."

"And you forget it, too."

"For tonight," he agreed with a twinkle in his eye. Leaning down, he kissed her cheek. "See you soon."

Bram's home was a two-hundred-acre ranch twenty miles out of town. Known in the area as the Colton Ranch, it had a big rambling house, a couple of barns, and fertile soil—soil rich enough to produce a nutritious grass ideal for raising quarter horses. The ranch had belonged to his parents, Trevor and Sally, and had been passed to their five children after their deaths. None of the five wanted to sell the family home, but the only one who wanted to do any ranching and live on the place was Bram. Much as he liked his job as sheriff, there was something in his blood that demanded a portion of his life be lived outdoors.

And he loved horses, as his Comanche ancestors had, for history books touted the Comanche as the most skilled riders of the Southwest. Bram broke and trained his own horses, but he was so good at the craft that sometimes other ranchers asked him to break one of their wild young stallions. He did it willingly and free of charge. What he knew about horses, he believed, was in his genes and had come to him from his ancestors.

Bram also had a dog, and when he arrived home that night Nellie came bounding out of the smallest barn, barking a joyous hello and wriggling her hindquarters back and forth. Nellie was a black-and-white Border collie with pale blue eyes. She was a love of a dog, and her main goal in life was to herd sheep, cows, horses, chickens or anything else that moved. Anytime Bram wanted some horses brought in from a pasture he whistled to Nellie, and off she'd go to get them. Bram's best friend, his fishing and hunting buddy, Will Mitchell, had three wild little boys, and all three adored Nellie and would let her herd them around Bram's yard when Will brought them out to the ranch.

Bram knelt down now and gave Nellie a hug, then scratched her ears. "Did you get lonesome today, girl?"

She wriggled again and licked his face. "Hey, that's going too far," Bram said with a laugh, rising to his feet. "Come on, let's go and scare you up some dinner."

It had been a long, busy day, and when Bram went to bed he was ready for sleep. But as he closed his eyes he promptly saw an image of Jenna Elliot. Punching his pillow in frustration, he turned to his side and tried to relax. But Jenna was still there, glowingly beautiful and causing him all sorts of physical distress.

Bram always thought of Jenna as Black Arrow's golden girl. Her hair had been twisted on top of her head today, but he knew what it looked like cascading down her back—like a golden waterfall. Its color nearly drove him mad, and he was positive it would feel as silky as it looked. Even Jenna's flawless skin had a golden hue, as though sprinkled with gold dust. Add her deep blue eyes to that mix and she sparkled. In Bram's eyes, anyway, Jenna Elliot sparkled more brightly and more beautifully than any Fourth of July fireworks he'd ever seen.

He recalled how much easier he'd breathed when she went away to college, and how the world had begun spinning crazily again when Jenna came home to help care for her terminally ill mother. After Mrs. Elliot's funeral Bram heard that Jenna had left town again, but not to return to college; she had decided to become a nurse. That had surprised him. Nursing was a service profession much like his own, and he'd wondered about a golden girl working such long hours. It wasn't as if she had to earn a living. Old Carl owned half the town and almost as much of the county. Everyone knew he had more money than he could count, and that he doted on Jenna. Hell, she'd never have to work a day if she didn't want to.

So that nursing business confused Bram, and he'd decided it was nothing but rumor, until he heard Willow mention it. He never asked Willow about Jenna because his baby sister was sharp as a tack and would catch on in a heartbeat if Bram so much as hinted he gave a damn about anything Jenna Elliot might do or say. But every so often he would pick up a tidbit of information about her from Willow. She had no idea that Jenna haunted her big brother's dreams. No one had any idea about that.

Bram fully intended to keep it that way, too. In truth, he would give almost anything to have Jenna move away permanently. He'd sleep better, since every single time he'd seen Jenna—starting with the day he'd discovered, or admitted, how she affected him—was lodged in his brain and came roaring out too damned often, especially at night.

One of the memories driving him batty had occurred on a hot day last summer. He had been slowly cruising a downtown street when he'd spotted Jenna strolling along the sidewalk, looking into store windows. She'd had on white shorts and a blue tank top. The sight of her long, gorgeous, deeply tanned legs had made him forget all about being behind the wheel of his prowl car and he'd come dangerously close to running into a light pole.

He'd hit the siren and taken off so fast that his tires had squealed, but he was pretty sure Jenna hadn't seen his embarrassingly narrow miss with that pole.

It was a memory Bram actually hated, for invariably it was followed by sexual contemplation of how it would feel to have those incredible legs wrapped around him, which led to other erotic thoughts that never failed to cause him more misery than he believed he deserved.

Sucking in a ragged breath, he forced himself to think about something else. The first topic to come to mind was the odd events occurring around town—the fire at the courthouse, for one, and the burglary of the local newspaper office for another. It appeared the fire had been arson, which made little sense, for why would anyone want to destroy Comanche County's courthouse? Of course, arson was usually senseless to everyone but the person who actually lit the match. It was too bad Jared and Kerry hadn't gotten a look at the arsonist that night. It was almost inconceivable that they had been in the very next room when the perpetrator had lit those candles. Thank God they'd seen the glow of the fire once it had gotten started, or there wouldn't even be a shell of the courthouse left. But the whole thing was as disturbingly mysterious tonight as it had been from the start.

And why in hell would someone break into the newspaper office and then leave without taking anything, when there'd been computers and other costly items throughout the place? That reporter had been right to question the motivation for that seemingly senseless crime.

There was one more thing nagging at Bram. He'd heard rumors about two *different* strangers asking questions about the Colton family. They had to be connected to the courthouse fire and possibly the *Chronicle* break-in, but why didn't they simply contact him? Or his grandmother? No one knew Colton history better than Gloria, or Great-granddad WhiteBear. But there were plenty of Coltons to confront if someone wanted to know something of their ancestry. Even so, Bram couldn't make heads or tails of the whole thing, for why would any outsider give a whit about any of the Coltons, none of whom had anything to hide? It was a damn weird mess, Bram decided again, having reached that conclusion quite a few times in the past few weeks.

Then, even through that maze of thoughts, Jenna's image threatened again, and Bram groaned and sought another subject to dwell on until he fell asleep. Fishing was a good nerve-settling topic, and Bram grasped at it, pondered it for a while and then decided to ask Will if he could go fishing this coming weekend. They had a couple of favorite fishing spots, and Bram never cared if Will took one or more of his sons with them. Maybe they could leave on Saturday and camp out that night. He would check his work schedule at the sheriff's station in the morning, and if he was free this weekend, he'd give Will a call or stop by his place.

The next day Bram checked the duty roster and saw that he had the weekend off. Feeling good about it, he drove by Will's house on his way home from work that afternoon. Will's three boys, nine-year-old Billy, eight-year-old Stevie and six-year-old Hank came running from the backyard yelling, "Bram! Bram! Daddy, Bram's here!"

Bram grinned. Dressed in cutoff jeans and T-shirts, the trio were barefoot and dirty. Before bed Bram knew that their mother, Ellie, would see to baths and fresh pajamas, but during the day there was no keeping her wildcats clean.

"Didja shoot your gun today, Bram?" Hank asked.

"Not today, Hank."

"Aw, heck," the youngster said.

Will had come out of the house and approached the group. "Hi, Bram. How're tricks?"

Will Mitchell was as fair as Bram was dark. Will had straw-colored hair, pale hazel eyes and skin that never tanned. The two had been friends since high school.

"My tricks are nonexistent," Bram said dryly. "You're the man with the tricks…three of them, to be specific."

Will grinned. "Boys, your mother asked me to tell you to go in and wash up for supper."

"Aw, heck," Hank said again. But he raced to the house only a step behind his older brothers, shouting, "Bye, Bram. See ya later."

"Want to come in and eat with us?" Will asked.

"Thanks, not tonight. I've got this weekend off and I was thinking about a fishing trip. With two days, we could go to Ridge Reservoir and camp out overnight. The boys would like that."

"Hey, they sure would. So would I. Let me talk to Ellie and see if she's got anything planned for the weekend. I'll give you a call. Two days at the reservoir would be great, wouldn't they?"

"Yeah, they would."

"I wish Ellie liked camping and fishing." Will paused, then grinned again. "She said to not say a word to anyone until she's certain, but I don't think she meant you. Bram, she's pretty sure she's pregnant. She says this time it *has* to be a girl. You know how she longs for a daughter."

Bram looked at his friend's excited face and felt the strangest ache in his gut. He covered it with a teasing wisecrack. "You're just full of tricks, Mitchell."

"You could be, too. There isn't a gal in the county who wouldn't jump at the chance to marry you and you know it."

"Bull," Bram exclaimed. "No one's pining to marry me. Hell, I can't even get dates for the Saturday night dances at the Grange Hall."

"You're so full of it, it's coming out of your ears, Colton. You don't have a girlfriend only because you don't *want* a girlfriend. You're afraid she'll rope and hog-tie you, and you're scared spitless of commitment and a wedding ring."

"Will, blow it out your ear." This was a common conversation for them. Will thought Bram—at thirty-seven years of age—should be married, and when Bram got tired of the subject he ended it with that one directive—"Blow it out your ear." Will always laughed and that was the end of it...until the next time.

Ellie called from the front door of the house. "Supper's on the table, hon. Hi, Bram, come on in and eat with us."

"Thanks, Ellie, but can't do it tonight. Some other time, okay?"

"Anytime, Bram."

Will said, "I'll call as soon as I know about the fishing trip."

Bram nodded and climbed into his car. "Great. Talk to you then."

As he drove away he thought about Will and Ellie having another child and Will being so thrilled about it. Bram wanted kids, too, but not with just any woman. And since he couldn't have the one woman he wanted, he'd probably never have kids.

He muttered a curse, then told himself to cool down. What made him think he needed kids of his own? When his parents were killed in that plane crash in 1987 he'd been twenty-two and had taken over as head of the household. He'd seen to it that his four siblings—Ashe, Jared, Logan and Willow—finished their education and continued to live as good, decent citizens, just as their mother and dad had taught them.

No, he didn't need kids, and he sure as hell didn't need a wife he didn't love. He would take bachelorhood for the rest of his days over *that* sort of mess.

He ate dinner with his grandmother, and it was only after he left and was driving out to the ranch that he realized she had looked a little peaked. Or maybe it was just his imagination; Gloria had bustled around her kitchen as always, hadn't she?

Will phoned the following evening, which was Friday. "Ellie's got a quilting thing—some kind of craft show at the fairgrounds—tomorrow. She said to take the boys and go fishing, with her blessing." Will chuckled. "Sounds like she's looking forward to a quiet weekend."

After they hung up Bram began gathering his camping and fishing gear. He grinned when he realized that he was probably as excited about the coming weekend as Will's boys undoubtedly were. Nellie was in the house, sniffing the sleeping bags and fishing poles Bram piled on the floor in the middle of the living room, and it was apparent to Bram from the collie's happy gyrations that she knew a fishing trip was in the making. Bram always took her along, and she wore herself out trying to herd chipmunks, squirrels and gophers. The boys would wear her out, too, but that was a two-way street, for Nellie wore them out, as well. Truth was, they would all have a great time.

Bram finally had everything in a pile, except for the food he would take with him. He'd get up early, pack the three ice chests with ice and food, and load his SUV. Then he'd drive over to Will's house and pick up him, the boys and all their gear. Eyeing the mound of items, Bram was about to go for a down-filled jacket—just in case the weather changed over the weekend and it got cold—when the telephone rang.

He picked it up. "Hello?"

"Bram...oh my Lord...Bram, Gran's on her way to the hospital. I found her—"

"Willow, slow down!" Bram's heart leaped into his throat. "What happened?"

"She went upstairs early, and I figured something was wrong then. But I was busy with customers, and when I finally had a moment to check on her I found her on the floor. The ambulance driver said something about a stroke. I'm hoping he was only guessing, but oh, Bram..." Willow began weeping.

"Okay, take it easy. Have you called the rest of the family?"

"I called you first."

"Good. I'll leave for the hospital as soon as we hang up. You stay there and call everyone. They all should be told."

"What about Great-grandfather? Should I try to reach him?"

George WhiteBear wouldn't permit electronic gadgets in his small, simply furnished house on a hundred sixty acres of land about thirty miles southwest of Black Arrow, and that included a telephone. Reaching George by phone meant calling his closest neighbor and asking her to drive over to George's place to pick him up and haul him back to *her* place. Annie McCrary would do it—she had in the past during family emergencies—but Bram was worried about imparting this kind of bad news over the phone to his aged great-grandfather. He made a decision.

"No, don't call Annie. If it's necessary, I'll drive out to Great-grandfather's place later on. See you at the hospital, Willow." Bram put down the phone and hurried out to his SUV, relieved that he hadn't already loaded it with camping gear.

He'd gotten out of his uniform the second he'd arrived

home, which was standard procedure, and he was wearing
faded jeans and a black, short-sleeved T-shirt. Thinking of
nothing but Gran, and praying she was all right, he pushed
the speed limit all the way to the hospital. He parked close
to the emergency room entrance and ran from his vehicle
to the door. Immediately he saw Coltons everywhere, all
but taking up the entire waiting room. He went over to
them.

"Do we know anything yet?" he asked.

He got teary answers from everyone. No one knew anything, except that Gran was in the emergency room.
Thomas, a twin to Bram's father and Gloria's only living
child, said, "Maybe they'll let you in there, seeing as how
you're the sheriff and all." Thomas had married Alice Callahan in 1969, and they had had six children. The way the
waiting room was overflowing, Bram was pretty sure that
every Colton in the area had come to the hospital.

"I'll see what I can find out," Bram said, and walked
away. He simply pushed open the door that bore a Keep
Out sign and then checked the curtained cubicles until he
found Gran. A doctor and nurse were with her. Bram's
heart sank when he looked at Gran, whose eyes were
closed. She looked small and old and gray, and at that
moment Bram knew that whatever had befallen her was
serious.

Dr. Vadella motioned for Bram to follow him, and he
took him to a quiet corner of the ER. "She suffered a
stroke, Bram. What we don't know at this point is its severity."

"But it doesn't look good, does it? Is she going to be
paralyzed? Is she going to live?"

Dr. Vadella looked him in the eye. "Bram, don't ask
me questions I can't answer tonight. To be perfectly honest
we won't know the extent of the damage the stroke in-
flicted for several days, maybe longer. Look, I know the

family is in the waiting room. Do them and yourself a favor and tell everyone to go home. Mrs. Colton is going to be taken to Intensive Care. We'll start running tests tonight, but most of them will be done in the morning. The family can see her tomorrow in between tests, but only one person at a time and each for only a few short minutes.''

Bram looked away. His chest ached and his eyes burned. He wanted to take Gran from that gurney, carry her out to his vehicle and drive her home. She hated hospitals. Always said that people died in hospitals and no one was ever to bring her to one. He felt like a traitor because she was here, and he also felt the same kind of pain he'd suffered when his parents died, the kind of pain one couldn't eradicate by good-intentioned doctors with common-sense explanations.

There was nothing Bram could do except long for the way things had been only hours before. Gran was now seriously ill and he *had* to leave her here. He brought his gaze back to Dr. Vadella.

''I'll tell the family what you said. Thanks for talking to me.''

Nodding, Dr. Vadella left to return to his patient. Bram went out to the waiting room and his family. He knew now that the fishing trip was off and that he would have to drive out to Great-grandfather's place and tell him that his daughter was in the hospital.

Life had fallen apart very suddenly, very quickly.

Chapter Two

Will and Ellie offered sympathy and any help Bram might need when he told them about Gran. There were so many Coltons, though, that assistance from anyone outside the family wasn't likely to be needed. Still, the Mitchells' gesture was heartfelt and genuine, and Bram appreciated their concern.

Bram put work and everything else out of his mind and spent almost the entire weekend at the hospital. The rest of the family came and went, each spending a few minutes in Gran's room and hoping to hear some good news. Actually, there was no news at all, either good or bad. The doctors and nurses that Bram waylaid in the halls and in Gran's room had only one message to impart: there would not be a credible diagnosis or prognosis until all of the test results came in, which would occur sometime on Monday or Tuesday.

Time had never moved so slowly for Bram. He drank

too much bad coffee and worried. He walked the floors of various waiting rooms and worried. He sat slouched on one uncomfortable chair after another and worried. And he took only an occasional break from his self-imposed post to dash home to the ranch for a shower, shave and clean clothes.

He kept putting off that drive out to Great-grandfather George's place because merely telling him that his daughter was in the hospital, obviously seriously ill, wasn't enough. It would be much better to convey the news with some concrete information from the doctors about her condition, Bram rationalized, which he would have along with the test results in a day or two. Sharing incomplete and possibly false information based on Bram's own fears might extinguish the small light still burning in George WhiteBear's ancient chest, and Bram wouldn't take that chance.

On Monday he had to tend to his job. He talked to the family and made sure that there would always be at least one Colton at the hospital, around the clock. Most of them worked, too, but they coordinated their hours off, which should have eased some of Bram's concern but didn't. Monday was a bad day for him, yet he ran to the hospital every chance he got just to look in on Gran, to make sure she was still breathing. He had a horrible feeling in the pit of his stomach, which he tried to ignore or at least minimize, and couldn't.

It was while Bram was with Gloria on one of his quick stops that she opened her eyes and tried to speak. He jumped up from the chair he'd been anxiously perched on, and took her hand. "Gran," he said gently, though his heart was in his throat and unshed tears stung his eyes.

She tried to speak again, failed, and he saw painful understanding in her eyes. "It's okay, Gran."

She made angry noises. It *wasn't* okay, and Bram didn't

have to hear the words to know what she meant. And then she got out a word. "Home!"

Bram sucked in a breath. "I know. You want to go home. I'm working on it, Gran."

Gloria's eyes closed again and Bram held her limp little hand for a while longer, then returned to his chair. He swore on all that was holy that he would take her home to either live or die. She would do neither in this or any other hospital.

Finally, on Tuesday morning, the Colton family heard what they already knew in their hearts. Gran had suffered a serious stroke. They also heard details that made them weep. Gran was partially paralyzed, her speech was impaired and her short-term memory was possibly eradicated, or no longer in chronological order. Her vision was cloudy and she would suffer bouts of dizziness and confusion. Full recovery at her age should not be expected, but speech and mobility could be greatly improved with physical therapy.

Bram spoke for the group. "Can she be cared for at home?"

The doctor nodded. "Yes, and I highly recommend home care. Stroke patients respond much better when they are with loved ones. However, she should remain here for at least a week, as not all symptoms of stroke are immediately discernible. Also, you all should understand that she will require a full-time nurse for an indefinite period, which is not inexpensive. Medicare covers—"

"The cost will be taken care of," Bram said curtly. He stood up and faced his family. "I want her brought to the ranch. Any objections?" A buzz of conversation swept through the group. "I know many of you want her, but I'm determined on this. You can drop in anytime to see her, and if you truly want to help, there's housework, cooking, laundry and errands.'' He turned back to the doctor. ''So, I can take her home when?''

''In about a week.''

''Next Monday?''

''Probably. Shall I arrange for the nurse?''

''Yes, please do. Okay, Doctor, thanks. We'll get out of your hair now.'' Bram urged his relatives outside, where a few of them told him what they thought of his tactics.

''She's *my* mother,'' Uncle Thomas said indignantly.

''When she's better you can take her,'' Bram replied. ''But I'm taking her first.''

The family began dispersing, going off to their cars, talking among themselves. Willow hung back and squeezed her brother's hand.

''I'm glad she'll be with you,'' Willow said. ''Everyone says they want her, but caring for an invalid is not easy. I know you'll follow through.''

''That I will,'' Bram said with that stern, determined look on his face that Willow knew very well. When Bram set his mind to something, it got done.

The rest of the week flew by because Bram was constantly busy, juggling caring for his horses and Nellie, getting the house cleaned and ready for Gran's arrival, seeing to his job and squeezing in as many trips to the hospital as he could manage.

It was Friday before Bram realized that he hadn't run into Jenna even once. As often as he'd been at the hospital that week, it was odd that he hadn't stumbled across her at least one time. His nerves had settled down some and he began watching for her, thinking that he'd been so focused on Gran's condition during those first awful days and nights that he might have walked right past Jenna and not seen her.

But even on the alert now he didn't see her. Of course, she might have weekends off, he told himself.

Monday morning finally dawned, and Bram jumped out

of bed, anxious for the day to begin. His beloved Gran was coming today, and he was thrilled to have her, ill or not.

When Jenna awoke to her alarm clock Monday morning, she stretched and yawned. She'd spent a marvelous week in Dallas with Loni, but her vacation was over and it was time she got back to her own reality. Smiling slightly, she got out of bed and headed for the shower.

Three hours later, on duty at the hospital, she heard two doctors checking a patient's chart and discussing it at the nurse's station. Obviously the patient was one of Dr. Hall's. "Mrs. Colton will be taken by ambulance to Bram's home. Now all I have to do is decide which nurse to send with her. There aren't many nurses that can move in with a patient and give her their undivided attention. Most have family of their own, and—"

"Excuse me," Jenna said. "Dr. Hall, may I speak to you for a moment?"

Bram went to work Monday morning but was back at the ranch again at noon. Nellie greeted him and followed wherever he went. The ambulance was scheduled to arrive around one, and Bram was nervous as a cat waiting for it. He walked through the house again to make sure everything was ready. Unquestionably, his home was cleaner than it had ever been, and the master bedroom, which Bram had assigned to Gran because of its private bathroom, had been scrubbed down with disinfectant.

Bram had taken the bed completely apart, scrubbed the frame and thoroughly vacuumed the springs and mattress before putting it all back together again. He had purchased a supply of white bed linens, including a soft white blanket and bedspread. It had been an expensive purchase, as he'd bought the best he could find in Black Arrow and had discovered that the ''best'' in sheets and pillowcases didn't come cheap.

He peered into the bathroom, which contained new, freshly laundered white towels and washcloths. The fixtures gleamed from the scrubbing and polishing they had received.

The kitchen contained foods recommended by the hospital dietitian, who had given him lists of proper and improper foods for a stroke victim, along with a small book of recipes and hints on how to make a salt-free, fat-free, sugar-free meal appear tempting enough to actually eat.

Everything was as ready as he could make it, Bram finally decided, and went outside. With Nellie on his heels, he walked down to the wooden fence surrounding one of the pastures, put a booted foot on the bottom rail and leaned his forearms on the top. He had built this particular fence himself. It was good and sturdy and he knew it would last for many years. But it was about due for another coat of sealer, he decided, mentally putting that on his list of chores to do when time allowed.

Narrowing his eyes, he watched the horses nibbling grass on the far side of the field. Sometimes he thought of resigning from his job, going into debt for a bigger spread and doing nothing but breeding and raising horses. But he wasn't a man who took debt lightly, and he was doing just fine with the status quo. He made a decent salary as sheriff, and his siblings asked for no rent for his use of the family ranch, as they were grateful to have their parents' home and their heritage being kept in such good condition. Along with that, Bram had always been a practical man as far as saving for a rainy day went.

For some reason his thoughts went from there to Carl Elliot, who had to be worth millions, if not more. There were folks in the county with enormous fortunes, of course, some of them oil families from way back. But no other millionaire that Bram knew of had Carl's less-than-sterling reputation. Bram would admire Carl's ability to amass wealth if there weren't so many rumors about his methods. *Crafty* was the kindest word used by some in describing Carl's way of doing business, and some called him corrupt and worse.

Bram was still watching his horses, still musing about Carl Elliot, when he heard an approaching vehicle. Turning away from the fence, he saw the ambulance nearing his driveway. Bram's heart skipped a beat. He was going to make Gran well, so help him God. He was going to spend every spare minute bringing her back to her former active, energetic self. He would see to exercising her legs and arms and eventually getting her out of that bed, and he would help her with the speech and facial therapies explained to him at the hospital, so she could speak with clarity.

The ambulance pulled up next to the house and Bram began striding toward it. Two paramedics got out of the front of the red-and-white vehicle and called hellos to Bram. He said hello as he walked up to them, and all three walked around to the back of the ambulance.

"So, how is she doing?" Bram asked.

"Just fine," one of the young men said reassuringly.

Bram stood by while the medics opened the back doors. And then the bottom fell out of his stomach. Getting out of the ambulance was Jenna Elliot. She was wearing white slacks and a white top, her glorious hair was pulled back from her face and restrained with a clip at her nape, and she smiled at Bram as though they had always been the very best of friends.

"Hello, Bram," she said.

He was too stunned to answer, to move or even to look as though he had a brain somewhere in his stiff and benumbed body.

Jenna became intent on assisting the paramedics in moving Gloria from the ambulance as gently as possible. She held the IV bottle and kept the tubing from getting twisted or in the way while the two young men did their job. When everything was ready to take Gran into the house, one of the paramedics said, "Lead the way, Bram."

"Uh...uh, sure," he stammered, and somehow managed to get his feet walking and heading for the house. This was unfathomable. Jenna was Gran's nurse? My God, Jenna was going to be staying in his house? Sleeping under his roof? In plain sight everywhere he turned? Hovering over Gran whenever he went into her room?

Bram led the way to the master bedroom, which had been his room before this tragic event.

"I gave her this room because of the bathroom," he mumbled, wishing to hell his tongue would cooperate.

Jenna walked in and looked around. The whole house— or what she'd seen of it on her way in—was spotless and bore the unmistakable odor of disinfectant. Someone had done a thorough cleaning job, or was this almost sterile condition the norm for Bram's home? She would never have thought so, but since she really didn't know him in spite of her long-standing friendship with his sister, she could only guess at his housekeeping skills.

The paramedics were about to transfer Gloria from the gurney to the bed when Jenna said, "Wait a minute, please. Where will I be sleeping?"

Bram nervously shifted his weight from one foot to another. "The guest bedrooms are on the other side of the house." Lord above, she'd be sleeping in the room next to his!

"Let me take a look." Jenna handed the IV bottle to one of the paramedics and left the room. "Bram? How about giving me a quick tour?"

"Yeah, sure," he said, again having trouble with the

simplest words. He walked past her, got a whiff of her clean, mildly floral smell and felt his face grow hot. Clenching his teeth, he led her through the house to the other two bedrooms.

Jenna took a quick peek into each and declared, "I'm sorry, but this won't do. I need to be much closer to your grandmother at night. How about moving one of those twin beds into her room for me? I'll keep my things in here and use the other twin when I think she's doing well enough for me to sleep away from her."

"Great," Bram muttered.

"I beg your pardon?"

"Nothing. Tell the guys to put her to bed. I'll move the twin."

"And I'll bring in my suitcase."

"Uh, I'll get it for you."

Jenna smiled sweetly. He was unbelievably rude, but she wasn't going to let him beat her up over nothing. After all, *he* didn't know that he had the starring role in the sexual fantasies that occasionally passed through her brain.

"Thank you." She left him standing there and returned to the master bedroom. "Put her to bed," she told the two young men. Seeing that Gloria's eyes had opened, she took her hand and smiled. "Do you know where you are, Gloria? You're at the ranch, at Bram's house. We're going to move you to what looks to be a very comfortable bed now. Are you all right with that?"

"Ho…ho…home," Gloria whispered hoarsely.

"Yes, Bram's home."

"N-n-no! Ho…home."

Jenna sighed internally. It was always the same with patients released from the hospital. They always wanted their own home.

The men easily and expertly moved Gloria to the bed, and then made sure her IV was working and she was as comfortable as they could make her. They left then and Jenna was alone with her patient.

On the other side of the house, Bram had taken one of the twin beds apart. Tossing the bedding on the other twin, he shoved the mattress and then the box spring onto the floor and picked up the bed frame. He wore a scowl because this whole setup was almost more than he could handle, and he hated feeling helpless about anything. How dare Jenna come barging into his life like this?

Carrying the bed frame into the master suite, Bram set it down long enough to move a dresser over a few feet to make room for the twin.

"May I help?" Jenna asked.

"No, thanks," Bram said curtly.

"Fine, do it all yourself," she retorted.

Bram's head jerked around so he could look at her. She looked back, and it was a stare-down that shook Bram's very foundation. He wanted to tell her that he didn't like her being there, and to ask her how in hell she expected him to sleep at night with her only a few feet and a thin wall away. But he couldn't reveal the secret passion he'd harbored for her for so long, and what rational excuse did he have for not wanting her to be Gran's nurse?

"I'll get the spring and mattress," he muttered darkly, finally breaking that unnerving eye contact and leaving the room.

Jenna took in a huge gulp of air and realized that she'd been holding her breath. Not only that, but her entire system was in chaos, all tingly and reminding her in the most erotic ways of her femininity, caused solely from looking directly into Bram Colton's incredible black eyes.

Shivering from so much sexual energy charging through her body, she busied herself unpacking a bag containing a supply of hospital gowns and the medications for Gloria.

Bram hauled in the box spring and left again without a

word or a glance. In a minute he was back with the mattress. Immediately he walked out again.

Jenna was surprised by the animosity she felt from Bram. He'd never been friendly, that was certain, but his attitude today bordered on actual dislike. Had she inadvertently trod on his toes at some time? She couldn't think of an incident where they were ever together long enough for either of them to injure the other's feelings. And heaven knew that she'd been open to a better relationship between them. At least she had tried smiling at him. If he ever deigned to show her a genuine smile, she'd probably faint dead away.

Bram returned once more with an armload of bedding. "It's clean," he said gruffly.

"Did you think I would accuse you of giving me soiled bedding?"

He couldn't believe her icy tone of voice and insulting question. "No," he said with heavy sarcasm. "I merely pointed out that this is clean bedding."

"Anyway, we're disturbing my patient."

"Who just happens to be my grandmother," Bram snapped, but in a husky whisper. He walked over to the bed Gran was occupying and looked down at her. She seemed small as a child in his big bed, and he'd never seen her as a tiny woman before the stroke. That shook him, for it was visible evidence of the changes in her.

He said brusquely, "Do you want me to make up the twin for you?"

"I'll do it. I know there are going to be a lot of family members dropping in, which is as it should be. But I must insist on one rule."

Bram's eyes got even darker. "You brought your own set of rules to *my* house?"

"One for now. And don't act so put-upon. It won't kill you or anyone else to follow it. When that door is shut, no one is to come in. I will close it only during baths or other episodes of personal care. Now, is that really asking too much?''

Bram was embarrassed but would die before showing it. "I can live with that.''

"Well, thank you very much.'' Disgustedly, Jenna turned away.

Bram wanted to pull a chair over to the bed and sit with Gran for a while, but with Jenna hovering and puttering— making up the twin bed, for one thing—and his every cell attuned to her every movement, he abandoned that idea.

"I'm going to work,'' he growled as he walked out. "Call me if you need anything. You'll find the phone numbers where I can be reached listed on a pad under the wall phone in the kitchen.''

"Thank you,'' Jenna said stiffly. She couldn't help feeling glad that he'd decided to leave, for he wasn't being one bit nice, and a grouchy distraction—even the sexiest guy she'd ever seen—she didn't need. She probably shouldn't have acted so impulsively when she'd heard Dr. Hall saying that he needed a nurse to care for Gloria Colton in Bram's home. What on earth had Jenna hoped would come from her actually living in his house?

Sighing when she heard Bram's vehicle start up and drive off, she finished making the bed, checked Gloria's pulse rate, temperature and blood pressure without waking her, and wrote the data and the time on the new chart started in the ambulance.

Gloria's eyes were closed and she seemed to be sleeping peacefully. Jenna took that opportunity to check out the kitchen and the food it contained. She would be preparing Gloria's meals, and her own, of course. But she was not going to cook for Bram. He could eat at the greasy spoon café, for all she cared.

* * *

Two hours later Willow walked into the house carrying a covered pot of something that smelled good. The young woman had black hair like her brother, but her eyes were gray and she was tall and slender and quite lovely.

"Jenna!" Willow exclaimed, obviously taken aback. "No one told me you were Gran's nurse."

"No one knew until this morning. What's in the pot?"

"Some homemade chicken broth for Gran."

"You used very little salt, I hope."

"*Very* little. Just a tiny pinch."

"Wonderful. Take it to the kitchen and then come say hi to your grandmother."

Willow returned in a minute and asked, "Is it all right if I sit on the bed next to her?"

"Of course."

Jenna watched Gloria's eyes follow her granddaughter until Willow was sitting on the bed. "Willow's here, Gloria," Jenna said gently.

"Hi, Gran," Willow said, and took her hand. "Are you happy to be out of the hospital?"

"Ho…home." Gloria slurred the word.

"Gran, you can't go to your home yet. Here you have Bram…and Jenna. You remember Jenna Elliot, don't you?"

Gloria turned her head and closed her eyes. Willow bit her lip and looked at Jenna. Then she mouthed, "What's wrong?"

Jenna motioned her from the room, and when they were out of Gloria's earshot she said quietly, "She's not happy, Willow. She wants to be in her own home."

"But she can't be. Does she understand that she must get much better before she can go back to that apartment?"

"I don't know what she understands," Jenna said with an apologetic sigh.

"Jenna, is she really going to get better?"

"I don't know that, either," Jenna said softly. "I do know that she can improve speech and mobility through exercise. She's not quite ready to begin that regimen, not today at any rate, but soon she should be. Right now she's feeling terribly discouraged and…and lost."

"How can we cheer her up?"

"By visiting as often as you can and talking to her. Tell her what you're doing and what the rest of the family is doing. If she had any special interests, talk to her about those. If she read a lot, read aloud to her—the kind of books or magazines she enjoyed before this happened. Be yourself with her, and above all, don't ever talk down to her, as though she's now incapable of grasping what you tell her. She might not be as quick on the trigger as she was, but we still don't know how affected her memory was by the stroke. And gradually, you'll see some improvement in her attitude."

Willow wiped away a tear. "I hope so."

Before the afternoon was over, nearly every Colton had come by, each bearing a gift of food Gloria could eat in her present condition—homemade broth or a bowl of custard or a dish of raspberry gelatin, her favorite flavor.

But some also brought things for Bram and Jenna to eat. There was a delicious-smelling beef stew, a baked ham, several cakes and pies and numerous salads and casseroles. Jenna realized that neither she nor Bram would have to do any cooking for days.

At five Jenna warmed some of Willow's chicken broth and prepared a tray for Gloria. She couldn't quite manage to feed herself yet, and Jenna sat on the bed and gently spooned broth, gelatin and custard into her patient's mouth. After a few bites of each, Gloria turned her head.

"You really must eat more than that," Jenna said in a genuinely kind voice.

But Gloria closed her eyes, and that was the end of dinner for her. Frowning and troubled, Jenna carried the tray back to the kitchen. She was rinsing dishes for the dishwasher when she heard Bram's SUV drive in and park.

Jenna had spotted Bram's dog through various windows several times that day, and when she heard joyous barking, she went to the kitchen window to see what was happening. Bram had knelt to hug his black-and-white dog, a pretty little thing, Jenna thought, and Bram's obvious affection for his pet revealed a side of him that Jenna had never seen. Actually, it made her wonder if her previous opinion about Bram avoiding her because of her father's intolerance was on the mark or if he simply didn't like her and never had.

But if *he* didn't like her, why in heaven's name was she so smitten by him? Couldn't her hormones tell the difference between an interested and an uninterested man? Shouldn't her own reactions to the opposite sex be more accurate than they apparently were with Bram?

Bram stood up and Jenna ducked away from the window so he wouldn't catch her watching him. She heard him come in and then call, "Jenna!"

Leaving the kitchen, she hurried to the front door entry. "What?"

"Can my dog come in the house?"

"Why are you asking me?"

Bram thinned his lips. "Because you've got rules. Nellie is used to coming inside, but if you don't want a dog in the house because of Gran—"

Jenna broke in. "Is Nellie going to jump on the bed and give Gloria fleas?"

"She doesn't have fleas!"

"I was only kidding. Pets are very good medicine for people in Gloria's condition. By all means, let Nellie come in."

Bram opened the door and Nellie came bounding in. "Settle down, Nellie," he said quietly, and the collie immediately obeyed.

"She's awfully cute," Jenna said. "Is she friendly with strangers?"

Nellie was, but Bram wouldn't give Jenna the satisfaction of saying so. Her nervy intrusion on his quiet life galled him, especially when he was with her again and seeing those glorious blue eyes and that golden hair.

"Sorry, but no. I recommend you give her a pretty wide berth until she gets used to you being here."

"All right," Jenna said with a soft sigh that ripped through Bram like a buzz saw cutting wood. The cut was just as sharp and jagged, and he wished he hadn't lied to her.

But it was done, and if Jenna had any backbone at all she'd discover Nellie's love of mankind in very short order.

"What breed is she?"

"Border collie. They're natural-born herders. What smells good?"

"Most of your family brought something to eat with them when they dropped in to see your grandmother. It's all in the kitchen. Help yourself."

So, she didn't intend that they eat together. Fine, he didn't want to eat with her, anyhow. "I'm not hungry," he said gruffly. "I ate in town." Bram walked off, leaving Jenna to cautiously keep an eye on his vicious Nellie, who was lying down with her nose on her front paws, closely watching Jenna. How was Jenna to know that the collie was so watchful because she never missed a chance to herd, and maybe this nice lady would run around the house and let Nellie herd her from room to room?

"Bram Colton," Jenna whispered, "I absolutely, positively loathe you."

Right at that moment, it was the truth.

Chapter Three

The chiming of the doorbell startled Jenna, who'd been so involved with Bram and his watchful dog that she hadn't heard the arrival of another vehicle. But all afternoon the visiting Coltons had merely rapped once and walked in, some of them not even bothering to announce their arrival with that cursory knock. Thus Jenna was pretty certain that whoever had rung the doorbell was not a Colton. She glanced toward the master bedroom to see if Bram had heard the chimes, but it appeared that either he hadn't or he was ignoring the caller.

Giving Nellie a warning look that Jenna hoped the dog would interpret to mean, "Don't you dare move from that spot," Jenna went to the door herself. Opening it, she could hardly believe her eyes.

"Dad!"

Carl Elliot's face was dark red with anger. "What in hell do you think you're doing?" he demanded. "Staying in a damn Indian's house. Don't you have any pride?"

"I'm working! I'm taking care of Mrs. Colton."

"You're living with an Indian man! This is his house!"

"I am *not* living with anyone, not in the way you're inferring. I explained my job assignment in the note I left for you, which you must have read or you wouldn't have known where I was. I'm very upset over this…this intrusion, Dad."

"And I'm so embarrassed by your behavior I can't hold my head up or look friends in the eye! Get your things and come home with me this instant."

"I most certainly will not!"

"Jenna, I'm warning you…"

Jenna felt Bram's presence behind her before he said a word. He stepped so close that her whole body became tense.

"What's going on?" he asked, using that lethally quiet tone that never failed to deliver a thrill to every erogenous area of Jenna's body. She took a quick, nervous breath and tried to ignore his overwhelming sexual magnetism so she could concentrate on minimizing the situation.

"I don't want my daughter staying here," Carl Elliot said coldly, proving that he was unafraid of Black Arrow's sheriff, or any other man, for that matter.

"Well, I'm not all that keen on your daughter staying here, either," Bram drawled, shocking the breath out of Jenna and possibly doing the same to Carl, who suddenly looked confused. "But Dr. Hall assigned her to care for my grandmother, and until another nurse appears on this doorstep to take her place, your daughter is working for me. Take it or leave it, but don't come here looking for trouble or you just might find it." Bram strode away with Nellie on his heels, heading, Jenna saw, for his bedroom.

"This is not the end of this," Carl said angrily, shaking his finger at his daughter. But to Jenna's immense relief, he left the front porch and walked—obviously in a huff—to his car.

"Dad," she called, having second thoughts. She ran after him.

Carl stopped as he reached his car. "Did you change your mind?"

"No, but there's no reason for anger between us. Try to understand. I'm only doing my job."

"Your wonderful job embarrasses me, shames me. Thank God your mother isn't alive to see how you've disgraced the Elliot name."

Jenna gasped. "How can you stand there and say something like that? Mother didn't have a biased or prejudiced bone in her body and you know it."

"Yeah, well, she wasn't always right, either. I'm not going to forget this, Jenna. How long are you planning to live with that big breed?"

Jenna's spine stiffened. "I won't listen to that kind of talk another second. Good night." Spinning, she walked back to the house with her head held high, went in and closed the door.

But her courage was mostly bluff. Shaking all over, she leaned back against the door and fought tears.

Bram walked in. He had changed from his uniform to jeans, a blue cotton shirt and soft leather cowboy boots, and he looked so handsome to Jenna that her heart actually ached. If there had been the slimmest chance of him liking her before this, her father's angry appearance just now had destroyed it.

"Why *did* Dr. Hall assign you to this job?" Bram asked brusquely.

Jenna's anger, normally so controlled, flared up. Right at the moment she didn't much care for Bram Colton *or* her father. "Because I'm the best nurse in town," she snapped, and ducked around Bram to go to the kitchen.

Frowning, he pondered her answer and decided to believe her. In the first place, why would she make up something like that? In the second, she had no idea of his feelings for her, so why *wouldn't* she take the assignment? As for Carl Elliot, he could go take a flying leap at the moon, for all Bram cared.

"Moronic jackass," he muttered as he headed back to Gran's room.

In the kitchen Jenna heated up a bowl of stew for her dinner and then could hardly get a bite down her tightly constricted throat, even though it was a delicious concoction of lean beef and vegetables. When was her father going to realize that she was a grown woman? she wondered. She was thirty years old and certainly intelligent enough to make her own career decisions.

This was really the final straw, she thought, exhaling a sorrowful sigh. She would start looking for her own place, and when she left this house she would also leave her father's. He had gone too far this time. As for Bram, he had made it clear as glass what he thought of her, the big jerk. He didn't like her and wasn't at all happy that she was the nurse sent by Dr. Hall. What was the word he'd used so insultingly? Oh, yes—*keen*. He wasn't *keen* on her staying in his house.

Well, she wasn't particularly keen on Bram Colton anymore, either.

They moved as shadows around each other, never eating together, barely speaking, and when they did, only about Gloria. Jenna felt empty, as though something crucial to life itself had vanished. At the same time she knew that reaction was utterly ridiculous. She'd never *had* Bram, so how could she *not* have him now?

On Thursday morning, after Bram left for work, Roberta Shane arrived. She was the relief nurse and would care for

Mrs. Colton on Thursdays so Jenna could have a day off. Roberta was around fifty, Jenna estimated, and had been in nursing all of her adult life. Rumor had it that Roberta had been very attractive when she married Jake Shane in her early twenties, but Jake had been a lazy good-for-nothing, and after supporting the bum for over twenty years, Roberta had kicked him out. She'd come out of the divorce a bitter, unsmiling, overweight woman with grown kids who had moved away and rarely came back to Black Arrow to see her. She was an excellent nurse, as far as the mechanics of the profession went, but she didn't even try to hide her contempt for the human race, and very few patients warmed to her.

Jenna turned over Gloria's chart to Roberta with a worried frown. Roberta would not have been her choice of relief nurses. Gloria wasn't responding to much of anything, and Jenna did everything with kindness and smiles. The small gains Jenna *had* made—whether real or in her imagination—could be wiped out by one unsympathetic person. Jenna sighed quietly; she had to rely on Dr. Hall's judgment.

Dr. Hall had phoned yesterday, and Jenna had given him a verbal report on Gloria's progress—or in this case, lack of progress. The doctor had told her he would be out to see Gloria and check her over sometime during the coming weekend.

At any rate, Jenna hated leaving her patient in anyone else's care, but especially Roberta's. But there were things Jenna needed to do, and a day off was necessary. She'd had friends bring her car to Bram's place within a day of her own arrival, so she had transportation. But when she got in her bright red sedan today and drove away, that frown of worry over Roberta Shane being the relief nurse was still furrowing her brow.

Jenna had to be back by eight that evening. Roberta

never took home-care cases that entailed twenty-four-hour duty, and she'd made it clear that twelve hours was her limit. Jenna had told her to relax, that she would definitely be back by eight, if not sooner.

"Make sure you are," Roberta had said coolly.

Truth was, Jenna didn't like leaving Gloria for long, anyway. She had started trying to teach Gloria simple facial exercises that would strengthen the muscles needed for speech, though most of the time Gloria simply looked away and closed her eyes.

Every evening after work Bram sat in Gloria's room and talked to her. Jenna wondered if he got more response from his grandmother than she did, but since she and Bram were hardly speaking themselves, and certainly avoiding all eye contact, she hadn't intruded on his time with Gloria to see what went on during those sessions.

The other Coltons were in and out all the time, at least during the day, and Jenna *did* hover and listen and watch for signs that Gloria even cared that they were there. Willow seemed to spark something in Gloria's eyes, Jenna noticed, and instinct—or practical experience—told her that Bram probably did the same. But there was no question in Jenna's mind that Gloria could not be more despondent. Jenna had seen it before, where the victim of stroke or some other destructive malady had lost his or her will to live. No matter how often Jenna or some other nurse or doctor explained the power of proper diet, rest and exercise, the patient simply faded away. Jenna could see it happening with Gloria, and she planned to visit Dr. Hall today and talk to him about it.

Bram got home around six that afternoon and was surprised to see Jenna's red sedan gone and a dark green one parked in his driveway. Concerned and curious, he didn't stop to pet Nellie, but hurriedly walked to the house. He let Nellie come in with him, then told her to stay. The collie obeyed and lay down near the door while Bram strode directly to the master bedroom.

At once he saw the strange woman sitting in the rocking chair and knitting. "Where's Jenna?" he asked.

"It's her day off. I'm Roberta Shane. I'll be working relief while she's here."

"You're a nurse, too?"

Roberta looked indignant. "Of course I'm a nurse."

"Sorry, but why didn't Dr. Hall send you here instead of Jenna in the first place?"

Roberta put down her knitting. "Because I don't take full-time cases like this. Not many nurses do."

"Oh." Wondering why Jenna Elliot, golden girl, would take a demanding case like this, Bram went over to the bed and smiled down at his grandmother. "Hello, Gran. How're you doing?"

"Sheriff, she's never going to answer you, you know," Roberta said.

The cruel comment angered Bram, and he turned hard eyes on the relief nurse. "Don't you ever say something like that in her presence again."

Roberta looked affronted, but she didn't say another word. Bram didn't care if she was affronted or not. Thank God that Dr. Hall *hadn't* sent a cold woman like her to care for Gran, he thought as he headed to his own room.

"Come on, Nellie," he said as he passed the pretty collie, who happily got up to follow her master. In his bedroom, Bram felt the sting of anger, and he almost went back to Gran's room to tell Roberta Shane to never set foot in his house again.

But Jenna had to have time off, and maybe Roberta was the only nurse available to take her place.

"Damn, damn, damn," Bram mumbled thickly as he removed his badge from his shirt and then took off his leathers, including his holstered gun, and put everything in a dresser drawer. He hated what had happened to Gran and he didn't like how out of control his life was now. Out of *his* control. He was a man with a penchant for routine and organization, great traits for a law enforcement officer to have. But those same traits made unexpected bumps in one's personal life tough to take.

He wondered when Jenna would be back. Tonight? Tomorrow morning? Clenching his teeth, he sat on the edge of his bed and thought about her. No man deserved to suffer the way he did over Jenna. Just her image in his mind made him so saturated with longing that even his bones hurt. He hadn't been sleeping well, just because she was in the house. He never ate at home anymore because he might have to eat with her, and he couldn't bear the thought. How much more of this torment could he take?

Jenna arrived at seven-thirty. She walked into the master suite, immediately went into the bathroom to wash her hands and then returned to say hello to Bram and Roberta. The relief nurse had already gathered her knitting bag and her purse.

She left after saying, "See you next Thursday."

Jenna let her find her own way out, and picked up Gloria's chart to make sure Roberta had done everything that was necessary that day.

Bram had gotten to his feet and he stood there wishing Jenna would look at him.

She finally did. "May we speak in another room?" she asked.

Surprised, and wondering what was going on now, Bram nodded, then followed Jenna to the living room. She turned and faced him.

"I talked to Dr. Hall today. We are both concerned with Gloria's lack of progress. I'm rarely blunt when discussing a patient with a family member, but in this case I feel I must be. She's not trying to help herself, Bram. She has given up.''

Bram flinched as though struck. "How dare you—"

Jenna cut him off harshly. "Don't start something you can't finish! Are you trained to recognize dangerous symptoms? Well, I am, and if we can't change her attitude she will die.''

Bram's voice was unsteady when he spoke. "How…how do we change her attitude?"

Jenna turned away and began pacing the carpet. "I've racked my brain trying to think of something to do that isn't already being done. She has a loving family, and some of them visit her every single day. I'm doing everything medically possible—everything Dr. Hall told me to do—and I'm sure she must appreciate all the time you spend with her every evening. Bram, she's never alone, except for brief moments like this. She can't possibly feel neglected. Her diet is restricted, of course. There are many things she might never be able to eat again, but are certain foods really that important? Plus, she absolutely will not concentrate on the exercises I've been trying to teach her. She just turns her head and shuts her eyes whenever I even mention exercise. I've been massaging the muscles of her arms and legs to keep them supple, but…''

"In other words, you're doing everything you can and nothing is working," Bram said dully.

Jenna's eyes misted and she could only nod. "I'm so sorry," she whispered huskily. She wasn't looking at Bram, so she didn't see him walk away. But she heard his footsteps, and when she turned around, he was gone.

A few minutes later she returned to Gloria's room, and there was Bram, telling corny jokes to his grandmother and chuckling over them himself.

All Jenna could think was that maybe laughter was the only medicine they hadn't yet tried, and maybe it would work. She mentally patted Bram on the back for his willingness to do anything to save Gloria from herself.

Jenna deliberately slept lightly, keeping attuned to her patient's slightest movement or sound. Even in a semi-slumber, though, she dreamed, and she had a nightmare around midnight that was so frightening that she jumped out of bed. Grabbing her robe, and taking a quick peek at Gloria to make sure she was asleep, Jenna left the bedroom and went to the kitchen.

Still shaken by the nightmare, she switched on lights and made a cup of cocoa, using a mix and the microwave. She was about to sit at the table to drink the cocoa when Bram walked in.

He stopped cold. The kitchen light had been on and he'd thought nothing of it, but seeing Jenna at the table was a shock he had trouble concealing. His mind grew fuzzy for a moment; he should turn around and get out of there while he could, he realized vaguely. But then he recovered some dignity. This was his house, after all, and Jenna was the intruder in this room, not him. He managed to say, albeit a bit thickly, "I can't sleep, either." He began preparing a cup of cocoa for himself.

Jenna watched his every movement with a heated sensation in the pit of her stomach. He had been so diligent about avoiding being alone with her that this unplanned midnight meeting felt like a tryst. Probably not to him, she told herself, but then he wasn't burdened with bittersweet longings the way she was.

She drank in the sight of him. He had pulled on his jeans, but that was the only clothing on his marvelously masculine body. His chest was smooth and hairless, his shoulders wide and muscular. He hadn't buttoned the waistband of his jeans, merely zipped the fly, and he was barefoot. His thick black hair, normally so neatly brushed, was tousled and looked so sexy to Jenna that she could barely swallow small sips of her cocoa.

With his cup in the microwave, Bram clenched his jaw and looked at Jenna. He could hardly pretend she wasn't there, after all. "I know why I'm having trouble sleeping, but she's my grandmother. Does every patient in your care cause you insomnia?"

My God, is he actually going to talk to me? Jenna was so surprised she nearly choked on a swallow of cocoa. She managed to answer him, though. "I was sleeping. A nightmare woke me."

The microwave went off and Bram took his cup to the table and sat across from her. Bram Colton joining her for midnight cocoa surprised Jenna so much that she wasn't sure how to deal with it.

"Tell me about your nightmare," Bram said after taking a cautious swallow of his hot drink. That was an innocent enough topic, he thought, even though he knew that he should have taken his cocoa back to his bedroom rather than risk even a few minutes in Jenna's company.

Jenna tried not to stare at this half-naked man whom she'd so often fantasized about having in her bed. But he was seated only a few feet away—all that darkly tanned skin, and that handsome face.

She dropped her eyes to her cup. "It's not worth talking about."

"But it scared you awake."

"Well, yes. That's what nightmares usually do. Don't you have nightmares?"

"Everyone does." Bram raised his cup to his lips and took in the truly glorious sight of Jenna Elliot sitting across from him at his very own table, with her golden hair loose and disarrayed around her beautiful face. Her robe was blue and he could see the neckline of a white gown beneath that. But it was very easy to envision her lush body under the gown. *That's the real reason you stayed in here instead of running back to your room the second you saw her—just to soak up the sight of her. Admit it!*

"Were monsters chasing you?" he asked as nonchalantly as he could manage.

"Monsters?" Jenna couldn't help smiling, and decided that he really must be curious about her nightmare, which was curious in itself. So why not tell him about it? At least they were talking, which just might qualify as a small miracle. "I guess there could have been monsters, but I don't recall seeing any. I was in a strange place—a rural setting—and I was walking down a dirt road. There were a few trees and I was wearing a red dress. Now, that's odd," she interjected thoughtfully. "I hardly ever wear red, and I don't even own a red dress." She paused for a swallow of cocoa.

"Anyhow, I could see a hill ahead of me and I began walking up it. It became steeper and steeper until I was clutching at the ground with my hands to keep from falling." She looked at Bram. "That's it."

"What scared you about that?"

"The fear of falling, I guess."

"Sounds to me like you might be afraid of reaching the pinnacle of something you've been trying to attain."

Jenna felt a wave of heat wash through her. *He* was the pinnacle, if there was any accuracy in his interpretation.

"When did you become an interpreter of dreams?" she asked pertly.

He grinned, surprising Jenna and melting her bones at the same time. Lord, he was handsome when he wasn't scowling! "Learned it at my great-granddaddy's knee," he said.

"George WhiteBear taught you how to read dreams?"

"Did you ever meet him?"

"No, but Willow's talked about him. His age is incredible."

"Ninety-seven is pretty incredible, all right. He says he will live to be a hundred and five. I can't doubt it."

"Does he still live alone and take care of himself?"

"He does." Bram frowned suddenly. "I expected Gran to have a long and healthy life, too. That stroke was a shock."

"For the whole family, apparently." Jenna couldn't believe it. They were actually having a normal conversation.

"I've got to drive out to George's place and tell him about Gran," Bram said, sounding as though he were talking more to himself than to Jenna.

"He doesn't know?"

"I didn't want to alarm him without cause. After what you told me earlier tonight, I think I'd better go out there very soon. I'm sure he'll want to see Gran."

Jenna's heart sank. "And what I said to you tonight is the reason you're not able to sleep. Do you understand that I only said what was necessary?"

"I don't understand a damn thing. She was always a live wire. What causes a stroke, anyhow? Why was she struck down like that?"

"Would you like me to explain the medical causes of strokes?"

"No." Bram turned his head, reminding Jenna of Gloria both from the action and from their physical similarities. "Hearing a bunch of medical terms I probably wouldn't comprehend isn't going to make me accept Gran's affliction. She doesn't deserve what she's going through, Jenna."

"I know she doesn't," Jenna said quietly, although a part of her rejoiced that her name had rolled off his tongue as though he said it all the time. She lifted her eyes and met his, and for the first time ever she thought she saw something personal gleaming in their black depths. Her pulse rate quickened, and when he suddenly looked away again her breath stopped as though trapped in her throat.

To alleviate the sensation she got up and brought her cup to the sink. She heard Bram getting up, too, and then felt him behind her.

"Just forming a line to rinse my cup," he said.

But he was standing a lot closer to her than he had to, and again Jenna couldn't breathe normally. "I—I'll only...be a minute," she stammered. "Give me your cup. I can take care of it and you can go back to, uh, bed."

He reached around her and put his cup in the sink in front of her, and she felt his long muscular body against her back.

"Jenna," he whispered, and placed his hands on the counter on each side of her. Her mind could hardly digest what was happening. He had never, ever touched her, not once, and now his entire body was pressed against hers and his arms were virtually enclosing her within a very sensual circle.

She didn't think, just reacted. Dropping her cup in the sink, she swung around, at the same moment raising her arms to his neck. She leaned into him and his arms tightened around her. She turned her face up and silently begged for his kiss, and he didn't disappoint her. His lips touched hers gingerly, then, in the next heartbeat, almost roughly. It was her fantasy come true, or at least the beginning of it.

She opened her mouth under his and kissed him back with all the desire she'd kept bottled up for so long. She knew she would do anything he wanted; all he had to do to get everything he could possibly want from a woman was to keep on holding her and kissing her.

She moved against him, an involuntary action caused by total surrender to Bram's will. She felt his hands moving on her back, up and down, and finally stopping on her bottom. The groan she heard deep in his throat as he cupped her buttocks excited her further, and she brought her hands down from his neck to explore his chest. More than his chest was hard, though, and that was the most exciting thing of all. He wanted her. He couldn't hide his desire or pretend it didn't exist, not when the proof of his feelings pressed into her abdomen. She was so thrilled and elated that she mumbled between kisses, "Wait…wait. Let me get out of some of these clothes."

He inched away from her and watched her shed the robe and let it drop to the floor around her feet. His black eyes devoured the sight of her in a rather sheer white nightgown with tiny straps, standing in front of him with all that long, golden hair draped over her shoulders.

"You are the most beautiful woman in the world," he said raggedly.

"Oh, Bram, do you have any idea how beautiful *you* are?" she whispered. And then fear gripped her, for something in what she'd said caused him to begin withdrawing before her very eyes.

He touched her cheek gently. "We can't do this."

She had no shame, not now, not when they'd been so close to something meaningful. "Why not?" she whispered.

"I think you know why not."

Jenna cleared her throat. She couldn't let this happen. Bram had crossed the line tonight and she couldn't stand the thought of him retreating behind it again.

"Because of my dad's attitude?" she said in a stronger voice. "Bram, you must ignore him. Prove you're the bigger and better man by overlooking his ignorance."

"How does anyone in Black Arrow overlook Carl Elliot?" Bram took a backward step, and Jenna quickly moved forward, wrapped her arms around his waist and laid her cheek on his chest. "Don't do this, Jenna," he said huskily. "I was afraid of this happening the second I saw you getting out of the ambulance. I want you to stay and care for Gran...you *are* the best nurse in town...but you and I can never be anything but speaking acquaintances." He grasped her arms and moved away from her. After one more yearning look at her beautiful face, he spun on his heel and walked out.

Jenna was devastated. He'd broken her heart, this time for real, for he'd given her just enough of himself to also give her a glimpse of paradise. Then he'd yanked it all away and told her it would never happen again. With tears burning her eyes, she pulled on her robe and dragged herself back to her lonely twin bed in Gloria's room.

Jenna thought she would cry her eyes red, but instead she stared at the ceiling and accepted the painful knowledge that she'd responded to Bram with the same fervor with which a starving person devoured food. She felt like a fool, a woman with no will of her own. She would never forgive herself for behaving like a tart, nor would she forgive Bram for treating her as one. He'd kissed and touched her intimately, and she would feel his hands on her body for the rest of her life. Damn him! She turned to her side and the tears finally came, and she wept quietly into her pillow until she finally fell asleep.

Bram never did go back to sleep. An immutable fact nearly drove him crazy: he could have made love to Jenna, his beautiful golden girl, in his own kitchen, and he'd turned her down. Dear God, he could have brought her to his bed and made love with her. The many places in his house where they could have made love haunted him, until he finally gave up on sleep and threw back the covers.

He was dressed and on his way to his great-grandfather's place before dawn broke.

Chapter Four

Traffic was light and Bram's thoughts naturally turned to Jenna while he drove. He despised himself for making that pass. He'd gone way past the line he'd drawn between himself and Jenna, and he knew he was going to pay a heavy penalty for acting without thinking, because nothing about that kiss had been ordinary. In fact, he was positive that what had occurred in his kitchen was one of those life-altering events that befell a person every so often. In its own way, that embrace was as destructive to his peace of mind as his grandmother's stroke. He actually gritted his teeth from mental anguish.

Out of self-preservation, his thoughts segued from Jenna to the Colton Ranch, and the contentment living there gave him. It had been home since his birth, and occasionally he thought of talking to his siblings about buying everyone out so it belonged only to him. And yet no one ever interfered with his use of the place, or gave him unwanted and unneeded advice simply because he or she owned as much of the land as he did.

He remembered growing up happy in a loud and boisterous household, with parents who laughed a lot and openly adored their five children. He thought of his brothers and sister, each one of them, and suffered again the agony of learning that their parents had been killed in a plane crash. It had been a terrible time, and he'd had to downplay his own shock and grief to comfort the others.

All in all, though, his life had gone relatively smoothly. He'd learned to live with grief and an ache for a woman he couldn't have, but it was funny that he had rarely thought of his Indian blood until falling for Jenna. There were so many mixed marriages and relationships between Native Americans and whites that most of the population in and around Black Arrow paid scant attention to ancestry. There were a few pure whites, like Carl Elliot—or so they claimed—and there were also a few pure Comanches, like his great-grandfather.

But George WhiteBear was the only pure-blooded Indian in the family. And he was one of the handful of Comanches who proudly clung to the old ways, to teachings handed down from generation to generation. It was George who had educated his offspring and *their* offspring in Comanche history. Bram remembered most of what he'd been taught.

The Comanche, like the Arapaho, Blackfeet, Cheyenne and Sioux, were considered Plains Indians. In the old days sign language permitted different tribes to communicate, and George had even shown his progeny some of the signs. George also boasted about the Comanches' amazing horseback-riding abilities and their ferocity in battle. Then there was the subject of counting coup—the act of touching a live enemy and getting away from him—which brought great honor to the brave warrior who managed that feat. That had always fascinated young Bram.

But then George would speak in a quieter voice, a sad monotone, about the Comanche people being forced onto the reservation in Oklahoma in 1867. "The government developed what might be called a conscience in the early 1900s and gave each Comanche still living—not many by then—160 acres of land. Many did not like farming, and sold or leased their land to whites. My father kept his and it is still my home," the old man declared.

But the stories Bram had always liked best were about the traditional vision quest that was so important to most of the Plains Indians, as their religion centered on spiritual power. Everyone had to find his personal guardian spirit, and would go off alone with a little food and water to search for it. George WhiteBear had stayed alone in the wilderness for eight days and nights, and then he'd heard coyotes communicating with each other all around him. One had entered the circle of light from his campfire and looked directly at him with eyes glowing amber from the fire, and it was at that moment that George had known that the coyote was his guardian spirit. To this day, George listened to the cries and calls of coyotes and knew what they were saying to him.

Sometimes, when life became more drudging than satisfying, Bram would cynically wonder if he should undress down to a breechcloth, find some wilderness and look for *his* personal guardian spirit. But he was more white than Comanche, if not by blood then by lifestyle, and he wondered if he would have a successful vision quest. After all, he'd been raised almost as white as Carl Elliot had raised Jenna, with a few notable exceptions, of course, mostly brought about by Great-grandfather George WhiteBear.

The sun was just beginning to bathe the landscape in a peachy-orange light when Bram reached the turnoff from

the highway that led to George's acreage. It was a dirt
road with a row of power poles along the side, accom-
modating George and Annie McCrary. Annie had become
widowed only two short years after she and her husband,
Ralph, bought their land. Annie and George weren't bosom
buddies, by any means, although Annie acted as if she
wished she were. She kept an eye on her neighbor and
dropped by George's place about once a week with something from her garden—fresh or canned—as an excuse to
check on him.

Annie's place was farther down the dusty washboard of
a road than George's, and Bram didn't anticipate seeing
her today. He felt sure George would want a ride to town
to see his daughter, which meant an immediate return trip
to Black Arrow.

Reaching the small wood house that was almost as old
as his granddad, Bram braked to a stop, turned off the
ignition and instantly felt the silence prickle the fine hairs
on the back of his neck. George's old pickup was parked
in its usual place, rusting away since the day George had
quit driving—at the stern advice of the police—after causing another fender bender. Everything about his great-
grandfather's place looked normal, but instinct told Bram
it wasn't.

For one thing, George had three mongrel dogs that normally rushed any visitor, barking up a storm. The noise
they made was their only contribution to guarding the
place, for they usually wriggled with pleasure when anyone came, and they had never chased off anything bigger
than a gopher.

There was no sign of the trio today. That unnerved
Bram. Frowning darkly, he got out of his SUV and walked
to the front door. He turned the knob and wasn't at all
surprised to find the door not locked, as he couldn't re-

member a time when any door or window of this house *had* been locked. "Granddad?" he called. "George?"

There wasn't a sound. Bram's uneasiness grew, and he hurriedly walked through the house, checking each room. George's possessions were simple and few, and he liked things neat and tidy. His bed was made and Bram could not detect anything out of place. And yet he knew, he *sensed,* that something was *very* out of place. What it was wasn't visible; nothing jumped out at Bram. But he didn't believe for a second that the old man had merely taken his three pets for an early-morning stroll. For one thing, George's daily walks these days were pretty much conducted close to the house, close enough that he or the dogs would have heard Bram arrive.

With his heart in his throat and suddenly beating anxiously, Bram went back outside and walked around the house, shouting every few moments, "Granddad? George?"

Nothing but the rustling of cottonwood leaves and the clucking of hens from George's fenced chicken coop could be heard. Bram made a run for the coop, opened the wire gate and entered the enclosure. He checked the nests of George's five chickens and found that each contained eggs. George had been gone for days! Bram's concern intensified tenfold.

He left the chickens to themselves, then stood halfway between house and coop and pondered the situation. Sometimes George rode to town with Annie, but not at such an early hour and never with the dogs. Still, it wasn't an impossibility.

Hurrying back to his SUV, Bram climbed in, started the engine and drove from George's yard with his tires kicking up gravel and dirt. He was alarmed and couldn't pretend otherwise. George was always home, unless some of the family drove out and hauled him to one house or another for a holiday dinner or get-together. No one in the Colton family was doing any celebrating these days. They were all too concerned about Gran's health to plan any festivities, and besides, Bram had put out the word that he would be the one to come out here and tell George WhiteBear about his daughter's stroke.

Bram turned left instead of right on the dirt road and in minutes was at Annie McCrary's little ranch. She heard his arrival and came out of the barn to greet him.

"Morning, Bram. You're out early," she called. She was a pudgy little woman with a warm, friendly face. She wore dresses to town, but on her ranch she favored bib overalls, and that was what she was wearing this morning.

"Morning, Annie. I've been to Granddad's place and he's not there. Have you seen him recently?"

Annie thought for a moment. "Four, five days ago, I believe it was. I brought over some onions and radishes from my garden, and also a quart of my canned peaches. He loves my peaches."

"And he seemed all right?"

"He seemed just fine. Would you like to come in and have a cup of coffee? I made a pot not too long ago. It should still be good."

Bram nodded. "Thanks, I'd love some coffee."

They went into Annie's house, and Bram sat at the kitchen table while Annie poured two cups of coffee.

"I can see the worry on your face," she said, joining him at the table. "George probably just went somewhere with one of your brothers or cousins."

"The dogs are gone, too, and the nests in the coop have at least three days' eggs in them."

Annie frowned. "Well, that's odd. I would have gone over and gathered the eggs if he had told me he was going to be gone. And where on earth would he go that he could take the dogs with him?"

"That's the answer I'm searching for, Annie. Did he say anything…? Let me rephrase that. What did the two of you talk about when you brought him the peaches?"

"Well, let me see." After a moment Annie's eyes lit up. "We talked about coyotes."

Bram's stomach sank. George didn't make small talk about his spiritual guardian. Annie wouldn't know it, she couldn't possible have known it, but George had been imparting seriously important information.

"Annie, try to remember exactly what he said about coyotes."

"Goodness, Bram, you sound just like a cop grilling a suspect," Annie teased.

Bram took a breath. "Sorry, Annie. Would you mind telling me as much as you can remember about that conversation?"

"Of course I wouldn't mind. I was only teasing you. Now, let me see. I gave him the little cardboard box with the things I'd brought over, and he said 'Thank you, Annie,' as he always does and then asked if I'd like to sit a spell. He offered a glass of lemonade and I accepted, and when he brought it outside, we sat on the bench under that big tree in his front yard to drink it. I asked him how he was feeling, which now that I think about it, was unusual. But he didn't look a hundred percent that day. Not that he looked ill—don't let me worry you on that point. But he looked like something was bothering him. And that was when he started talking about coyotes. I was rather surprised, I remember, because I hadn't seen or even heard a coyote in quite a while. Actually, I do believe he said the same thing, so I really don't know why the subject even came up."

"Are you sure he said he hadn't seen or heard a coyote's cry in quite a while?" Bram persisted.

"Very sure."

Bram slumped back against his chair. "There's the problem."

Annie laughed. "Surely you're not saying he *wants* coyotes skulking about his place."

"Annie, he's very dedicated to Comanche traditions, and when he was a mere boy he left the family home and went in search of his personal guardian spirit. All young Comanches went on vision quests—it was a rite of passage and necessary to their spiritual growth. Granddad connected with a courageous young coyote, and he claims to this day to understand their language. Their cries."

"Goodness," Annie murmured. "Bram, is that your belief, too?"

"Not for myself, Annie, but I can't doubt it for Granddad. He's predicted or explained too many events based on his guardian spirit's messages for me to doubt his beliefs. The last time we discussed it, his personal guardian had most recently taken the form of a big male coyote with a silver-tipped, dark gray coat. If that big fellow isn't around anymore, or if the whole pack moved on, then Granddad is without his spiritual guardian and feeling lost."

With a grim expression on his face, Bram got to his feet. "He took his dogs and went looking for his guardian spirit."

Annie rose, looking aghast. "He's wandering around looking for a coyote? Bram, that's crazy. A man his age?"

"No, Annie, it's not crazy, not to a Comanche. But you're right about one thing. At his age he shouldn't be wandering around alone. Damn, so many questions! Which direction did he go? How far did he get in four, five days? Does he have enough food and water with him?

"He did this before, about ten, twelve years ago. I was worried sick about him then, and he was only in his eighties. Now he's almost a hundred. Annie, thanks for the

coffee and information. I've got to be on my way. I've got
to do something.''

Bram hurried out, with Annie following and trying to
keep up with his long stride. "What will you do, Bram?"

"I don't know, but I can't just do nothing." Bram
climbed into his SUV. "Bye, Annie."

He drove away with his mind racing a hundred miles
per hour. He turned into George's driveway again, hopped
out of his vehicle and ran to the house. This time he
searched for scraps of paper, something, anything, that
George might have written a note on saying in which direction he and his dogs were going in search of that silver-
coated coyote.

There was nothing.

But Bram didn't give up, he couldn't, and he went back
outside and slowly circled the house with his eyes on the
ground. Close to the house, the grass was too trampled for
him to find any clues. But as his circles became larger and
larger, he finally found footprints and paw prints heading
southeast. The direction made sense to Bram, for about ten
miles southeast there was a forest of cottonwoods, syca-
mores and elms along a creek. That would provide the old
man with shelter and water, although Bram hoped he had
taken water with him and wouldn't drink from the creek.
It wasn't certain the water was polluted, but he felt that
people his great-granddaddy's age shouldn't take chances
like that.

Bram returned to his vehicle, got in and drove home to
his own ranch, deciding what to put in his backpack for a
ten-mile hike and possibly an overnight sleep-out. Of
course, he'd have George's stubbornness to contend with,
that was certain, and if the old man wasn't ready to go
home, Bram knew he couldn't force him. But what if he'd
taken a fall during that long trek, or gotten ill and was in
dire need of help? Bram *had* to find him.

He went into his house and saw the door of the master suite closed. Recalling Jenna's rule, but wondering if maybe she'd shut the door just to avoid seeing him, he sat at the kitchen table and used the telephone to call the sheriff's station.

Sergeant Lester Moore was the day's duty officer, and Bram asked if anything was going on that required his attention.

"That insurance investigator is in town, Bram. He came in and introduced himself, then went over to the courthouse. He said he wants to talk to you."

"Hell," Bram muttered.

"Something wrong, Bram?"

"I don't know. There could be. I was going to find out for sure, but now... I guess I can take the time to go by the courthouse. What's his name?"

"Just a sec, I've got his card here.... It's Robert Kirby. He said to call him Bob."

"Okay, I'll go and talk to him, but then everything's in your hands, Lester. I'm going to be out of touch for the rest of the day and possibly tomorrow."

"What the heck's going on? You on the trail of that arsonist or something?"

"Wish I were, but it's something else. Just hold down the fort, okay?" Bram could tell that he'd aroused Lester's curiosity, but except for family, this really was no one's business. "Did Bolling's report come in yet?" The state fire inspector's written report might be of some assistance to the insurance adjuster's investigation, Bram figured.

"Not yet."

"Okay. I'll probably see you late tomorrow afternoon." Hoping that was going to be the case, Bram hung up, and was getting to his feet when Jenna walked in with an armload of bed linen and towels.

"Good morning," she said, and went on through the kitchen to the laundry room.

Bram swallowed hard and mumbled, "Mornin'." Just the sight of her had always made him a little crazy, and now that he knew what kissing and holding her felt like, his former torment was small potatoes compared to what he felt now. If he had deliberately set out to inflict unbearable emotional torture upon himself he could not have done a better job. What on God's green earth had made him behave so heedlessly last night?

Jenna's hands shook as she put the bedding and towels in the washer. She'd been busy with Gloria and hadn't heard Bram come home. Walking into the kitchen and seeing him like that, without any warning whatsoever, had been a shock to her system, which wasn't functioning all that well to begin with. Where had he gone so early? Not work, for he wasn't in uniform. And why *hadn't* he gone to work? Why was he back home again? What if...what if he made another pass? What if he'd thought it over and decided that he shouldn't have been so hasty last night? Maybe he wished now that he hadn't put the brakes on during that runaway kissing session, and maybe he'd like her to know that.

With the washer running, Jenna returned to the kitchen, expecting to see Bram again. But the room was vacant, and an overwhelming disappointment instantly destroyed all of the foolish hopes she'd formed while taking care of the laundry.

Sighing heavily, and reaching for the composure that she always found so readily with anyone else—with *everyone* else—Jenna headed back to Gloria's room. But Bram was in there. The door was open and Jenna could see him sitting on the bed next to his grandmother. He was holding her hand and talking to her, and tears suddenly filled Jenna's eyes, emotional tears from seeing Bram's love of his grandmother so clearly. If only he could love *her* like that, Jenna thought sadly.

Why had he never married? She'd heard very few stories about Bram and women. Whatever he did in his private life must be conducted very discreetly, for she'd never heard any gossip being bandied about. For the most part, Sheriff Bram Colton was liked and respected by the community, with the most prominent exception being Jenna's own father.

It was a bitter pill for her to swallow. And there was nothing she could do to change Bram's attitude toward her, either. If she knew anything at all about him, it was that his stubbornness was as deeply ingrained as her dad's. Neither man would ever admit it, but they were very much alike in that regard, and apparently the women they knew either had to take them as they were or leave them be. But as sensible as banishing Bram from her heart and mind would be, Jenna wasn't sure she could do it. More to the point, she wasn't sure of *how* to do it.

She recalled something she'd read years ago about "a choice of difficulties," and the term seemed to fit her present situation so well that it remained in her mind as she watched Bram and Gloria. It was when Gloria closed her eyes and turned her face away from her grandson that Bram did something that brought tears to Jenna's eyes. He looked at his grandmother for several seconds, then covered his own eyes with his left hand. The line of his slumped shoulders and back conveyed grief and defeat, and Jenna's heart reached out to him.

She didn't stop to think, merely reacted, hurrying into the bedroom and putting her hand on Bram's shoulder. It was meant to comfort him, nothing more, to let him know she understood how bad he felt. She hadn't expected a simple gesture to startle him so. He practically leaped to his feet and, in the next instant, without a word, strode from the room. Dismayed, Jenna followed.

"I didn't mean to offend you," she said to his retreating back, speaking rather sharply.

He stopped and turned to face her. "You didn't offend me. I've just got a lot on my mind and didn't expect what you did."

"You looked ready to fold and I guess I was offering sympathy."

He knew he was staring, undoubtedly an embarrassment for her, but he couldn't stop doing it. If there was a more beautiful face to be found in Oklahoma, he had missed it. Jenna's deep blue eyes, so heavily fringed with long lashes, and her full lips and flawless complexion all had a hypnotic effect on him. As many times as he'd run across this golden girl in years past, he had never had an opportunity to fill his eyes and soul with her beauty. And now, while he looked and studied and memorized, his fingers itched to release her hair from its clasp, and his blood began moving faster throughout his body.

He had things to do that shouldn't be put off. Great-granddad could be in danger, and Bram knew he should have already filled his backpack and started back to George's place to begin a search for the old man. Then there was the insurance inspector, Bob Kirby, to see before he left town. And God knew his heart was heavy with fears for his grandmother. Yes, he had a lot on his mind.

But still he stood there with Jenna, and felt things he had no business feeling, while thinking thoughts he had no right to think.

Jenna suddenly found breathing darned near impossible. Her heart was racing because of what she was seeing in Bram's black eyes. He wasn't any more immune to her than she was to him, and that pass last night hadn't been an unexpected urge coming out of nowhere for him! He'd been feeling for her the same things she'd been feeling for him, and he had fought against any kind of relationship between them because of his Comanche blood.

She moistened her lips with the tip of her tongue and said, "Bram, darling, I do believe that I'm reading your mind."

"Jenna," he said in a hoarse, tortured voice. "Don't do this to me." Whirling, he rushed away, heading for his bedroom to get his backpack from the closet.

She stayed right behind him. "Don't do what, Bram?"

"Don't come into my bedroom, for one thing," he growled.

"I'm already in." She shut the door and leaned against it. "You're scared of me."

He gave a short, sharp laugh. "How'd you guess?" Bram went into the closet and came out with a good-size backpack.

"I always thought you were afraid of nothing," Jenna said.

"Guess you were wrong, huh?" He took two pairs of socks from a bureau drawer and put them in the pack.

Jenna wondered what he was doing, but didn't want to veer from the subject at hand.

"Are you afraid of every woman you're sexually attracted to, or am I a special case?" she asked.

Bram nearly choked. "You're pressing your luck, Jenna. I think you'd better leave. Gran probably needs you."

"She's resting and *doesn't* need me. But you do. I didn't know what to think last night, but I know now."

Bram narrowed his eyes on her. "Do you understand what you're saying?"

"I believe I'm saying yes. What does it sound like to you?"

Bram placed the backpack on the bureau and then stood

looking at Jenna. "You're making a big mistake," he said raggedly.

"Maybe," she admitted in a husky voice, and began walking toward him. "But let me be the judge of that, all right? You judge your mistakes and I'll judge mine. An addendum to that remark is that I do not consider it a mistake to make love with the man I've wanted since I was old enough to want a man." She put her hands on his chest and slowly slid them upward to lock together behind his head. "Are you going to do anything about this, or are you going to tell me again that we can't do it?"

He didn't have time to make love. That is, he shouldn't *take* the time to make love. But he couldn't stop himself, and he cradled the back of her head in his big hand, brought her closer with his other hand and then covered her mouth with his. It was a long, wet, hungry kiss for both of them. And they writhed against each other without one single sign of inhibition or objection. They had, it seemed, reached an understanding.

They managed to get undressed and over to the bed without letting go of each other. And then she was on her back and he was on top of her. He needed her immediately, and to appease his conscience he told himself that the next time they did this he would take all the time she needed and do all the things he should have done before the big step.

But he'd wanted her for too long to go slow this first time, and he was so driven to possess her that he rode her hard and fast. He came within minutes, and he could hardly believe Jenna's cries of release at almost exactly the same moment as his own.

Totally drained of all strength, he collapsed with his face buried in the pillow and her mass of golden hair.

Chapter Five

Bram raised his head and looked into Jenna's eyes. She smiled softly, touched his cheek and whispered, "That was beautiful, Bram. So very beautiful."

He studied the emotion in her eyes and the beauty of her face, her glorious hair pooling on the pillow, and his own head swam with foolish thoughts, such as wanting to hold his golden girl to his heart throughout eternity. He wanted to agree with her perception of their intimacy, to go even further and tell her that making love with her had been the most beautiful, most meaningful experience of his life.

But the reality of what they had just done was too severe to soften with pretty words, and he couldn't act as though everything was great when it wasn't. He'd committed an unpardonable sin against Comanche pride—seduced the daughter of a man who looked down on him—and not for a second could Bram doubt that he'd pay for it in some painful way.

He pulled away from Jenna and got off the bed. Hearing her gasp of surprise and forcing himself to ignore it, he began getting dressed.

Jenna sat up, became suddenly embarrassed at her nudity, and pulled the edge of the bedspread up to her neck. Why wouldn't Bram look at her? Talk to her? She didn't know what to think or do. His stony expression chipped at her pride and made her heart ache. But then suddenly, unexpectedly, anger entered the equation. How dare Bram make passionate love to her and then act as though it hadn't happened? No man had the right to treat a woman like that.

"Obviously you were hit by some sort of ridiculous remorse," she said in a voice that was icy enough to put frost on the furniture. "It's not as though you stole my virginity when I wasn't looking, you know. You're certainly not the first man I've slept with." She hoped that insensitive reminder would make him wonder how many men had come before him, as she wanted desperately to hurt him as he'd hurt her. But when she saw him wince, she felt no satisfaction. In fact, she felt like toppling over on the bed, burying her face in a pillow and crying her eyes out.

But she would die before crying in front of him. He'd just destroyed any privilege he might have had to learn the secrets of her heart.

Dressed except for his boots, Bram sat on the one chair in the room to pull them on. "Just so you know," he said, speaking without emotion or inflection, "I'll be gone until late tomorrow. At least till then, I should have said, and possibly longer, though I'm planning to be back by then. I just thought you should know because of Gran."

His flat, unreadable voice, so guarded, so distant, added insult to injury for Jenna. "Heaven forbid that you'd tell me something because you thought *I* should know it," she snapped.

The bitter sarcasm in her voice shook Bram. He took a chance and looked at her, and exactly as he'd feared would happen if he made eye contact, his entire system came alive again from the memory of their lovemaking. He could easily get up from this chair, undress again, go over to the bed and make love to her a second time, only this time slowly, doing all of the things he'd omitted in his haste to have her the first time.

Jenna's breath caught in her throat. The way he was looking at her...

But then, abruptly, he yanked on his second boot and got to his feet. "I'll be out of touch all night," he growled. "If you need anything, call Willow or any other Colton you can get hold of." He went to the closet for some shirts and jeans, which he stuffed in his backpack. Then he walked out.

Jenna chewed on her bottom lip and fought tears for a few minutes, then, furiously aflame with resentment, she got off Bram's bed. After a peek beyond the door to make sure the house wasn't full of Coltons, she gathered her clothes and made a dash for the bathroom.

In the kitchen Bram was trying to clear his head enough to use the remaining space in the backpack for food. The pack finally contained a variety of foodstuffs that wouldn't spoil without refrigeration, and Bram began filling two canteens with tap water.

He kept cursing himself for stupidity, for having so little control over his libido. Of course, Jenna wasn't just any woman, but there was an enormous wall between them, and trying to hurdle it with sex was just plain ludicrous. Not that he was doing any laughing. What he'd done wasn't even remotely funny or amusing, it was *crazy!*

Muttering curses under his breath, Bram gathered up his

things and left the kitchen. He could see down the hall into
the master bedroom, and Jenna was there with his grandmother. Saying goodbye to either one of them was senseless. Jenna would probably give him a dirty look for his
effort and Gran probably wouldn't even grasp that he was
going somewhere.

Heaving a massive sigh, he left the house. From there
he drove directly to the courthouse. He would try to keep
the meeting with Bob Kirby short so he could be on his
way back to George's place. How much time had he
wasted with Jenna?

Bram angrily slapped the steering wheel. How could he
even think that those remarkable few minutes with her
were wasted time? In fact, she should be steaming mad
that he'd gone so fast. He'd been much too hot and anxious
to go slowly, and he sure as hell hadn't expected her to
keep up with him.

Unless she'd faked her orgasm…?

But no, he would bet his life that her response had been
genuine. Which just might mean that she *did* sleep around
and he hadn't heard about it. After all, she'd made sure he
knew that he wasn't the first guy to hit the target. Maybe
she was a woman who needed sex on a regular basis, and
with her living with him, so to speak, he was the handiest
man around.

Grimacing, Bram mumbled another curse as he turned
onto the main avenue and wondered despondently if those
few minutes on his bed were going to tweak his conscience
for the rest of his life. Considering that Jenna had resided
in the back of his mind for years now, and that he had
finally gotten his hands—and much more—on her, he suspected that he was doomed to suffer at least until he was
too old to give a damn about the opposite sex.

Bram parked the car and walked into the courthouse.
The burned areas were cordoned off with yellow tape and

Keep Out signs, while it was business as usual in the un-
damaged sections of the building. Bram ducked under a
long strand of the yellow crime-scene tape and called,
"Mr. Kirby?"

"In here." A young man with sandy hair and wire-
rimmed glasses came from another scorched room. He was
carrying an impressive-looking camera and wearing cov-
eralls—smudged and soiled—over his clothing. "What
can I do for you?" he asked in a friendly way.

"I'm Sheriff Colton."

"Oh, guess I thought you'd be in uniform, like the deputies I talked to at the station." Kirby offered his hand.
"Nice meeting you."

"Same here. Lester said you wanted to see me about
something."

Kirby looked thoughtful for a moment, then nodded.
"This fire is particularly disturbing. Ever since Inspector
Bolling proved it was arson, the question of why anyone
would want to destroy a fine old building like this one has
nagged at me. Do you have any leads on the case?"

"That question is nagging everyone in the county, other
than the arsonist, whoever he or she is," Bram replied
grimly. "We have a few leads, but I'm sorry to say they're
not very solid. I'll tell you right now, Mr. Kirby, that there
have been some peculiar things going on around Black
Arrow for the past few months, and this fire was one of
them."

"Call me Bob."

Bram took a second look at Kirby and realized how
young he was. He could be thirty, but certainly no older.
The insurance adjuster was closer to Jenna's age than his
own, Bram realized, and for some reason the seven-year
difference in his and Jenna's ages suddenly seemed like
one more reason to stay away from her.

That conclusion caused a weakening sensation to wash

over Bram, as though the last of the air in his own personal
balloon had just been squeezed out. This was one of those
days when the weight of too many burdens was almost
more than he could carry on his broad shoulders and still
stay on his feet. He'd been spreading himself too thin, and
it was catching up with him. Knowing what was happening
didn't alter the situation. He had Gran to care for, his great-
grandfather wandering in the hills only God knew where,
and a weirdo—possibly a couple of weirdos—running
loose in *his* jurisdiction, setting fires, breaking into the
newspaper office and asking questions about the Colton
family that made no sense at all. And they were clever
weirdos, because Bram kept hearing about them nosing
around town, here and there, but had never once seen them
himself. And neither had any of his deputies. What in hell
were they—ghosts or specters that could appear and disappear at will?

On top of that mystery, which might be comical if no
physical damage had been done, he'd been neglecting the
training of his horses. Hell, he'd barely taken the time
lately to make sure the trickle of water constantly running
into their drinking trough from an outdoor spigot hadn't
clogged, and to scatter good alfalfa hay in their pasture so
their diet didn't consist entirely of green grass.

And then there was Jenna. God, what was he going to
do about Jenna? Bram ran his hand down his own face, a
weary gesture that would have told Bob Kirby, if he knew
him better, that the sheriff was reaching a dangerously explosive stage.

But ignorance was sometimes more appropriate to a situation than knowledge, and Kirby explained, "I've been
taking photos of everything in the burned rooms."

"For appraisal purposes?" Bram asked, calming his
nearly shattered nerves through sheer willpower.

"Precisely. But it's really sad. Furniture, woodwork,

paneling and flooring can all be replaced, but the contents of the burned rooms are gone forever. I can tell that some of the books on those wall shelves over there were really old. Things like that are priceless.''

Bram didn't enjoy standing there and lamenting lost causes. Yes, some of those books had been very old records of births, deaths, marriages and land ownership, and yes, historians would probably have deemed them priceless. But they were charred and curled and gone now, and he would do his utmost to bring the arsonist to justice. He was about to tell Kirby goodbye and good luck when the insurance adjuster spoke again.

''In that lower cabinet in the far corner are some things that weren't destroyed. I think you should take a look at them,'' Bob Kirby said.

Keeping a lid on the impatience badgering him, Bram followed Kirby to the cabinet. It was constructed of heavy metal and its dark green paint had bubbled and burned, but the cabinet wasn't destroyed as the wood fixtures had been. Kirby bent down and pulled open the door.

''The books in here are still intact,'' he said.

''And what are they?''

''Older than both of us combined and undoubtedly valuable. This is only a suggestion, but if I were you I would either appoint someone to get them out of here or take them myself. Put them someplace safe until the repairs are made in here, or maybe they should be in a museum.''

''They're that old?'' Bram hunkered down in front of the metal cabinet and carefully took out one of the large books with smoke-seared hardboard covers. He handled it gently and opened it to read notations dated in the early 1900s. ''This *is* old.''

''There are two others,'' Kirby said. ''I suspect that no one working in these rooms had reason to unlock this cabinet for a good many years. It's possible there wasn't even a key anymore. Yes, Sheriff, it definitely was locked. I had to photograph the contents, if there were any, so I pried it open.''

Bram didn't waste any time on a making a decision. "I'll take them out to my rig. You're right, they should be put in a safe place.''

"I'll give you a hand.''

Together the two men carried the heavy old books out to Bram's vehicle. Bram said, "I really appreciate this, Bob, and so will the other residents of Comanche County. Thanks for your help. I have to be going now, but I'm sure we'll run into each other again.''

"Possibly. I should finish up here by tonight, but if not, then I'll still be snapping photos in the morning. Drop by if you have a few minutes. We could have coffee together.''

Bram didn't want to explain what he would be doing for the rest of today and probably all day tomorrow, so he merely said, "Thanks, I'll do that if I can.''

He covered the books with one of the blankets he kept in the back of his SUV, then got into the driver's seat and drove away. Almost at once he forgot his cargo and began concentrating on finding his great-grandfather.

And praying to God that some mishap hadn't befallen the old man.

Jenna could call Bram "rat" and "snake" in her own mind, and she did, but she was still consumed with curiosity over his backpack. He was going to be gone all night and most of tomorrow, according to what he'd grudgingly told her. But what in heaven's name was he going to be doing that would require him taking food, water and a sleeping bag with him? Was this law enforcement or personal business?

Trying with all her might to eradicate everything she'd

ever known, thought or dreamed about Bram Colton from
her brain, she brought a bottle of lotion to Gloria's bed
and began massaging the weakened muscles of the elderly
woman's legs.

"We really must get you up and walking more often,
Gloria," Jenna said gently. "Your family loves you so
much, and wouldn't you enjoy feeling strong and able
again? Please don't give up. Help me to help you."

Gloria merely watched her with dull eyes, and Jenna's
heart sank. But she couldn't accept Gloria's lethargic lack
of interest in her own recovery as though it didn't matter.
It *did* matter, not just because Jenna was a nurse and dedicated to doing the very best she could for any patient, but
because Gloria was so very important to the Coltons. Important to Bram. How could she, Jenna, care so much for
Bram and permit his grandmother to waste away before
their very eyes?

Realizing that she had just admitted how much Bram
meant to her caused tears to gather in Jenna's eyes and her
heartbeat to quicken. Only minutes ago she had decided to
hate him forever, and in little more than the blink of an
eye she *cared* for him? What in heaven's name was wrong
with her? Bram had used her—with her own damn help—
and she *cared* for him?

If she had half a brain she would phone Dr. Hall and
ask him to find another nurse to care for Gloria. Biting her
lip to keep from crying again, Jenna continued to massage
her patient's arms and legs. She felt as helpless as Gloria
truly was, Jenna thought sadly. She wasn't physically dis-
abled like Gloria, but emotionally she didn't have the
strength of a gnat. Not where Bram was concerned. Was
she doomed to suffer indignities of this nature ad infinitum
because her father and Bram were at opposite ends of a
tiresome, pointless spectrum?

Jenna could tell that her hands were trembling, though

she managed to keep them functioning and doing their job. She felt shaky internally, as well. This thing with Bram was far more serious than anything she could have imagined before the episode in his bedroom. If an acceptable replacement nurse magically materialized this very minute and she could leave this house forever, she would still shiver and quake every time she thought of Bram Colton.

Sighing hopelessly, Jenna got up from her perch on the edge of Gloria's bed and went into the bathroom to wash her hands.

It hurt terribly to recognize and admit her own weaknesses, which when added up really constituted only one catastrophic flaw: feelings for a man who would use her sexually but never even consider anything more between them. Even with that hanging over her head, though, Jenna knew she would not be phoning Dr. Hall about a replacement nurse anytime soon.

One thing was certain, however. If some course of action occurred to her that would make Bram suffer even a fraction of her torment, she would carry it out in a New York minute.

He didn't care how badly he hurt her, did he? Well, he just might find out that her once soft heart had hardened to pure granite.

In the meantime she was going to do her utmost to incite and stir Gloria's desire to live. It really was the only thing that would halt or at least slow her downhill slide.

Bram turned onto the familiar dirt road leading to George's place, feeling anxious to get started on his search for the old man. Bram had confidence in his tracking ability, which, in this case, was amplified by the fact that George had taken his three rowdy dogs on his own search for his guardian spirit. Those mutts would leave all sorts

of signs for a tracker, and since George had no reason for
stealth in his hike, he, too, would leave signs.

So Bram's scope of confidence also included finding his
great-grandfather rather quickly. His main concern was
that the old guy might have taken a fall. George
WhiteBear's tall, lean, straight body and barely lined
face—not unusual in older Native Americans—gave
strangers a false impression. He looked much younger than
he was, and it was often hard for Bram to believe George
had lived for almost a century.

But the truth was that George WhiteBear *was* elderly,
and a hell of a lot more fragile than he'd been during
Bram's adoring childhood years. A hard fall could easily
break brittle bones, and he could be lying out there suffering. Bram prayed that wasn't the case, but it was a possibility he couldn't erase from his mind.

He drove as fast as he dared on the washboard road,
and he was about half a mile from his great-grandfather's
place when he saw a plume of dust ahead, created by an
oncoming vehicle. Annie must be on her way somewhere,
he thought, and then frowned, because Annie's pickup
truck was red and what he was catching sight of
was…white!

"My God, it's Granddad's old truck!" he exclaimed out
loud. Had someone stolen it? To Bram's knowledge it
hadn't been driven or even started in years. But with
George gone so long, a thief could have tinkered with the
engine, poured gas into the tank and just driven it away.
Whoever he was, he was going to be one very surprised
car thief when he was stopped by the county sheriff!

Bram turned the steering wheel of his big SUV and
parked it crosswise on the road, effectively setting up a
roadblock. He took the gun he always carried under the
seat and got out, tucking the weapon into the back waistband of his jeans. Then he waited and watched his poor

old great-grandfather's stolen truck, a truck George still valued highly even though he couldn't drive it, coming closer.

It was moving slowly, Bram realized with an angry scowl. Unusually slowly, in fact. Of course, the thief had probably spotted the makeshift roadblock and was trying to figure out a way around it.

"There *is* no way around it, jerk," Bram mumbled. "This is it, the only route to the highway, and you're going to the lockup. Count on it."

The pickup kept coming at the same snail's pace, and as it got closer Bram could see the form of the driver through the windshield. Then it was closer still and Bram could see details—long hair, black hat...long *gray* hair and black hat. "My God, it's Granddad!" Bram exclaimed, too shocked to do anything but stare.

George stopped the truck and he, too, stared—straight ahead, with not even a glance at his great-grandson. Bram nervously cleared his throat and walked over to the opened window on the driver's side.

"Uh, where are you going, Granddad?" he asked.

"Did your car break down across the road?" George asked.

"My car's fine. I parked it that way to stop...well, when I saw this truck I thought someone had stolen it."

"Why would I steal my own truck?" George still wouldn't look at Bram, and Bram was catching on that the old man was angry with him, angrier in fact than Bram had ever seen him.

"I had no idea you still drove. I thought a stranger...a thief...had taken your truck."

"As you can see, *I* took my truck. I suppose now you're going to arrest me for driving without a license."

"Granddad, I would never arrest you for anything."

"You're the sheriff, aren't you? I'm breaking the law, aren't I? Go ahead and get out the handcuffs."

"Granddad!"

"If you're not going to haul me to jail in handcuffs, please move your car so I can be on my way."

Bram flinched internally. He owed this old man, the eldest member of the Colton family, the highest, most sincere respect he could muster. And truly Bram did respect his great-grandfather. He always had. But this whole thing was trying Bram's patience, which had already been pushed pretty much to the limit today. He drew a calming breath, or one that he hoped would steady his nerves.

"On your way where, Granddad?"

"You didn't tell me which one of my family is dying, so I'm not sure I should be telling you anything," George said.

Bram exploded. "Dying! Where in hell did you get that idea?"

For the first time George turned his head and looked at his great-grandson. "Are you speaking to me?"

"I'm sorry, but today has just about done me in. Listen, I came by your place early this morning and you weren't there. I talked to Annie and figured out you had gone looking for coyotes, your guardian spirit. I went back to my place to get a backpack, food and water, and here I am again, all set to hike the hills and look for you. Instead, here you come down the road in this old truck, which I didn't even know still ran."

"Why wouldn't it still run? It's a fine truck."

"That's beside the point. Granddad, would you please turn this fine truck around and drive it back to your place? I will take you wherever it is you want to go. Besides, I have something to tell you. It's the reason I came out here this morning."

"Oh, you were finally going to tell me who in my family is dying?"

"No one is dying!"

"Either you don't know about it or think *I* don't know about it." George put the truck in reverse and stepped on the gas. The pickup shot backward, swerved to the left and ended up in the ditch.

Bram ran after it, suddenly scared to death. He breathed freely again only when he saw George getting out of the cab, apparently uninjured.

George called, "That old truck has more power than I remembered." He calmly walked to Bram's SUV and got in.

Bram looked at the old truck in the ditch and then back to his great-grandfather, now sitting calmly in Bram's rig. Shaking his head, he walked over to his SUV and got in.

"I take it you want to leave your pickup in the ditch for now?" he said to George.

"It's a good place to park it."

"Fine." Bram started the engine, then decided to get the worst of this meeting over with. While he drove he glanced at his great-grandfather and felt a swelling of love in his chest. "Granddad, it's Gran. She had a stroke."

George didn't respond for a long moment, then said sadly, "Gloria, my dear child. I will outlive my daughter."

"She isn't dying, Granddad."

"Not today, but soon," the old man said.

Bram knew arguing was futile. Besides, he wasn't so sure himself that Gran wasn't dying. She wasn't even close to being the grandmother he had adored all of his life. She had no sparkle, no life in her eyes, no laughter just waiting to erupt, and she displayed no will at all to recover and return to even a semblance of her former self.

"Where were you going?" Bram asked quietly.

"To town. Didn't I already tell you that?"

"Maybe you did, but where in town?"

"The feed store. Since no one bothered to tell me who had fallen ill, I decided to find out for myself."

Bram drove in silence for a while, then brought up the subject that he knew was on his great-grandfather's mind. "Apparently you located your guardian spirit."

"I did," George confirmed.

"And he conveyed the message of illness in the family."

"Death in the family," George corrected.

A chill went up Bram's spine. George's premonitions, wherever he got them from, were usually much too accurate to ignore.

"Something quite unusual occurred when I finally found coyote," George said then, surprising Bram, for his great-grandfather seldom detailed meetings with his guardian spirit. "He wasn't alone. He brought fox with him, and she was a golden fox, so beautiful to behold that my eyes watered."

Bram recalled stories of fox, raven, bear, coyote and other animals that represented guardian spirits, heard many times in his youth. This was the very first time Great-granddad had actually seen fox, and Bram couldn't remember ever hearing about a golden fox.

"Does fox's color have significance?" Bram asked.

"I believe it does, although I haven't yet deciphered it," George replied. "Is Gloria in the hospital?"

"She was. I had her brought to my place when the doctor said she could receive home care. She has a full-time nurse."

"Then we are going to your place now?"

"Yes, Granddad," Bram said with a catch in his voice. As sad and difficult as seeing Gran in bed and helpless was for him and the rest of the family, it was going to be doubly so for her father. "I'm sorry I didn't tell you sooner," he added softly. "But when it first happened the doctors weren't certain of the severity of her condition, and I saw no sense in worrying you unnecessarily. I can see now that I should have told you right away."

"Yes, you should have."

They finally reached the ranch, and Bram was relieved to see Jenna's car parked in its usual spot. In the back of his mind he'd worried that she might arrange for a different nurse and leave because of this morning. He wanted her to care for Gran, true, but he also just plain wanted her, and he suffered over a dilemma that he feared he would never be able to solve.

After parking near the house, he got out and walked around the front of his vehicle to offer assistance to his aged great-grandfather. But when Bram reached that side of the SUV, he was already standing on the ground and required no assistance.

Together the two men walked to the house. Jenna knew the sound of Bram's SUV by now, and her heart actually skipped a beat when she heard it arrive. Obviously his plans had changed, she thought nervously, because she hadn't been worried about seeing him until tomorrow.

She was in Gloria's room, where she had every right to be, and so she stood her ground and prepared herself to face Bram with a stiff upper lip and a challenge in her eyes that just dared him to say something rude to her.

She was taken completely by surprise when she saw the tall, dignified older man with Bram.

"Jenna, this is George WhiteBear, my great-grandfather," Bram said without quite meeting her eyes.

But George turned *his* dark eyes on Jenna, and she smiled at him. He was a wonderful-looking old man, and she liked him on sight. So what if his great-grandson was the jerk of the century?

"Hello," she said. "I'm very honored to meet you."

George stared for a long moment, then said softly, "The golden fox."

Bram heard him distinctly, and Jenna thought she did. But when she left the two men alone with Gloria, she frowned and decided she couldn't possibly have understood what George WhiteBear had really said. After all, why would he say something to her about a golden fox?

That was just too bizarre.

Chapter Six

Brewing a pot of tea in the kitchen, Jenna's thoughts kept returning to her introduction to George WhiteBear. If he *had* said "the golden fox," which was what his words had sounded like to her, what would it mean? Surely he wasn't using the word *fox* in the same context some men did when referring to an attractive woman. That dignified old gentlemen? No, she couldn't believe George WhiteBear would talk that way behind a woman's back, let alone to her face.

His remark could have had something to do with her blond hair, she mused. Maybe she had heard the word *golden* correctly and misunderstood the others. Maybe he admired light-colored hair and had complimented her.

Still pondering the incident, which seemed rather mysterious to her, Jenna poured tea from the pot into a cup and then carried the cup to the table. Sitting down, she sipped her hot tea and listened to the unintelligible rumble of male voices coming from Gloria's room.

Jenna actually prayed that a visit from her father would lift Gloria's spirits. Maybe he was the one person Gloria had longed to see all this time.

Sighing, knowing she was merely engaging in wishful thinking, Jenna found her thoughts going back to the morning and the urgency with which Bram had made love to her. It was a memorable event, however she looked at it. Even though he'd retreated into that rude shell of his practically the second it was over, being in his arms, his bed, having him naked and holding her, having him inside her and joined in the most intimate act possible between a man and a woman, was something she would cherish forever.

Emotionally she was in Bram's bed again when he walked into the kitchen and said, "Oh, there you are."

Jenna's cheeks got warm because of where her thoughts had taken her, but she cleared her throat and did her best to look composed. "Yes, here I am," she said.

Bram looked rather uncomfortable. "Listen," he said, "don't pay any mind to Granddad's remark."

"What remark?" Jenna asked, becoming strangely positive, in light of Bram's discomfort, that she had heard George WhiteBear correctly.

"He only said one thing to you when I introduced him," Bram said, speaking more sharply than he'd intended, to cover his embarrassment over having to talk to Jenna about a Comanche ritual she couldn't possibly comprehend.

Obviously this was really bothering him, Jenna realized. Very well, she thought. She would stop pretending she didn't know what he was talking about.

"Yes, he said only one thing," she said calmly. "What did it mean? How should I take it?"

"I could talk about it for three days and you still wouldn't grasp its meaning."

Jenna's blood began boiling. "Why not? Did my brain

suddenly disintegrate? Or maybe you just see 'stupid' written across my forehead.''

Bram's dark skin became even darker as embarrassment flooded his system. "I've never thought of you as stupid. If you got that impression from what I said, then I'm sorry.''

"Fine. Since we both agree I'm not stupid, tell me what your great-grandfather meant when he said 'the golden fox.' Those were his exact words, I believe.''

"Jenna, it's a Comanche…uh, thing. You really wouldn't understand, and that doesn't make you stupid.''

Jenna held her cup to her lips and glared at him while she took a swallow of tea. "It makes me white, doesn't it?''

"We are what we are. Neither of us can change that.''

"I wonder if you would if you could. Don't you enjoy being part Comanche so that you can strut around in your sheriff's uniform and rub it in to people like my dad?''

"I don't strut and you're deliberately twisting the situation to taunt me. Remember one thing, Jenna. Your dad could have me fired if he took the notion.''

Jenna scoffed. "My dad's not your boss.''

"He has powerful friends in high places, and if he pulled the right strings, believe me, I wouldn't be sheriff for long.''

Jenna frowned. Was that true or just another of Bram's ruses to keep the two of them apart? He'd had her this morning, and if that was enough for him…? Jenna had to swallow hard to keep from breaking down before Bram's eyes, which would destroy every speck of pride she possessed. She picked up her cup and realized it was empty. Rising, she walked over to the counter where she'd left the pot, and brought it to the table.

Bram watched her every move. Her grace had a hypnotic effect on him, and he knew he was staring, but couldn't seem to break the spell.

Jenna sat again, refilled her cup, then looked at him. "What?"

Bram fought his way back to reality and mumbled, "I have to go out and see to the horses. If Granddad wants anything, I would appreciate your telling him that I won't be long." Before Jenna could do more than nod, he hurried from the room.

Again Jenna heaved a sigh. Bram was the most discombobulating man she'd ever known. It wouldn't have killed him to explain what George had meant with that golden-fox remark. And if she hadn't completely understood its Comanche meaning, so what?

And yet, despite Bram Colton's many faults, she was crazy about him.

"Oh, no," she moaned, for that was the first time she'd admitted her feelings in such a down-to-earth way.

A tear seeped from the corner of her eye. How could she be crazy about a guy who believed heart and soul that they lived on opposite sides of a fence?

After a few minutes of silent suffering, Jenna got up and went to a window to catch a glimpse of Bram down at the pasture with his horses and Nellie. But neither Nellie nor Bram was anywhere in sight and, wondering what else Bram might be doing outside, Jenna went to another window, this one overlooking the driveway. Sure enough, there he was, fiddling with something through the opened back door of his SUV. Nellie was there, too, sitting as close to Bram's boots as she could get.

Jenna sipped her tea and speculated on what he might have in his SUV that required so much attention. His back-pack, which he obviously hadn't used, was a possibility, but why on earth didn't he just bring it in the house and unload it?

Bram was wondering what to do with the three old books he'd taken from the courthouse for safekeeping. Actually, he'd forgotten about them until he'd left the house a few minutes ago to tend the horses. Now, looking at them, he frowned and pondered their worth. Maybe they had no value at all, beyond their age, which didn't necessarily make them of any use to anyone.

Turning around, Bram sat on the downed tailgate of his SUV to think about the books. Bob Kirby thought the three heavy old things might be valuable to historians, so Bram figured he should take that into account. After all, the man was an appraiser of all sorts of goods, wasn't he?

From the window, Jenna watched Bram sitting there motionless. Was he thinking? she wondered. Maybe about them? Remembering the morning? Reliving their kisses and their passionate lovemaking, as she'd done again and again throughout the day? Had this morning meant something to him, after all, and he'd merely been pretending it didn't?

Her body began tingling when she thought of him naked. She wanted him again with a surprising desperation. If only they were alone, she thought. She would knock on the window and motion for him to come in, and when he did, she would meet him at the door, kiss every inch of his incredible body and—and…

Her fantasy evaporated and her eyes widened when she saw him get off the tailgate, turn around, reach inside the SUV and come out with a blanket-wrapped bundle. From the way he was holding it, she guessed the blanket concealed something heavy.

With Nellie on his heels, Bram began walking to the house. After only a few steps he heard a car and looked to see who was coming. His brother Jared drove up and got out with a grin.

"Hey," Jared called.

"Hey," Bram said. "I've got to get this inside."

"Need some help?"

"No, I've got it. Just open the door for me."

"What're you carrying in that blanket?"

"Three old books from the courthouse records room that miraculously escaped the fire. The insurance appraiser recommended they be put someplace safe for the time being. Today's been nuts, Jared. Granddad's inside with Gran, and I forgot about the books until just a few minutes ago. Anyhow, I'm going to store them in my bedroom for now and figure out what to do with them when I have more time. Where's Kerry and Peggy?"

"They're at Kerry's mom's. We've got company, some of Kerry's family. I stole away before dinner to check on Gran. How's she doing?"

"Not good, Jared." They were on the front porch, and even though burdened with the old books, Bram stopped to talk a minute before they went in. "I'm really worried about her now. Granddad's guardian spirit told him about a death in the family. It's a long story, but that's the gist of it. Plus, you gotta hear this before we go in. When I was getting close to his place this afternoon with the express purpose of telling him about Gran, I saw his pickup coming down that dirt road. I thought someone had stolen it, and prepared myself to arrest the thief. But it was Granddad driving again, heading for town and madder than hell that no one had told him who in the family was dying."

"Has he ever been wrong in his predictions?" Jared asked somberly.

"Not that I can remember. Sometimes they're hard to figure out, but what he said today was clear as glass."

"Well, let's not panic," Jared said. "Wasn't his last prediction before this one about you? Something about your not hiding behind your heritage, and listening for the coyote's cry that would change your life?''

"Now that one *is* tough to figure.''

"I haven't given it a lot of thought, but you have to wonder if it isn't something simple and we just don't see it,'' Jared said. "Oh, well, have any of us kids ever *really* understood our great-grandfather?''

"I thought so. Are you saying you never did?''

"Hell, I don't know what I'm saying. Ready to go inside? That looks really heavy.''

"It is.'' Jared opened the door and Bram went in first. "Thanks.''

Jared saw Jenna and said, "Hello, Jenna.''

"Hi, Jared. Isn't Kerry with you?''

"No, I came alone this time.''

"Did you know your great-grandfather was here?''

"No,'' Jared replied, and Jenna saw the strangest look come over his face. "But something told me I should come here.'' Jared tried to grin, but it came off pretty feeble, Jenna noticed. "A psychic message, maybe?'' he said in an attempt to joke about his unexpected visit.

Jenna noted that Bram had gone immediately to his bedroom, and when he came back he no longer carried the bulky bundle.

"Well, I'm going to go say hello to Granddad and Gran,'' Jared said, and walked away.

Jenna ignored Bram and went into the living room and sat down. Much to her surprise, he followed her.

"What is it?'' she asked, thinking that he must need something from her. Certainly he hadn't followed just to be in the same room with her.

"I wanted to, uh, say something.''

He looked embarrassed again, Jenna saw, which made her wonder what his next words of advice would be, since telling her to ignore what George had said upon their introduction still made no sense to her. "Go ahead and say it," she said with some caution.

"I just wanted to, uh, thank you for sticking around. I mean, after, uh, this morning, I wondered if you would still be here when I got back."

"After this morning," Jenna repeated quietly. "So you actually remember this morning?"

Bram's spine stiffened. His thanks had been genuine and heartfelt, and she should have known that and not started to pick a fight about this morning.

"I remember it," he said flatly.

"Astonishing," she retorted. "I never would have guessed."

"Jenna, damn it, you know how things stand for each of us. Why can't you accept the facts of our lives?"

"Because your interpretation of the facts of our lives is totally ridiculous," she snapped much too loudly. Instantly she calmed herself. "I'm sorry. I don't yell at people and I certainly wouldn't want your family hearing me screeching like a fishwife. But I'm so opposed to your biased point of view no matter *who* spouts it that it's difficult to maintain my equilibrium. My hold on sanity," she mumbled as a frustrated afterthought.

"My interpretation of the facts of our lives is realistic," Bram said through gritted teeth. "You live in a damn fairy tale, where all the little princes and princesses are white and given everything money can buy. Lady, that ain't life in Black Arrow! Grow up and smell the coffee."

Jenna jumped to her feet. "My mother's death was a fairy tale? My father's intolerance is a fairy tale? You insensitive clod, my life was no easier than yours was. At least you had a large loving family to kiss your bruises every time you fell down!"

"I don't intend to fight with you."

"Well, you're doing a damned good imitation of it."

"You have one quick trigger finger, lady, which I don't mind telling you I never would have believed about you before this." Bram turned and began heading for the door.

"What did you think I was, a doormat for men to wipe their feet on? I stand up for myself because there's no one else to do it for me. Unlike you, you jerk, who has more protective relatives than he can count!"

Jenna stared at the empty doorway that Bram had just gone through. Then she slumped down on the sofa and wished the earth would just open up and swallow her whole.

After a while she told herself to try to remember that he had expressed thanks for her staying to care for Gloria, considering the way he'd treated her this morning.

That was what he had thanked her for, wasn't it?

She was still sitting in a forlorn heap on the sofa when Jared came in. Quickly pulling herself together, she got to her feet.

"No need to see me out, Jenna," he said. "I have to get to my mother-in-law's for dinner."

"Yes, it is getting close to the dinner hour. Jared, help me out, would you? Should I ask your great-grandfather if he wants to eat dinner here or should I just go ahead and prepare something?"

"Don't do either, Jenna. He won't stay."

"He won't? Are you saying he never eats with any of his family?"

"No, of course not. He enjoys holiday get-togethers as much as any of us do, but he's already in mourning. He will want to go to his own home, most likely within the hour. And part of his ritual for the dying is a special diet."

Stunned, Jenna gasped out loud. "He isn't mourning Gloria, is he?"

"I'm afraid so."

"But why? She's—she's..." Jenna's voice trembled

and faded to nothing, for she herself was deeply concerned about Gloria's frail condition.

"Jenna, Granddad knows things before the rest of us do. There's so much to it that I doubt I could make you understand how I know that. But from early childhood all of his grandkids knew that Granddad was special and different from everyone else, even from our parents."

Jenna couldn't doubt Jared's sincerity, and she appreciated his talking to her like an adult, an equal. Bram never quite did that. Of course, there was a lot more baggage between her and Bram than there was between her and Jared.

Tears filled her eyes. "If Gloria is truly that bad off, should I have her taken to the hospital, Jared?"

"Please, no. You're taking excellent care of her and I believe she likes you."

"How can you tell?" Jenna asked sadly.

"We all can tell. Leave her here, Jenna. She's better off."

"I...I know how much you all love her," Jenna whispered.

"Yes, we do."

"Is your great-grandfather in an agony of grief over it?"

"Granddad accepts death as he does life."

"But you said he's already in mourning."

"It's not the same as...Jenna, I hesitate to say white people, but that's what it amounts to. Granddad knows Gran's time is short, and he's been chanting softly in the Comanche language. He will not weep or carry on. He will carry sadness in his heart for a while, but outsiders will not know it. Privately he will carry out some very old rituals, and if we bury Gran in the Black Arrow Cemetery, he will not attend the funeral."

"Because...?"

"Because she will not have undergone the rituals of

death practiced by Comanches for centuries. Jenna, I really have to go. Talk to Bram. He can answer your questions as well as I can.''

She walked him to the front door. ''Thank you, Jared,'' she said quietly.

''You're welcome. See you soon.''

Jenna closed the door behind him just as Bram raced from Gloria's bedroom. ''Did Jared leave?'' he asked.

''Just now, yes.'' Jenna moved aside, as she could tell Bram wanted to go outside. Apparently he had something to say to his brother before Jared drove away.

Jenna liked the Colton family very much, and she could never deny how strongly Bram affected her. But for the first time in her thirty years of life in Black Arrow she grasped, at least vaguely, the many differences between herself and the Native Americans of the area. Obviously people such as her father could not deal with anything different from their own plodding path through life. How sad, she thought, feeling sorry for her dad instead of condemning his pitifully narrow point of view, as she usually did.

Outside, Bram talked with Jared through the driver's open window of his car. ''He wants to go home. I wish he would stay, at least for tonight. Maybe if you talked to him?''

''Bram, it wouldn't do any good. He has to do what he has to do. You know that. It's never been any other way. Damn it, man, you look like you're carrying the weight of the world on your shoulders. You should have let Uncle Thomas take Gran to his house.''

Bram shook his head. ''No, I wouldn't have rested a single moment if she was somewhere else. I'll get through this, same as everyone else.''

''Well, it's true the whole family is feeling the same pain,'' Jared said quietly. ''We're all lucky to have Jenna

Elliot on our team. She's an especially nice person, along with being an exceptionally good and caring nurse. Don't you agree?'' When Bram looked away and avoided his eyes Jared added, ''Hey, something's going on between you two, isn't it?''

Bram put one hand on the roof of his brother's car and let his head drop forward. ''She drives me crazy,'' he finally said.

''But in a good way?''

''A good way? Is there *anything* good about insanity?''

''Oh, come on. She's a stunning lady, and if you're smitten and she's not objecting, you should be thanking your lucky stars. Tell me if this is none of my business, but have you made love to her?''

''It's none of your business.''

Jared chuckled. ''That's what I thought you'd say. Well, good luck, big brother.''

''Oh, there's one other thing. Granddad said that when he found coyote, his guardian spirit, it wasn't alone. There was also a golden fox, and then when he met Jenna he said plain as day, 'the golden fox.' Jared, if I hadn't already been half-crazy before that, it would have done the trick all by itself.''

Jared let out a whoop of laughter. ''Looks to me like love and wedding bells are closing in on you, bro. Accept your fate. Go with the flow. Jenna's not only bright and intelligent, she's a beauty. How could you do any better?''

''The flow, you pitiful excuse for a comedian, leads directly to Carl Elliot. Would you want him for *your* father-in-law?''

Jared's expression sobered. ''Sorry for joking around. No, I wouldn't want Carl Elliot for a father-in-law. Bram, I gotta get moving. I promised Kerry to be back in time for dinner, and they're probably all getting ready to sit down as we speak. Catch you later, okay?''

Bram stepped back from the car and waved his brother off. Watching Jared's vehicle disappear down the road, he wished he hadn't told him about Jenna, and George's "golden fox" reference. His love life really *was* no one else's business, not even his brother's.

"Love life?" he muttered under his breath as he started back to the house. Was that what he should call the mess he was making of things between himself and Jenna—a love life?

Remembering his horses at the last minute, Bram whirled away from the house and walked at a fast pace down to the barns and pasture. "Go get 'em, Nellie," he said, and off the collie went, diving under the bottom rail of the fence and running hell-bent for the huddle of horses on the other side of the pasture.

Bram went into the barn and brought out a bale of hay. After cutting the strapping on it, he lifted it over the fence, then entered the compound and spread the hay with a pitchfork. He checked the water trough and spigot, and then reached down to pat Nellie, for she had brought in the horses and they were all eating hay.

"Good girl," Bram said to his collie.

He returned to the house, and this time let Nellie come in with him. He had no more than closed the door behind him when his great-grandfather shuffled out of Gloria's room and announced, "I'm ready to go home."

Bram didn't waste his breath in issuing an invitation to stay overnight, because he knew there wasn't a snowball's chance in hell of George WhiteBear veering from Comanche ritual at a time like this. Bram merely nodded, opened the door again and let his great-grandfather go out first. Catching sight of Jenna from the corner of his eye, he sent her a glance and said, "I'm going to drive Granddad home."

"Take that vicious dog with you," Jenna said, wide-eyed.

"Nellie? She wouldn't hurt a flea."

"Then why did you tell me to give her a wide berth?"

"I honestly don't know. To tell you the truth, Jenna, I honestly don't know much of anything these days. See you in about an hour."

He got George settled in his SUV and began the drive.

"I did not expect to meet the golden fox so soon," George said when they were away from Bram's house and on the highway. "These things usually take more time. Sometimes years."

"Yes, Granddad," Bram agreed, simply to sidestep a debate or argument. He really didn't want to discuss Jenna with his great-grandfather, especially since George believed heart and soul that he had just met the human form of the magical golden fox he'd encountered during the renewal of his original vision quest.

"But we must always be prepared for the unexpected," George said stoically.

"That's true."

"Even a golden fox could be sly enough to sneak up on a man."

"You're right."

"But Jenna didn't sneak up on me. I entered your house and there she was. I was very surprised to see her there. It indicates a very close connection to the family, but I haven't yet figured out what it could be."

Bram cleared his throat. "The connection is with Gran."

"And maybe you?"

Bram felt the old man's dark eyes on him. Lying to his great-grandfather was something he could never do, and he said, "There's a connection with me, yes, but it's not an unbroken chain, Granddad."

"Ah, problems. Too bad you will have to go through so much trouble to win her."

"Granddad, I'm not sure I *want* to win her!"

"That's rubbish. Of course you want to win her. She's the golden fox. It would bring great honor to the family to have her join her hand with yours in marriage."

"Marriage! Granddad, Jenna and I hardly know each other."

"I detect something not said in your voice, which leads me to believe you know each other much better than you can admit to me. Treat her honorably, for her heart is true and kind. I knew seeing the golden fox would bring good fortune to the family. Her first name is Jenna?"

"Yes."

"And her second name? Who are her father and mother?"

Bram hated telling his great-grandfather who Jenna's father was, for every Native American in the area had a very low opinion of the man, even though they shopped at his stores and banked at his bank. Carl Elliot had a monopoly on the area's banking and retail businesses, however, which left most of Black Arrow's residents very little choice in who they dealt with. People of means took most of their business to Oklahoma City and points beyond. It was the Native Americans who were more or less trapped into making Carl Elliot richer every day of every year.

"Bram?" George prompted. "Didn't you understand my question?"

"I understood just fine, Granddad." He drew a breath to answer.

Back at his house Jenna was warily eyeing Nellie. "So, my pretty little friend, what's the truth about you? Are you naughty or nice?"

Nellie lifted her head from her front paws and pricked up her ears.

"You look friendly," Jenna said, and took a step toward the collie. "But are you?"

Nellie got up suddenly and Jenna gulped. Hastily she held out her hand. "Go ahead and sniff me," she said nervously. "If you let yourself like me, I might even give you a nice piece of roast beef. You'd like that, wouldn't you?"

Nellie approached the dangling hand, sniffed it, then started licking it wetly. Jenna grimaced. "Are you resorting to kissing already? Well, you're no threat, are you?" She knelt down and petted Nellie, who was so delighted with the attention that she couldn't keep her hind end still. "In fact, you're a little love, a little sweetheart," Jenna said. "I should be much more afraid of your master than of you, shouldn't I? If you could talk you would agree, I just know you would."

With her newfound friend, Jenna went to the kitchen and opened the refrigerator. She couldn't think of a reason in the world not to feed both Nellie and herself a decent dinner.

Even with a deep breath inflating his lungs, Bram found it hard to say the words. But he knew he couldn't put it off any longer and so he just blurted it out.

"Jenna's mother is dead and her father is Carl Elliot, the whitest white man in Comanche County." He expected George WhiteBear to at least look disappointed, but that wasn't what happened at all.

To Bram's everlasting surprise, his great-grandfather smiled—a rare event on any day—and it wasn't an ordinary smile, either.

It was one so rife with mystery that Bram blinked to clear his vision, to take another look at it.

Too late, it was gone. But it was a smile that Bram knew he would never forget, nor ever get over wondering about.

Chapter Seven

Preparing her own dinner before Gloria's would be negligent, so Jenna set to work steaming some vegetables, which she then mashed and flavored with appropriate seasonings. Jenna tried the dish herself and found it to be quite tasty. Gloria just might like it, she hoped. Adding some apple juice and a small dish of lemon pudding she'd made earlier in the day, Jenna carried the tray into the master bedroom and put on a big smile.

"Here's dinner, Gloria," she said brightly. Setting down the tray, she tucked pillows around Gloria to put her in a better position for eating. Sitting on the edge of the bed for convenience's sake, Jenna scooped a small portion of the vegetables onto a spoon. "Here you go, Gloria. This is very good. I tried it myself."

Gloria accepted the bite, and Jenna said, "It's good, isn't it?"

She got no response from her patient, but Gloria accepted a second bite and also a drink of apple juice, which was very encouraging for Jenna.

"I'll bet you enjoyed your father's visit," she said, and scooped up a third helping of the vegetable dish.

Gloria turned her head and Jenna's heart sank. "Gloria, please, two bites of food are not enough. Here, try the lemon pudding."

But Gloria refused another bite of anything. Sick at heart, Jenna finally gave up, rearranged her patient into a more comfortable position, lying down, and then decided to postpone her and Nellie's dinner even further by getting Gloria ready for sleep. Gently she bathed the elderly woman with a soft washcloth, then massaged her limbs and back with soothing lotion and finally got her into a fresh gown. Gloria was no longer hooked up to an IV line, so Jenna offered a drink of water, and Gloria sipped it through a long straw. She looked at Jenna, and Jenna was positive she saw gratitude in the bedridden woman's dark eyes.

"Sleep well, Gloria," she said, affectionately touching her hand.

With tears clouding her vision, she picked up the tray of uneaten food and carried it back to the kitchen. Nellie appeared again, as if by magic, and Jenna absently realized that the little collie hadn't followed her into the sickroom.

"She won't eat, Nellie," Jenna said sadly, and then wondered if talking to a dog indicated some sort of mental abnormality. Feeling blue over Gloria's disintegrating health and the situation in general—heaven knows coming out here hadn't done *her* much good, nor was she doing Gloria Colton much good—Jenna took out ingredients for her own dinner.

She moved slowly, though, because she couldn't stop thinking about George's belief that his daughter would die soon. Even Jared had seemed to accept the old man's prediction, and probably so did Bram. She had to know Bram's position on this, Jenna decided. Did he believe, as Jared seemed to, that every word George WhiteBear uttered was gospel? If so, what had the old guy meant with that golden-fox remark? But that wasn't bothering her nearly as much as this other thing. All the Coltons loved Gloria, Jenna was positive of that, and they would mourn her passing when it happened. But why on earth was George so certain his daughter's death was imminent?

Well, even if everyone in the whole darn town was just waiting for the ax to fall for poor Gloria, *she* was not going to stand around and do nothing. Jenna marched to the wall phone and dialed Dr. Hall's number. Just talking to Dr. Hall about Gloria and this most peculiar business with her family would help her nerves, Jenna felt.

But she got his answering service, and all she could do was leave a message. "Please have Dr. Hall call me. It's not an emergency, but I'm a nurse and I need to speak to him about one of his patients." Jenna hung up with a heavy sigh.

Nellie let out one quick little bark, obviously issuing a reminder to the only human present that she was a very hungry pooch.

If it did nothing else, it made Jenna smile. "All right, girl, dinner's coming up." She went to the refrigerator again and set some things on the counter. One plate contained the remnants of a beef roast, which was now mostly bone. Jenna decided to throw it out, so when she brought some other dishes from the fridge and then accidentally knocked the old bone on the floor, she didn't get upset about it.

But in the next instant everything changed. Nellie, faster than greased lightning, rushed at the bone, picked it up in her mouth and ran from the room. Startled and worried that Bram might not let Nellie have bones—Jenna had friends who *never* gave their dogs bones—Jenna ran after the collie, calling, "Nellie, now you stop running! You can't have that bone, do you hear me?"

Nellie disappeared into Bram's bedroom, and Jenna raced after her. Bram had left the closet door ajar, and Nellie squeezed through the opening. Jenna pulled the door wide and switched on the light. Nellie was crouched with her precious bone behind a blanketed bundle.

Jenna stared at it. It was the bundle Bram had carried in from his SUV, the one she'd been so curious about.

She was *still* curious, and she got on her knees and carefully drew back an edge of the blanket. Books? Smoky-smelling books with hardboard covers? Why on earth would Bram be carrying around smelly old books?

The books were very large, very thick, she saw. What could they contain? She gave in to her curiosity, opened the top book without disturbing the others and saw a list of entries dated almost a hundred years ago, written in ink—faded but still legible—in a beautiful hand.

Jenna was truly stunned. These books had to have been in the courthouse! The ancient entries—why, they must be extremely valuable! Why had Bram been carrying them around in his SUV, and then hidden them in his closet? Jenna sat back on her heels. She had always thought of Bram Colton as scrupulously honest, but wasn't there an old saying that everyone had a price? Was Bram's price the value of three old books?

Wiping away a tear, wishing to high heaven that she had minded her own business and not seen these books, Jenna smoothed the blanket back in place, got to her feet, switched off the light and left the closet—leaving Nellie to gnaw on that bone till the cows came home.

She was in no mood for a big dinner after that shock, and she desultorily put together a salad and made a pot of tea.

Bram, on his way to his own ranch from George's, decided to drive into Black Arrow and make an appearance at the station. He should check in, let everyone know about his change of plans and that he would be on call, after all. He parked and walked in, and was greeted by everyone in the place.

He returned the greetings, but sought out the duty officer, who tonight happened to be Sergeant Roy Emerson.

"Hey, Bram," Roy said. "I thought you were out of town or something for the night."

"My plans got changed. How's everything?"

"Afraid we got a homicide on our hands. An anonymous caller used a pay phone and said there was a body down by the railroad tracks near the old depot. I sent a car to check it out and the deputy found a dead man with a small-caliber bullet wound in his head." Roy picked up some papers and handed them to Bram. "This is the first written report to come in."

Bram read that the man was approximately fifty years old, without identification or valuables, and after numerous photos had been taken of the crime scene, the body had been transported to the morgue.

"The autopsy will be done tomorrow," Roy said. "It looks to me like a simple case of robbery with a deadly weapon. No sign of the perp, of course."

"Probably was armed robbery, but this isn't common in Black Arrow. The first thing we have to do is find out the name of the victim. Were fingerprints taken yet?"

"Yes, but they haven't been processed. Lab's closed for the night, same as the coroner's office."

"Well, it was damned stupid of the victim to get himself murdered in Black Arrow, wasn't it?" Bram drawled. Unlike bigger cities, Black Arrow didn't have round-the-clock lab facilities. Frowning at the report in his hand, Bram added, "I wonder if he lives...or *lived*...here."

"Hard to say. So far, no one who's seen the body recognized the man."

Bram thought a minute, then said, "I'm going to drive down to the old depot and take a look at the scene of the crime. It's cordoned off, I hope."

"Supposed to be, yes. I've also got two men scouring the ground for anything suspicious in all directions from where the body lay."

"Good."

"Figured that's what you would've done."

"It is. I'm going to swing by the morgue on my way to the old depot. Talk to you later. Oh, I'll be taking a patrol car. Tell dispatch."

"Will do."

After plucking a set of keys from the vehicle board, Bram hurried out to a patrol car and drove to the morgue. The night watchman, the only person who was actually alive and breathing on the premises, let him in.

"Hi, Jake. I'd like to take a look at—"

Jake waved his hand. "I know, I know." He led the way and showed Bram the body. The victim was a stranger to Bram, a small man with pale blond hair. But what really caught Bram's eye was the man's clothing. It was good-quality stuff, obviously expensive.

"Do you have his shoes?" Bram asked Jake.

"Yep. They're in a bag over there."

"Let me see them."

The shoes were Italian leather loafers. This man had not been a transient, nor had his killer been, Bram concluded. Those shoes alone would feed a roaming criminal for at least a week. Unless the victim's wallet had been so fat the killer hadn't bothered with the shoes.

Bram heaved an internal sigh. A murder to solve before the killer got out of town was the last thing he needed right now.

"Okay, I've seen enough. Thanks, Jake."

Bram returned to the patrol car and drove down to the old depot, called "old" because it was early vintage, practically falling down. The railroad had constructed a smaller but much more modern depot to handle freight and passengers about eight years back. Bram had been pleading with the town council to insist that they raze the old structure for years, as it drew the dregs of society like a flame drew moths.

Not that Bram begrudged a decent guy down on his luck a place to sleep, but Black Arrow had several shelters for the homeless, and the town had never been so overrun with indigents that those charities hadn't filled the need.

When he drove up to the old eyesore of a building, he turned on the vehicle's flashing red lights and got out. Walking over to the crime-scene tape, he heard the approaching footsteps of the two officers sweeping the area for clues with high-powered flashlights.

They all said hello, and Bram asked if they had found anything. They each had a large plastic bag practically full of much smaller plastic bags containing heaven knew what. Bram soon heard what they contained, however.

"Just a lot of junk," he was told by both men.

Bram hadn't expected any glaring clues that would easily lead law officers to the killer, but given everything else going on in his life at present, he would have liked just one break.

"You guys got an extra flashlight? I'd like to look around some myself."

"Here, take this one. I've got another in my car."

Bram accepted the flashlight and began walking toward the old depot.

"We checked that out already," one of the young deputies called.

Bram stopped and turned. "Was there anyone in the old depot when the body was found?"

"Not a soul. My feeling is that anyone in there at the time of the murder got the hell away from here the second it happened."

"Which means there could have been witnesses."

"Yeah, but just try to find them."

"I intend to." Bram continued on to the old building and went in. There were no lights to turn on, of course, no electricity, and he slowly moved the flashlight's beam around what had once been a passenger waiting room. Old newspapers and paper cups and bits and pieces of rags lay everywhere. "More junk," Bram mumbled, but covered the area with the flashlight to make sure.

There were two other rooms, and he checked them both with equal caution. Something shiny in the third room gleamed in the sweep of the flashlight's beam, and Bram hastily returned the light to it. It was a small round object, and he walked over to it and peered down at it without touching it.

A chill went up his spine. It was a worthless metal medallion, but it bore the likeness of a coyote's head. Bram stared at it in utter amazement. Coyotes haunted him, through his great-grandfather, through things like this, through life itself. *And foxes, as well?* he thought dryly. George WhiteBear was convinced that Jenna was the golden fox he'd seen with his coyote guardian spirit, and that Jenna and Bram were destined to be together in this life and whatever came after. Bram knew differently, but he was still puzzled by that enigmatic smile on his great-grandfather's face after hearing that Jenna was Carl Elliot's daughter.

Pushing that from his mind and using a small piece of paper from the floor, Bram carefully picked up the medallion. It *might* bear a fingerprint. Wouldn't it be something if he solved a murder with a coyote medallion?

It was after midnight when Bram finally got home. He was so tired he could barely drag himself into the house, but once inside he knew that he had to check on Gran before he went to bed. There was always a night-light burning near Gloria's bed, and he peered down at his beloved grandmother and felt a telltale burning in his eyes. He couldn't possibly be ashamed of crying over this sad event, but still he glanced over to make sure Jenna was sleeping.

She wasn't. She was watching him from her little twin bed, her beautiful eyes smoky-looking in the shadows created by the night-light.

"Did your car break down or something?" she whispered.

Her whisper was the most sensual sound Bram had ever heard, and he couldn't stop himself from tiptoeing over to her bed and kneeling beside it to answer.

Much to Jenna's surprise, he put his mouth very close to her ear and whispered, "I don't want to wake Gran. I stopped at the sheriff's station and...and there was some work I had to do." The scent of her hair and the warmth he felt emanating from her brought his blood to life so fast he actually got dizzy. "Jenna," he whispered brokenly. "Oh, Jenna, if you only knew." He slid his hand under the blankets to touch her, and she took his head between *her* hands and looked deeply into his eyes.

"If I only knew what, Bram?" His hand was caressing her body under the blankets, first just her waist, and then her breasts. She suddenly couldn't breathe very well. "You're only going to regret this later," she whispered. But when he managed to reach under her pajama top and stroke her nipples, she attempted no more sensible words of caution. Instead she closed her eyes and savored the incredible sensations running rampant through her body. Her fingers twined in his hair and she brought his head down so their lips would meet, and then, when they did, and he was kissing her as though he might never stop, she knew she was his forever, to do with whatever he wanted. She could never deny him anything, especially this.

He finally broke the kiss long enough for her to whisper raggedly, "We can't do this in here. Let's go to your room."

He nodded in agreement, but couldn't stop touching her long enough to make the move. And he slid his hand under the waistband of her pajama bottom and found what he needed to touch so badly he hurt.

"Bram...not in...here," she gasped as quietly as she could, but she spread her legs farther apart for him.

He kissed her lips again while his fingers circled and tantalized her most sensitive spot. She felt the needful pleasure building in the pit of her stomach and knew if he didn't stop she would finish without him. She worked her hand down between Bram and the edge of the bed and began stroking the bulge in his jeans.

"That's what I want," she said thickly. "Inside me, Bram. Filling me."

Her boldness thrilled him so much he wanted to shout, and knew he didn't dare. "Come on," he whispered feverishly, and got to his feet.

Together they stole from the master bedroom, and once away from the door they raced through the house to Bram's room. He switched on the light and shut the door.

"I want the light on. I have to see you," he said.

She answered by kicking off the bottoms of her pajamas and unbuttoning the top. He was undressing so fast it was almost funny, but she wasn't in a laughing mood. Her mood, in fact, was one she'd never quite experienced before. Not in the same way she was feeling it now. Her desire was so powerful it was overwhelming. She threw back the covers on his bed, lay down and reached for him.

"You are the most beautiful woman alive," he said hoarsely. He was down to his jeans, and practically tore them off, along with his underwear. Naked then, he fell upon her and kissed her with such hunger they both lost the last shreds of control either might have been trying to maintain.

"I should use protection," Bram groaned.

Somewhere in the far recesses of her mind Jenna wondered why he hadn't stopped for protection the first time they had made love. But she knew, even though it was a thought blurred by intense sexual desire, that they should do so now.

"Yes," she managed to whisper. "Do you have it?"

"Yes. Don't move." Bram reached into the small drawer of the nightstand and fumbled around. "I'm sure I put them in here when I changed bedrooms."

"Hurry," Jenna said breathlessly.

"Jenna, they're not in here." Groaning again, he buried his face in the pillow next to her head. He was so hard he was in agony, and Jenna wanted it all, same as he did. But the condoms he'd thought he had put in that drawer weren't in it, so obviously he'd put them somewhere else. But where? There was no way he could get up and start searching the bedroom for them.

Jenna moved her hips under him, creating a friction that brought each of them to the brink. Bram knew then that Jenna wasn't going to let him stop, nor could he, even though he should. His goose was cooked for sure when she whispered, sounding sexually frenzied, "Now, Bram, now!"

He did it—pushed into her—and they both forgot all about being sensible and using protection. His movements in and out of her hot, velvety depths were blowing his mind. He could think of nothing but her and how perfect they were together. Maintaining his rhythmic thrusts, he kissed her mouth and deemed it perfect. He lowered his head to kiss and suckle her breasts and deemed them perfect. He felt her fingernails lightly scoring his back, and the rise and fall of her hips moving in tandem with his own, and deemed her responsiveness perfect. She was perfection itself, every part of her—everything she did and said, her physical beauty and her tender care of the sick— and he would worship her till the day he died.

The realization wasn't new, it just wasn't permitted to surface very often. Making love to her with so much heat and passion between them removed all the self-protective measures he'd devised since he'd first seen her—the most incredibly beautiful, desirable woman in all of Oklahoma—and known at once that he could never make her his. He'd done his best to avoid her, and fate or some damn thing had intervened. How could he ignore her when she was everywhere he looked, in his own home yet? He was, after all, a mere mortal, strong in some ways, weak in others. Where Jenna was concerned he couldn't be weaker.

"Jenna," he mumbled. "Jenna…Jenna."

She wrapped her legs around his hips and drew him deeper inside of her. "Tell me what you're feeling," she whispered, longing to know what he was so efficient at concealing. Did anyone really know Bram? Even any of the Coltons? He bore much of the same dignity as George WhiteBear, but his handsome face and strong, muscular body were all his own. Dazed from all they were doing, all they were sharing, she could easily say right now, "I love you…I've *always* loved you."

But even without clarity of mind, she knew that saying something like that out loud would scare Bram to death, and that the best way to lose him forever was to even mention words like *love* and *commitment*.

But she knew now that she could have him in bed. She could have his physical side, and maybe, given the strength of her feelings for him, sex would be enough. But it was painfully hard not to say what was in her heart and causing her body to tremble from head to foot. For her, making love with Bram wasn't just for sexual pleasure, and she knew it never would be.

"Tell me," she whispered again.

"You know what I'm feeling. Aren't you filled with the same excitement?"

"Excitement," she echoed, with a disappointed tear in her eye. If he had even hinted at having special feelings for her, she might have blurted her own. But he couldn't, and she couldn't, and almost roughly, in a mild form of vengeance, she yanked his head down and devoured his mouth with hers, wondering if a woman had ever *made* a man fall in love with her through sex alone.

That wild, ravenous kiss was the finish line for Bram. Riding her harder, faster, he brought them both to a mind-boggling completion that left them breathless and gasping. They lay entwined for a long time, and finally their heartbeats slowed to normal.

Drained and exhausted, Bram could hardly lift his head to look at her. "You're fantastic," he said softly.

"Not without you I'm not."

Bram probed the dark depths of her eyes and became concerned at what he thought he saw in them. She couldn't fall for him, she just couldn't! Granted, the sex was great between them, but it was all they could ever have.

"You know how things are, same as I do, Jenna. Let's not talk about it," he said almost gruffly, and rolled off her.

Jenna's first reaction was fury, but what good would

fighting with him do? Arguing about his blood versus hers
was never going to change his attitude. Maybe loving him
as much as she could without actually saying it was much
smarter.

She moved over until she was nestled against him, and
then she laid her head on his chest. It took Bram by surprise, but he couldn't push her away, and his arm rose to
encircle her. When he felt tears on his chest, though, his
heart began hammering.

"Don't cry, sweetheart," he said softly.

She loved the endearment, but it only made her cry
harder. "There's a lot to cry about," she managed to say
between sobs. "Bram, I tried to give you the impression
that I sleep around, but I don't. And your Gran is fading
away right before our eyes and everyone seems to just be
taking it in stride. You're not, are you? Say you're not."

She felt a tear that wasn't her own and knew it had come
from Bram. "Love for one's family is the same in my
world as it is in yours," he said huskily. "No, I'm not
taking Gran's ill health in stride."

"And this…you and me? Are you taking us in stride?"

"I can't do anything else. Jenna, I can say one thing,
and please believe it's heartfelt. You and I might never be
able to build a bridge between your life and mine, but I
can't deny my need of you."

"It's all sexual for you then."

"It's all it *can* be. Can you accept that, live with that?
If you know right now that you can't, tell me and I swear
I'll never touch you again."

Jenna wept quietly, then whispered, "I can live with it."

"Oh, my sweet, sweet Jenna." Teary-eyed himself,
Bram wrapped both arms around her and held her close to
his aching heart. "I don't want to hurt you. You have to
believe that."

"I do." In her heart, Jenna was saying that "I do" to

a minister. In her heart she was committing herself to Bram forever. It would have to do for now, she thought sadly.

But somehow, some way, she was going to rid Bram of prejudice, for that was all it was. Prejudice as strong and indestructible as the garbage her dad clung to.

She felt Bram's hands glide down her back and cup her buttocks, and when he brought her closer still she felt his renewed arousal.

"I can't hold you like this and not want you," he said.

"I'm glad."

"Are you, Jenna? Are you really glad?"

"Kiss me and let me prove it." Her hands crept up his chest to lock behind his head.

"How about my kissing you like this?" He started dropping kisses on every part of her he could reach, and soon the blankets were bunched at the foot of the bed and he was kissing her breasts, her abdomen and then the inside of each thigh.

"Got enough strength left for one more?" He shifted back on top of her and brushed his mouth gently over hers.

"Anything for you," she whispered weakly.

He entered her and moved slowly and gently, and she was astonished when she felt heat and thrills coalescing in the pit of her stomach again. Never had she reacted to a man like this before, and her love for Bram became so huge in her chest that she thought she might burst.

They reached fulfillment together, and almost too exhausted to keep on breathing, Bram rolled to her side and immediately fell into a comalike sleep.

Utterly amazed at her intense response to Bram's intimate attentions, Jenna lay still until her heart stopped pounding. Then she propped herself up on her elbow and looked at him. He was sleeping so soundly he appeared to be unconscious. She touched his face with her fingertips and whispered, "I love you more than I can say. Please love me back."

She wanted to snuggle down and sleep with him for the remainder of the night but she knew she couldn't. Getting up quietly so she wouldn't disturb him, although she doubted a tornado ripping off the roof would do so, she pulled on her pajamas and tiptoed from the room.

She went to the master bedroom, peered at Gloria to make sure she was sleeping normally, then went to her little bed and lay down.

She fell asleep with a soft smile on her face. She was in love, and nothing and no one, not even Bram himself, could change her feelings.

Chapter Eight

Despite getting very little sleep, Bram woke up at his usual early hour. For the first time since Gran had begun occupying his master bedroom, Bram didn't go into that room first thing after getting dressed. The omission was deliberate. He simply did not want a confrontation, friendly, sensual or otherwise, with Jenna this morning. In fact, he was going to do his best to avoid even thinking about her.

Before leaving for work he checked on his horses and then filled Nellie's food and water bowls in the small barn. All the while he rued the fact that he hadn't allotted even a minute's time to the breaking and training of his young horses for weeks, and with all that was going on in his world he wasn't apt to have any free time in the near future.

Bram wore a grim expression while tending to chores. He hated what was happening in his town—robbery, arson and now murder. What's more, he didn't much care for what was happening in his own home. Last night he had sensed that more than sex was happening in his bed; Jenna was burrowing into his very soul. And considering the things she'd said to him, even though he knew she hadn't confided *everything* in her heart, she was becoming much too attached to him.

It was his fault, all of it. He never should have touched Jenna, never kissed her, caressed her, buried his face in her glorious golden hair to breathe in its magical scent. Never taken her to bed. He would pay for his loss of control, make no mistake. He didn't know exactly what form punishment would arrive in, but it would come, and it wouldn't be pleasant.

Hell, he thought as he tossed a half bale of hay over the pasture fence, he was already paying through memory alone. *Avoid thinking about Jenna? So much for good intentions,* he thought in wry self-denouncement. He might as well face the truth: he would *never* be able to avoid thinking about her. What's more, anytime he dared to feel happy or lighthearted about something long into the future, an image of any segment of last night with Jenna would be enough to destroy his good mood.

Finished with chores, and with his mind stuck on Jenna and the incredible highs of last night, Bram absently put his hand in the pocket of his jeans and took out the coyote medallion. He'd had it checked for fingerprints at the station yesterday. All that had been found on it was dirt, without so much as a minute smudge proving contact with a human hand. Frowning, Bram had studied the coinlike object, pondering its reason for existence. Some person or company had forged it, but for what cause? Bram felt certain that it wasn't made of a precious metal, certainly none that he recognized at any rate.

Officially established as worthless as far as evidence

went, Bram had cleaned off the dirt and closely studied the medallion with its raised configuration of the head of a coyote. It wasn't thin and weightless, rather it felt substantial in his hand, and without its former layer of grime, it gleamed bright as polished pewter. For some deeply rooted reason Bram didn't quite comprehend, he had put it in his pocket instead of the trash.

Now, turning it over and over in his fingers, vaguely aware of its smooth surface and weight, he questioned his ability to do anything right anymore. In retrospect, life had been pretty darn sweet not too long ago. He'd had this ranch, which couldn't be a finer home, in his estimation. He'd had a job that he was good at, and a clear conscience. Now he had criminals running all over town, a sick grandmother, no time to give to the ranch *or* his livestock. And the only woman who had ever gotten under his skin was actually living in his house.

Not that he blamed Gran for anything; people didn't become ill because they wanted to. But the hospital was full of nurses. How come Jenna had been the one chosen to take care of his grandmother?

"Aw, hell," Bram muttered, and dropped the medallion in his front shirt pocket. He felt tired and stretched too thin. If things were normal, he would hang around the ranch for a few hours and work with the horses, which had always perked him up. But that was before Jenna, and hanging around now would just dig him into an even deeper pit.

Bram finally got in his rig and drove from his ranch to town. His jaw was granite hard and determined. He might not be able to do much of anything about Jenna right now, but he could work like crazy and clean up Black Arrow.

Seated at his desk an hour later, Bram began going through the papers and reports filling his "in" basket. He made quick work of everything until he came to a hand-

written memo from one of his older deputies. It read:
"Bram. Sheila at the Crossroads Café told me about a guy
asking questions about the Colton family. Thought you
should know. She described him as tall and well dressed,
with dark hair and blue eyes. Around thirty years old. She
added that he was a 'classy guy'—her exact terminology,
if that means anything. Maybe you should talk to her yourself. Fred."

Since Bram hadn't yet had breakfast, he decided to eat
it at the Crossroads Café and told the duty officer where
he would be for the next hour or so. Then he drove to the
café and went inside. He waited a moment before choosing
a booth to make sure he sat in Sheila's station.

She walked up with a big smile. "Morning, Sheriff.
What can I get you?"

"Coffee, scrambled eggs well done and whole-wheat
toast." Bram looked up at Sheila. "And when you have a
minute, I'd like to talk to you about the 'classy guy' asking
questions about the Coltons."

"Sure thing. I'll get your coffee." Sheila whisked away
and was back with a large mug of coffee in seconds.
"Your breakfast will be ready in about five minutes."

"Thanks, Sheila." Bram sipped coffee and stared out
the window on his right. The café was busy and numerous
cars were parked outside. He thought of staking out the
place, putting a deputy in regular clothes and having him
watch for that "classy" guy. With so much traffic in and
out of the café, a stakeout was feasible.

Sheila delivered his breakfast, refilled his coffee mug,
then sat across from Bram in the booth, with a mug of
coffee for herself. "I have a ten-minute break. This place
has been crazy all morning." She took a sip of coffee. "I
told Fred all about the guy, Bram, but I don't mind repeating the story to you. Anything in particular you'd like
to ask?"

Bram had started eating and he lowered his fork. "Does he come here regularly?"

"You mean like some of these guys who are in and out of here almost every day? No, I only saw him that one time. I just thought his questions were odd, which was the reason I told Fred about him."

"Well, I appreciate your concern. Sheila, do you remember the gist of his questions, what exactly he was trying to find out?"

"Well, let me see. He sat at the counter, which I was working that day, and only ordered coffee. He was real friendly and made a remark every time I walked past him. Finally I had a slow minute and so I talked to him. I said something about his being a stranger to Black Arrow, or at least I hadn't seen him before, and he said yes, he was a stranger to the area, but it sure was a nice little town. We chatted about that for a bit, then he asked if I knew any of the Coltons. I said, 'Heavens, yes, the county's full of Coltons,' or something like that. Just a wisecrack, you know. He's a good-looking guy and, well, I'm not exactly tied down, if you know what I mean."

Bram smiled. "Go on. What else did he say?"

"He asked for some names. No, wait, first he asked if I knew Gloria Jones. I said, 'Who in the heck is Gloria Jones?' and he said, 'Apparently you don't know her by that name. How about Gloria WhiteBear, or Gloria Colton?' Well, of course I said yes, and I was about to tell him she wasn't well and was staying at your ranch, when he asked if I knew Thomas. I couldn't say yes. Although I certainly know who Thomas Colton is, I've never met him."

"Did he say why he was grilling you?"

Sheila looked surprised. "Was that what he was doing?"

"What would you call it?"

"I...don't know. Should I be worried? I mean, he seemed really nice, but so do some serial killers, I've heard."

Bram rushed to reassure her. "I don't think the guy was asking about Coltons just to put you off guard, Sheila. And you're not the only person he's talked to about my family."

"I'm not? Well, that might not be good news for you, but I'm relieved. Gosh, you just never know who might come walking in when you're working in a public place. Guess I shouldn't be quite so friendly to people I don't know."

"Don't be *un*friendly, Sheila. Your personality is what earns you the good tips."

"Yeah, right, like I'm rolling in big tips." Sheila got up. "If I think of anything else he said, I'll let you know."

"Thanks, Sheila. Oh, one other thing. Did you happen to see what he was driving?"

Her eyes widened. "Yes! Bram, he got into a gorgeous pale gray Lincoln. I remember thinking that not only was he good-looking and charming, he must have money." She grinned rather feebly. "A girl alone thinks that way a lot of the time."

"Don't apologize for being yourself, Sheila, and thanks for the information."

Sheila went back to work, and Bram finished his breakfast. He had a solid lead on one of the strangers nosing around town about the Colton family, and he felt considerably better when he left the café than when he'd gone into it.

Before returning to the sheriff's station, he drove past several of the motels. The driver of that Lincoln had to be staying somewhere, and his car would be easy to spot in any parking lot in Black Arrow.

But Bram had other things to do, and after an hour or

so he put his search on hold for the time being and went back to his desk and the much more serious crime of homicide awaiting his attention.

Jenna smiled a lot that morning while caring for her patient, even though she wasn't altogether floating on air from overwhelming happiness. But even with a noticeable helping of fear tainting the joy that seemed to have taken up residence in the vicinity of her heart, Jenna couldn't help smiling. Yes, she was torn. One second she was positive Bram loved her, and the next she was wracked with confusion and indecisiveness. But weren't actions stronger than words? And hadn't he proved his feelings for her with his passion last night?

Right after lunch, Willow arrived. As always, she brought something good to eat with her, and today it was a homemade chocolate cake with fudge frosting for Jenna and Bram, and tapioca pudding for Gran.

"She always loved tapioca pudding, Jenna. Do you think she can eat it without too much trouble?"

"I'm sure she can…if she wants it," Jenna replied quietly.

"She—she's still not showing signs of improvement then?" Willow looked downcast.

"I'm so sorry, Willow." Jenna wondered if Jared or Bram or someone else in the family had told Willow about her great-grandfather's prediction, but decided not to mention it unless she did. Jenna's heart went out to her childhood friend, and she said in as cheerful a voice as she could manage, "I'd love to try that cake. How about some tea? I'll make it while you see your grandma."

"Yes, thanks."

"But don't hurry, Willow. We can drink tea together anytime. Spend as much time with Gloria as you'd like."

"I will."

In the kitchen Jenna wiped away a tear and put the tea-kettle on the stove. She had always liked Willow so much, and she knew how her friend had to be suffering over this terrible blow to the Colton family. It was much too reminiscent of those awful months prior to Jenna's mother's death, unquestionably the worst period of Jenna's life.

And yet something good had come from that heartbreaking tragedy—her decision to become a nurse. She loved her profession and was extremely relieved that she hadn't pursued the art history career that had once seemed perfect for her. Jenna sighed. If only her dad would realize how much caring for people who so desperately needed professional nursing meant to her.

But he never would, she thought sadly. Nor would he ever give an inch on his biased attitude toward Native Americans. Why he believed he was so much better than people who weren't a hundred percent white truly eluded Jenna. It was so unreasonable, especially when she thought of the fortune he had made—and was *still* making—from the very people to whom he felt so superior.

The teakettle whistled and Jenna prepared a pot of tea. She wouldn't cut the cake now, but a cup of tea wouldn't hurt. She sat at the table and sipped hot tea, and immediately became dreamily immersed in memories of last night with Bram. Gazing into space, she wondered exactly when she had fallen in love with him. She had been profoundly attracted to him since her teen years—she knew that—but physical attraction wasn't necessarily love.

"Oh, well," she said under her breath.

Willow walked in and Jenna jumped to her feet. "I'll get you a cup of tea," she said. "Go ahead and sit down."

"Thanks," Willow said wearily, and gladly took a chair at the table. "She doesn't even seem to care anymore that I come to see her. Why has she given up? And what's maybe more frightening, why did she give up so quickly?

Jenna, Gran was always a fighter, stronger than all the rest of us put together.''

"It's possible that's the very reason she can't accept being an invalid," Jenna said gently. "I've explained to her at least a dozen times that she could regain strength and mobility and even her ability to speak legibly if she would just cooperate and try. She doesn't want to hear it." Jenna set a cup of tea on the table in front of Willow. "Be careful. It's very hot."

"Thank you." Listlessly, Willow picked up the cup and took a sip.

Jenna resumed her chair and picked up her own cup. "You're looking a little peaked yourself, Willow. Haven't you been feeling well?"

Willow heaved a sigh. "I…I'm not sure how to answer that. I'm not physically ill, but I've really been down in the dumps, Jenna. Gran's part of it, of course, but I…" She hesitated, then blurted, "I'm tired of my brothers watching every move I make! They're not my keepers and I'm hardly a kid. Why can't they live their own lives and leave mine to me?"

Jenna was stunned. "I had no idea you felt that way. Actually, I had no idea your brothers made such demands on you. Bram does it, too?"

"Lately he's been too busy to harangue me, but he used to all the time."

"What does he expect from you?" Jenna hated hearing anything negative about Bram, even something as normal as big-brother overprotectiveness for his baby sister, and she felt a strong urge to tell Willow just how wonderful Bram really was. In fact, she would like nothing better than to tell Willow everything going on between her and Bram. She took a big swallow of tea instead.

"That's a darned good question," Willow said. "What do any of them expect from me?"

So filled with her own wild and wonderful emotions for a man, Jenna couldn't help thinking that Willow needed the same thing—a man that gave her goose bumps and more physical pleasure than she'd even known existed.

"I think you should get out of town for a few days and let your hair down," Jenna said.

Willow's cheeks got pink. "I...I already did that, Jenna. Now I'm worried about..."

"About what?"

"Oh, forget it. It's probably nothing. Let's have some of that cake now."

It was after Willow had gone that Jenna realized no one had told her about George WhiteBear's dire prediction of an impending death in the Colton family. Then something occurred to Jenna that gave her a chill. Why was everyone so positive the prediction was about Gloria? There were a lot of other Coltons, and accidents happened all the time.

However, worse than everyday accidents was what Bram did for a living. "My God," Jenna whispered, shaken to her soul. Law enforcement officers worked every day in the line of fire. What if Gloria wasn't the endangered Colton, and Bram was?

It was almost four that afternoon when the medical examiner, John Burnam, surprised everyone working in the sheriff's station by delivering his autopsy report in person.

John laid the report on Bram's desk, then sat down. "That's a surprise package," John said. "I'll wait while you read it."

Bram read quickly, then sat back, stunned. "Powder burns on his right hand?"

"Bram, all things considered, it looks like that man shot himself."

Bram got up for a cup of stale coffee. "Want some?" he asked Burnam.

"No, thanks. I've got some battery acid in the car."

John's droll sense of humor usually brightened Bram's day, but at the moment he was in a state of shock over the autopsy results and barely heard the man.

Resuming his chair, coffee cup in hand, Bram went over the report again. Then he sat back and regarded John somberly. "Your conclusion isn't the only possibility, John. He could have had a gun of his own and shot at the person who killed him."

"That would make a fine plot for a movie, but it's a bit far out for Black Arrow. Suicide makes the most sense."

"Since when has a homicide made sense?"

John shrugged. "I've given you my opinion—based on scientific fact, of course, and my many years of experience with violent death. But you interpret that report any way you wish."

"You know damned well I respect your opinions."

John grinned. "Of course you do. We all do."

Bram shook his head. "Burnam, you're a case all by yourself." Then his face took on a faraway, thoughtful expression and he murmured, "Suicide. If that's what happened, then the gun and his valuables were stolen *after* his death. And I've run the department ragged looking for an unclaimed car parked anywhere near the old depot. How in heck did he get down there?"

"You have nothing conclusive on his identity?"

"Not yet. His fingerprint data—hopefully there is some—should be coming in at any time. I've been waiting for it most of the day."

"You need direct access to that kind of information."

"Tell that to the county bigwigs at their next meeting," Bram said dryly. "More powerful computers just don't hit that group's hot button. They immediately start talking about raising property taxes or something else that the voters would nix."

"And yet everyone expects fast action from county and city employees." Burnam got to his feet. "Oh, well, such is life in the trenches."

Bram rose. "Thanks for the personal delivery of your report."

"Kind of you to say that, but I'm afraid it was strictly for my own benefit. I wanted to witness your reaction to it with my own eyes." John grinned. "But I did make your life much easier, didn't I? Instead of a homicide to solve, you now only have to ferret out and arrest a morbid thief. Good luck."

"Thanks a lot," Bram drawled as John walked away. The medical examiner waved his hand in farewell without turning around, and Bram slowly sank back into his chair.

He sat there thinking for a long time. What in the devil was happening to Black Arrow and Comanche County? Until a few months ago there'd been few crimes to solve, very few thieves to ferret out and arrest, few mysteries to puzzle over. Now they seemed to be popping up everywhere he looked.

After muttering a curse under his breath, Bram shouted, "Lester, check on those fingerprint requests again! And don't be nice about it!"

Jenna dealt with one Colton after another all day. The family was in chaos, each member seeking confirmation that their beloved Gran was still alive. Obviously George WhiteBear's prediction had been making the rounds.

Jenna felt for each one of them, she truly did, but she also wanted to say, "Why are you all so certain the prediction is about Gloria? Haven't you considered that it could be about one of you...or about Bram? My Lord, think of what he does day after day, night after night."

In truth she was worried sick, and though she did everything for her patient that she did each day, same as always, and spoke nicely to the arriving and departing Coltons, her thoughts were with Bram, wherever he was, whatever he was doing. Jenna looked out a window at every opportunity, praying to see his SUV or prowl car, whichever he was driving today.

The dinner hour arrived and she made a tempting tray for Gloria, which, as usual, was returned to the kitchen virtually untouched. Jenna warmed some soup and made a sandwich for herself, and then realized that her own appetite wasn't much better than her patient's.

By eight o'clock Jenna's thoughts were almost too painful to bear. She was living and breathing for someone else, for a man who didn't care enough about her to pick up the telephone and call her. She would have been overjoyed to receive a thirty-second phone call just to hear Bram's voice saying, "Hi, how are you today?"

If this awful heartache was love, did she want it?

The fingerprint reports finally were faxed in late in the day, and Bram and several of the deputies read with great disappointment that the dead man's fingerprints were not on file with any law enforcement agency.

"He wasn't a criminal," Bram said. "So who is he?" If they didn't find out his identity in a reasonable length of time he would be buried as a "John Doe," which Bram always felt bad about. A person should be buried with his or her loved ones, or at least among friends.

And there were so many other unanswered questions. Given the good quality of his clothing the man hadn't been poverty stricken, so had he worked somewhere in the county right under Bram's nose? Or owned a business? Inherited from his family?

But if he'd been a county resident, wouldn't someone have filed a missing person's report by now?

Bram sat down and placed a call to the local radio station. "This is Sheriff Colton. Would you do me a big favor and broadcast the description of an unidentified man who died in Black Arrow last night?"

The station manager said that he would be happy to cooperate in any way. After thanking the man, Bram phoned the newspaper and made a similar request. "We have a John Doe in the morgue. Would you please publish his description?"

"I'll send a reporter by in the morning."

Bram stayed at his desk long after the shift change. He took the medallion from his shirt pocket and absently toyed with it while he thought about the many convolutions his life had taken in recent days. Would things ever get back to normal? Was there any connection, even a tiny one, between John Doe and the other events rocking Bram's world of late?

And then there was Jenna. Bram heaved a mighty sigh. What in God's name was he going to do about Jenna? Fire her? Call Dr. Hall and request another nurse?

Keep your hands off her and everything will even out, you moron!

It was a simple solution to a complex problem, and maybe he could go one better by having a heart-to-heart with Jenna. *"I'm sorry, but nothing is ever going to come of you and me sleeping together. It has to stop. You have to stay in your bed and I have to stay in mine. Alone. That's it. The end. Finito, finished."*

Feeling an abnormal burning sensation on his palm, Bram dropped the medallion onto his desk and looked at his hand. "What in hell?" he muttered, and touched the medallion with one fingertip. It wasn't at all hot. In fact it was downright cool.

So what had burned his palm? he wondered, and then realized it wasn't burned at all. His imagination must have gone wild.

Still, he sat and looked at that medallion without touching it for a long spell, marveling again at the odd coincidence of him, George WhiteBear's great-grandson, stumbling across a medallion with a coyote's head embossed on it.

Bram shook his head. This sort of thing was his great-grandfather's specialty, not his. He had no psychic powers, nor did he have a guardian spirit. Doggedly he turned his attention back to his work, only to worry about John Doe's suicide gun. Someone had it, and did that make Black Arrow a more dangerous town in which to reside?

And dare he forget that *two* men had been asking questions about the Coltons? The second one had been described as a fairly forgettable character, except he seemed out of place in Oklahoma. He had medium brown hair and eyes, and seemed like a sneaky sort of fellow. It was, in Bram's estimation, a pretty poor description, but it was all he had. At least after talking to Sheila, he knew with certainty that he *was* dealing with two different men.

Feeling as though he was spinning his wheels whichever way he turned, Bram checked out with the duty officer and left the station. Driving his own vehicle, he made the rounds of Black Arrow's motels, this time missing none of them.

Completely worn out, Bram finally headed home. He tiptoed into the house and went directly to his bedroom. He moved so quietly that he was sure Jenna couldn't possibly have heard him come in.

But he was wrong. She heard his SUV drive in, then heard Bram enter the house with barely a sound. And she knew why he was being so silent. He wanted to avoid seeing her, just as he had early that morning, when he'd gotten up and left the ranch.

Jenna stared at the shadowy ceiling for a very long time. She could hear Gloria's labored, raspy breathing, but she was able to listen to every tiny sound her patient made and still think about Bram.

And she finally had to admit, heartbreaking though it was, that Bram Colton was carrying around too much baggage to let himself love Carl Elliot's daughter.

Chapter Nine

Bram sat on the edge of a table to talk to his deputies, some of whom were seated at desks, while others leaned against file cabinets or walls, coffee in hand. They were a fine group of dedicated officers, and Bram was proud of his staff. He didn't usually speak to them en masse like this, but today he felt that he had to convey the importance of their mission.

"We're all familiar with the medical examiner's autopsy report. John Doe wasn't murdered, as we first thought—he committed suicide. Why he chose that particular place to end his life we might never know, but I suppose he could have chosen it because of its isolation from family and friends. If he had family and friends, that is. The man's description is being aired and published as we speak—I'm sure you've heard it on the radio and read it in the *Chronicle*—but no one's come forward.

"Does that mean Mr. Doe wasn't from around here, or

does it mean he lived quietly, maybe off in the country somewhere, and had no family? So we have that problem to deal with. The county will bury him, we know that, but his only crime was illness or whatever drove him to suicide, and he deserves a proper ceremony with folks who cared about him in attendance…if we can find them.

"A more serious problem is the gun he used. It's a .22 caliber handgun, and someone took it that night. It's debatable whether John Doe was carrying valuables, although I've been considering a wallet and a watch—the watch because of the slight indentation on his left wrist indicating longtime usage of one. But maybe he carried nothing, because he didn't want his identity known, in which case the gun would be the only stolen article.

"That gun worries me. Who took it? Who has it now? I want that gun found. The people hanging out at the old depot are transients, and it's entirely possible that whoever grabbed that weapon is long gone by now. But maybe not, and I want all of you to talk to every stranger on every street, in back alleys, in the homeless shelters and anywhere else you run across them. We're not rousting out the homeless, not by any means, and every officer should keep that in mind. But if anyone has something to say about that night, I want to hear it."

One of the men spoke up. "We've been keeping an eye on the old depot and haven't seen anyone hanging there since the incident."

Bram nodded grimly. "Doesn't surprise me. Word travels like quicksilver among the homeless, and no one would want to be connected to the theft of that gun. Remember, though, that any number of people might have seen who walked away with it. There's information out there—we just have to find it."

The meeting broke up and Bram returned to his office. As was becoming a habit when he was thinking, he took the medallion from his shirt pocket and toyed with it, agilely moving it from finger to finger on one hand as some people did with a coin.

Mentally he ran down his list of problems. Gran was number one, Jenna number two and the gun number three. Then there was his great-grandfather, who somehow seemed to overwhelm everything else on the list, and the two different strangers asking questions about the Colton family. And last but certainly not least was the courthouse fire. Oh, yes, there was also the break-in at the newspaper office.

It shook Bram that he wasn't making much headway with anything on his list, although he had been pretty successful in avoiding Jenna lately. He left the house before she and Gran awoke in the morning and didn't get home again until midnight or later. He was working sixteen-hour days and using the other eight to catch a little shut-eye, spend time with Gran and worry about the next day's agenda. He had not eaten a meal at his own table for...well, since Jenna showed up as Gran's nurse. He didn't much care for his avoidance routine, but it was the only way to keep them apart. He loved her, and...

Bram winced. He had been trying so hard to keep from saying or thinking that, and now the words seemed to be printed on his forehead for all the world to see.

"Damnation," he muttered, and got to his feet. There was always paperwork to be done, but he would rather drive around and interview people about John Doe and that damned gun. He glanced down at the medallion in his hand and sank back into his chair. Could this shiny little object, which he'd assessed as immaterial to the tragedy at the old depot, in reality have a story to tell, if only he had the wits to decode it? Should it be locked in the evidence room instead of residing in his pocket?

Bram decided to take another look at the items picked

up by the two officers the night of John Doe's suicide, and headed for the evidence room. Everything gathered had been gone through, examined and labeled "Junk," but they still kept it and would until they could stamp the word "Closed" on John Doe's file.

Bram checked each item again—empty cigarette packs, candy wrappers, torn bits of old newspapers—and finally shook his head. There was nothing there. The most valuable piece of junk picked up that night was the medallion he carried in the pocket of his shirt. He took it out and looked at it again. Was it evidence? It had no fingerprints—other than his own now—and nothing on it to identify its origin. But how in heaven's name had it found its way into the old depot? And why had whoever transported it there left it behind?

A final—and recurring—question had actually been haunting Bram. Why had he been the officer to find the medallion? The other guys had searched the old building. Why hadn't *they* spotted it gleaming in the beam of a flashlight?

Frowning in serious thought—had the medallion been destined for his eyes alone?—Bram returned to his office, dropped the medallion in his shirt pocket and tried to forget it. Immediately he thought of something else that needed doing.

He dialed Annie McCrary's phone number and waited through six rings before she answered.

"Annie...Bram Colton here. Sorry to bother you, but have you seen anything of Granddad lately?"

"I saw him only yesterday, matter of fact, and you're not bothering me, Bram. Call anytime. I know you're concerned about the old fellow."

"You must have gone by his place, then?"

"He came by here. Surprised the heck out of me, I don't mind admitting. Actually, Bram, I think he was going to walk on by, but I spotted him and his dogs and called out to him.''

"He was on the road? Annie, that road comes to a dead end less than a quarter mile past your place. Did he say where he was going?''

"Bram, I've been hearing coyotes howling every night this week, and George said he was going to talk to them. I probably shouldn't be saying this, but are you sure he's all right? I remember what you said about coyotes being some kind of spiritual thing to him, but...''

"Annie, talking to coyotes, or believing he talks to coyotes, is perfectly normal for Granddad. I'm more concerned with his physical health. How did he look to you? I mean, did he appear to be his usual hale and hardy self?''

"Well, yes, but... Bram, he's so old. Should he be living all alone? I realize this is your business and none of mine, but I can't help worrying about him.''

"I worry about him, too, Annie. So does the rest of the family. But no one could get Granddad to live anywhere else no matter what they did. I honestly believe you couldn't pry him from the place with a crowbar. I've told him many times that he's welcome to move in with me and he won't even consider it. So all I can do is keep an eye on him. I wish he would let me have a telephone put in his house so I wouldn't have to bother you, though. I would have driven out there and seen him for myself but things are kind of crazy in town right now.''

"So I've gathered. What about that dead guy? Has anyone contacted your department with information about him yet?''

"No, we haven't had one single call about him. Annie, I would appreciate your calling me if you happen to see Granddad wandering off again. He...he's in mourning, and apt to do some things that you would find strange. But the one thing I'm afraid of is his taking a fall and no one knowing about it until it's too late.''

"He's in mourning? Oh, my goodness! Who passed away, Bram?''

Bram cleared his throat. "No one yet. It's a Comanche thing, Annie. Thanks for talking to me.''

"Call anytime,'' Annie murmured, and Bram could hear the puzzlement in her voice because an old man was mourning the death of someone who hadn't yet died.

Bram set down the phone, thanked his lucky stars for Annie's kindness and wished he knew how to explain George WhiteBear's beliefs in a way that she would understand. It simply wasn't feasible.

Jenna awoke angry and stayed that way all morning. How dare Bram treat her in such a callous, cavalier way? He was deliberately leaving at an impossibly early hour every day and not coming home until late. She was usually asleep, but even if she sometimes did hear him come in she knew he didn't want to see her, so she stayed in bed and felt bad about being in love with a heartless oaf. She suffered over him and he didn't give a damn about her. It wasn't fair! She resented the very air he breathed...and *still* loved him. Was she mad?

Gloria ate a few bites of breakfast and another two or three around noon. In the interim Jenna did all of the things she was supposed to—bathing her patient, seeing to Gloria's medications and finally attempting to convince her to work on facial exercises. Gloria's response to that request was always the same: she simply turned her head and shut her eyes.

It was around two that Jenna heard an approaching vehicle, and her heart leaped crazily because just for a moment she thought that maybe Bram had come home.

But it wasn't Bram, nor was it any Colton. It was, Jenna saw from the kitchen window, Dr. Hall.

She went to the front door and let him in. "Hello, Doctor."

"Hello, Jenna. How's Mrs. Colton today?"

"She's slipping away before my eyes," Jenna said quietly. "I'm glad you're here."

Dr. Hall surprised her by laying his hand on her shoulder. "I'll take a look at her and then we'll talk."

"Uh, yes…fine," Jenna stammered, and then watched the doctor walk to the master bedroom and go in. It occurred to her, not for the first time, that Dr. Hall was young—no more than forty—and quite nice looking. He was also a divorced man, she recalled from rumors that had titillated several of the single nurses about six months ago.

The gossip hadn't thrilled Jenna, for the only man on her mind had been Bram. Now, hurting from Bram's ambivalent treatment—he slept with her when the mood struck, apparently, and then deliberately ignored her very existence—she wondered about Dr. Hall's gesture. Was he just being kind because of her downcast expression over her patient's failing health, or had he meant something personal by laying his hand on her shoulder?

Should she find out? Wishing for a way to repay Bram for the hurt he kept inflicting upon her was rather dangerous business, Jenna knew. But Bram Colton deserved to be taken down a notch. And if dating another man while sleeping under Bram's roof would cause him the slightest bit of anguish, she'd be a spineless wimp not to do it.

And she was tired of being spineless. Tired of being dressed down by her father for having become a nurse and for liking people of all colors, races and creeds. She hated bigotry so much that she could make herself nauseous just thinking about it, and it hurt terribly that her own father was the worst bigot she'd ever run into.

It was all so senseless—her dad's rigid attitude and Bram's pigheaded pride. Se was caught in the middle, and neither man cared that his silly self-righteousness hurt her.

She should never speak to either one of them again, she thought bitterly while preparing a pot of tea in the kitchen.

The tea was beginning to cool a bit before Dr. Hall walked in. Jenna rose and gestured at the table. "Join me for tea and cookies?"

Dr. Hall smiled and looked pleased. "Why, thank you. This is a most pleasant surprise." He pulled out a chair and Jenna served the tea.

"How did you find her?" she asked.

The doctor's forehead creased with a concerned frown. "She's listless and losing ground. Jenna, I know you're doing everything you can, but I'm beginning to think she should be back in the hospital."

Jenna frowned as well. "I'm not sure her family would permit it. Would it benefit her to be hospitalized? I mean, would she have a greater chance of recovery?"

"Maybe. It's possible. But it could also be detrimental. Jenna, to be honest, I can't give you a positive answer to that question with any real confidence. She seemed glad to see me, but it was only a moment before her eyes became dull again."

"She's been doing the same with her family."

"She's giving up, Jenna. She's tired of living."

"But she had a good life! And she was very active and full of fun. I've heard about her from members of her own family, and they're truly devastated by what's happening to her. They love her, and she always loved them."

"But still she's tired of living. Jenna, I've seen it before and so have you. I know it makes no sense to a beautiful young woman like yourself, but serious illness changes people.''

He'd said she was beautiful, and she couldn't help responding to the compliment. Then and there she decided to give Bram a run for his money, the jerk, and she did it in a flirtatious way, blushing a little and saying, "Goodness, I'm not beautiful, Doctor. Wherever did you get such an idea?''

"I'd rather you called me Richard," he replied with an admiring gleam in his eyes and a sexy half smile. "And you *are* beautiful. I've never seen another woman with hair like yours.''

"I guess I'll just have to accept your compliment and say thank-you," Jenna murmured, assessing his nicely cut dark hair and gray eyes. But could she really go out with him? Let him kiss her? Lead him on while wishing every second they were together that she was with Bram instead? Misery suddenly shaped itself into a ball in her midsection and extended clawlike tentacles throughout her being. She couldn't deceive this nice man just to get back at Bram. How could she even have thought of something so disgusting?

She completely erased all signs of Southern-belle coyness from her expression and got up. "I'll talk to Sheriff Colton about hospitalization for his grandmother when he comes home. There's something else I have to say before you leave. I embarrassed myself by flirting with you, and I apologize for being so shallow and silly when I'm in love with someone else.''

Dr. Hall slowly rose. "Doesn't he know you're in love with him? I mean, if you *are* in love, why would you flirt with another man?''

"Because I know it and he doesn't. At least he won't let on if he does.''

"Jenna, he doesn't deserve you. Tell him I said so.

Goodbye. Call me if the Colton family decides to hospitalize Gloria.''

Jenna followed him to the door. "You're a nice man."

Dr. Hall smiled wryly. "I just take rejection well." He started to leave, then stopped and looked back at her. "Maybe I'll give you a call one of these days. Dinner and a movie is an innocent enough date, don't you agree?"

"I can't leave Gloria, Doctor."

"Richard. And I'm sure we could arrange for a substitute nurse for a few hours."

Jenna couldn't help smiling. "You might *think* you take rejection well, but from where I stand it appears it merely makes you more determined."

"Could be...could be." Chuckling, Dr. Hall continued on to his car.

Neither Bram nor his deputies learned anything helpful from any of the people they talked to for the rest of the day and far into the night.

Discouraged, Bram threw in the towel and drove home around two in the morning. He wasn't getting enough sleep and he was beat. It was an effort to walk from his car to the house, and he merely glanced to his left, into the dimly lit bedroom occupied by Gran and Jenna, before heading for his own room and bed. The house was as silent as usual, and he'd been able to see Gran in bed during that one brief look he'd taken, which pacified his worry for her enough to let him sleep. He wouldn't let himself think of Jenna, whose much smaller bed wasn't visible from the front entrance.

Yawning, he approached his bedroom and realized that he must have forgotten to turn off the lamp on the bedstand that morning, because it was still on and casting light on the hallway carpet. He stepped into the room and stopped dead in his tracks. Jenna was asleep on his bed.

He blinked and prayed he was hallucinating, for he didn't have the strength to deal with Jenna at this unholy hour and at a time when exhaustion threatened to knock him off his feet.

But he knew he could stand there for the remainder of the night and she would *still* be sleeping on his bed, and damn, she was beautiful. He actually felt like bawling. She was the woman he should have. Because he couldn't have her he would remain a bachelor for the rest of his life. It wasn't fair.

But had anyone ever said that life was fair? Leaning against the frame of the door, Bram drank in the sight of Jenna. She was covered to the waist with a blanket, breathing evenly and shallowly, obviously in a deep sleep. Her glorious mane of golden hair was spread over the pillow, and she was wearing something pink and pretty.

Then bitterness twisted Bram's mouth. He loved this woman and couldn't make her his wife. He'd crossed way too far over the line with her and shamed both her and himself. And still he loved her—in such a powerful, all-consuming way that he knew nothing else in his life would ever compare.

Heaving a self-pitying sigh, he pushed away from the door frame and walked over to the bed. "Jenna?"

She didn't budge. He leaned over and spoke a little louder. "Jenna?"

"Umm," was all she said, but she opened her eyes to tiny slits and saw him. Her arms went up. "Come to bed, darling."

She was still sleeping! He *knew* she wasn't awake, and yet her words delivered such a potent thrill to his system he reeled from it. He also knew that he should shake her shoulder and fully waken her, then tell her to get the heck out of his bed and go to her own.

But she looked soft as a kitten and so womanly and

beautiful that he merely stood there, clenched his jaw spasmodically and suffered the torment of the damned. What
had he done, he wondered, to deserve this kind of torture?
If he lay down with her he knew exactly what would happen, and it wouldn't be the sleep he needed so much. It
would be hours of kissing her, undressing her, touching
every inch of her incredibly lush body and making love to
her for as long as his strength held out or dawn broke,
whichever came first. No, he couldn't let it happen again.
How much misery could a man cause himself, anyway?

"Jenna!" he growled loudly.

"Wha-what?" Eyes wide-open, she sat up with a start.
"Did you just yell at me?"

"What're you doing in my bed?"

She was getting her wits about her. "I have to tell you
something, and since you never come home at a respectable hour anymore, I figured sleeping in here until you
showed up was the only way to see you." Feeling vul-
nerable on his bed, she slid from it, making sure she didn't
come close to him, and padded barefoot to the door in case
she needed to make a quick getaway. That man was not
going to have his unscrupulous way with her again, however much her body yearned for his touch.

He didn't miss her cautionary tactics and felt rather
wounded by her obvious determination to avoid contact.
He wasn't a threat, for hell's sake. All she would have had
to do was to say no and nothing would have *ever* happened
between them. So which of them bore the most blame? He
was willing to accept his own, but she had been just as
eager to make love. Both times!

"So say what you have to say and get it over with. I'm
dead on my feet," he growled.

"Oh, you're just the sweetest thing, aren't you?" she
said with heavy sarcasm.

Her queen-of-the-prom tone really fried him. He was too

damn tired to play games. "Jenna, I'm going to bed. If you have something to tell me, do it." He started unbuttoning his shirt.

"Don't you dare undress in front of me."

"Like you haven't seen it all before?" He removed his shirt and dropped it on the floor.

"That doesn't mean I want to see it again!"

"Well, if you stand there and watch, you're going to."

Jenna rushed into her little speech. "Dr. Hall was here today—I should probably say yesterday, seeing as how it's already tomorrow—and he thinks Gloria should be hospitalized."

Bram had been unbuttoning the fly on his jeans, and he stopped to glare at her. "Why? Did he just now stumble across a miracle cure for stroke victims?"

"Of course not. Don't be absurd."

"Did he guarantee her recovery if we put her in the hospital?"

"No one could do that."

"Then why in hell should we take her there so she can die in a strange place that she already hates?"

"*I* didn't say you should take her anywhere! Dr. Hall said it."

"Oh, I get it, your precious Dr. Hall merely makes the bullets. You shoot 'em."

"You perfectly odious person! Don't you know I love Gloria? Don't you know I only want to see her live and be active and happy again? And while I'm walking around sad and weepy and praying for a miracle, you Coltons are already planning her funeral! Well, you can go straight to hell, all of you!" Jenna whirled around to leave.

"Jenna!" Bram made a dive for her and caught her by the arm. "What you just said is how you snow-whites see Comanche ways, and the precise reason you and I could never make a go of it!"

"So who *wants* to make a go of it, you conceited…egotistical…" Her voice trailed off as tears flooded her eyes. "Damn you," she whispered hoarsely.

Bram gathered her into his arms and brought her head to his chest. "We're forever making each other miserable. I'm sorry…I'm sorry."

Jenna sobbed against the smooth skin of his bare chest. "You exaggerate our differences because of my dad."

"I know."

Jenna leaned her head back and looked up at his face. "You *do* know it, don't you? And still you let bigotry run your life. Bram, you were elected to office by the people of Comanche County. *All* the people, not just the Native Americans. Doesn't that mean something to you? Don't you realize that you're as prejudiced as Dad is? You just called me a snow-white, and I just might be the least prejudiced person you know."

She stood in the circle of his arms and waited for him to answer, and when he didn't she knew he didn't *have* an answer. Escaping his embrace, she said wearily, "I'm going to bed. Good night."

Bram was too tuckered out to lie awake and worry about anything, but he drifted off thinking about Jenna and the things she'd said to him, her point of view on their impasse.

There was no question about her getting the last word in that particular argument, and his only defense on that score was a question: did it matter who had won the argument? All it had accomplished, after all, was more pain for both of them.

He awoke three hours later remembering Dr. Hall's recommendation that Gran be hospitalized.

"No way," he muttered while dragging himself out of bed. "No damned way is she going to die alone in a hospital!"

But this wasn't a decision he could make all on his own. He would contact his brothers, his sister, his uncle and his cousins later on today and get everyone's input. It was the only fair thing to do about a family problem this serious.

He deliberately omitted George WhiteBear from that list because he knew the old man would be appalled at the mere thought of his daughter being shuffled off to a hospital during her final days. Death was part of life, just as birth was, and George could deal with that. But he strongly believed in a family's responsibility to care for its sick and dying.

He would not only vote no, Bram knew, he would recite Comanche rituals and customs to every one of his descendants until the day of his own death, possibly fearing that if they would put his daughter in a hospital to die they would do the same to him.

Bram left the house feeling like the dregs at the bottom of a barrel. It was a feeling that was becoming much too commonplace lately.

Chapter Ten

Around eleven in the morning, with Gloria resting, Jenna had a little time on her hands. Using it to curl up on the sofa in the living room and worry wasn't all that bright, but she couldn't help herself. *Would* Gloria be better off in the hospital? Dr. Hall couldn't guarantee it, but a doctor was only a person with a medical education, not the Almighty.

And neither was Bram omnipotent and all-knowing, Jenna thought resentfully. As for Mr. WhiteBear, wasn't it rather callous of him to predict his own daughter's demise and scare the living daylights out of the rest of his family?

Jenna couldn't shake the doldrums this morning. If Bram had come home at a respectable hour last night she would not have been in his room, sleeping on his bed. But she had felt duty-bound by her profession to relay Dr. Hall's recommendation, and after trying to keep her eyes open for hours, she'd finally lost the battle and decided that the only way she was going to see Bram was by waiting for him in his room. And, of course, she'd gotten chilly lying down, had pulled up a blanket and eventually fallen asleep.

The phone rang, and Jenna got up with a frustrated sigh to answer it. "Colton Ranch."

"This is Bram."

She could hardly believe he'd called, and couldn't begin to guess at the reason. "I'm surprised you know your own phone number."

"I didn't call because I was longing for another argument with you. How's Gran this morning?"

"The same."

"Well, 'the same' is a lot better than 'she's much worse,' wouldn't you agree?"

"You'll get no argument from me on that point. However—"

"No, don't say it. Let *me* say something. I've made at least a dozen calls this morning and talked to almost every Colton. They all agreed that Gran should not be put in the hospital. We'd lose her within the week if she thought no one wanted her."

"Even if everyone took turns staying in her room with her?"

"Do you really find her fear and dislike of hospitals that unusual? I can't believe Gran is the only person who doesn't like being surrounded by strangers."

Jenna heaved another sigh. "No, she's not the only person who doesn't like hospitals. It would be moronic to argue that issue, but most people have to spend time in a hospital at some point in their life."

"So you think that's where she belongs?"

"I didn't say that."

"Would she get better care than you're giving her?"

"I...can't say that, either."

"Well, I can say that she wouldn't. You're constantly there for her, and I know how clean you keep her and how hard you try to make her meals palatable. She wouldn't receive one-on-one care in the hospital. She couldn't. The hospital has just so many nurses on staff, and I've heard they're overworked as it is. One elderly lady is not going to be given preferential treatment—you know it, I know it."

"You're never here and yet you know all that."

"I've been home enough to know what's going on, Jenna. There's something else, too. I've been thinking about what you said about Granddad last night, and—"

"Don't you mean this morning?"

"Yes, I mean this morning. Sorry I can't keep my working schedule in line with yours."

Jenna bit down on her lip for a moment. Haranguing Bram wasn't going to accomplish anything, except maybe to cause him to stay away from his own home even more than he already did.

"Sorry," she said quietly. "I'm not anxious for another argument, either, despite evidence to the contrary. What did you want to say about your great-grandfather?"

Her change of attitude and gentle apology warmed Bram through and through. They shouldn't be on opposite sides of any issue, real or imagined, not when there were so many good feelings between them. His feelings for her were not only a very big part of him, but he was beginning to believe that Jenna was falling in love with him. Yes, he'd been fighting against that very thing, but it was damn tough for a man to keep shoving happiness out of his life.

He realigned his thoughts. "I think you have a wrong impression of Granddad. I know it's not your fault," he hastened to add. "You formed it from the little you've seen of him and from things I've said about him."

"You and others in your family. Bram, he's a very old

man and often advanced age causes, uh…'' She couldn't say it, couldn't suggest that George WhiteBear no longer possessed all of his faculties.

But she didn't have to say it. Bram knew exactly what she was thinking. ''Granddad's mind is as clear as mine, Jenna, but he lives by some very ancient ways that you've probably never even heard of. I'm sure you've wondered why he didn't stay with me so he could be with his daughter. But the family didn't wonder because everyone knows that twenty years ago—maybe even ten—he would have demanded that his daughter be brought to *his* house so *he* could care for her. He didn't desert her, Jenna, and I know he's performing all sorts of rituals that will take her from this life to the next in peace and serenity.''

''How can I put stock in ancient rituals? I was trained to believe in science and the dependability of modern medicine and technology.''

''And I believe in your training, even while understanding and accepting Granddad's methods and beliefs. Jenna, there's always more than one way to do something, and you said last night…or early this morning, if you prefer…that you're the least prejudiced person I know. Isn't your opinion of Granddad just a bit biased?''

''Bram, it's not easy to reconcile science and messages from coyotes and golden foxes. *You* don't live that way, and from what I can deduce from talking to your cousins and siblings, neither does anyone else in your family.''

''We've all been homogenized,'' Bram said dryly. ''Jenna, it wasn't too many years ago that almost all Native Americans in the area leaned a lot further toward Granddad's style of living than yours and mine.''

She took in a big breath and released it slowly. ''I suppose you know a lot more about it than I do, but coyotes, Bram? Golden foxes?''

"One golden fox, Jenna. In all of his life, he's seen only one golden fox. Until he met you, that is."

"He did say what I thought he said, didn't he?"

"Yes, but don't take it to mean that he thought you were a very foxy lady—which you are, of course. Only Granddad hasn't noticed foxy females for quite a few years now."

"Then what *did* he mean?"

"Uh…" Bram didn't want to tell her about his great-grandfather's interpretation of meeting a human golden fox, and what Bram should do about not letting her get away. "When I drove him home he said you have a good heart."

"Meaning a heart attack is still a ways off?"

"Possibly, but I think he was referring more to your generous spirit and kindness."

"He sensed those things about me from one brief meeting?"

Bram grinned. "Probably made fast work of determining your personality because of your being a golden fox."

"It concerns me that you actually might be serious about that."

"Well, I think you're a golden fox, too, only the term means something much different to me than it does to Granddad."

Jenna's pulse quickened. Was he actually flirting with her? Did she *want* him flirting with her? Considering his erratic treatment of her, she shouldn't even be talking nicely to him. And yet there was no way she could deny the anticipatory thrills building within her.

"If I'm a fox, does that make you a coyote?" she asked. She'd never been overly fond of coyotes, so her question was more of a dig than a compliment.

He caught on and played along. "I'm not a coyote, I'm

a bear. A grizzly.'' Almost lazily he swiveled his desk chair so he could see out the window of his office.

"Liar. You've never even seen a grizzly. They're all up north.''

"Neither have I seen a golden fox before, but that doesn't mean they don't exist.''

"Foxes are red, not golden.''

Bram was enjoying the banter. He didn't ordinarily hang on the phone and flirt with women; in fact, this could be classified as a first. But this was Jenna, the love of his life, and he knew now that he was capable of behaving as giddily as any other guy in love.

"Yes, but…'' Bram suddenly got to his feet and stared out the window. Driving into the visitors' lot and parking was a pale gray Lincoln. "Jenna, I have to go. See you later.''

Putting down the phone before she could even say a quick "Bye,'' he stepped outside his office door and waited for the tall, dark-haired driver of the luxury car to enter the station.

The man walked in and stopped at the counter. "Is Sheriff Colton in?''

"Yes, sir, he is,'' the duty officer replied. "Do you want to see him?''

"Yes, thanks.''

"Give me your name and I'll let him know.''

"My name is Rand Colton.''

Bram was thunderstruck. The nosy but classy guy driving a Lincoln—as described by Sheila at the Crossroads Café—and asking questions about the Colton family, was a Colton himself?

Bram walked over to the counter. "I'm Sheriff Colton. Did I hear your name correctly?''

"I'm sure you did. Rand Colton.'' He extended his hand.

Bram shook it. "Come on back to my office." He led the mystery man into the room and gestured at the chairs in front of his desk. "Have a seat."

"Thanks." Rand sat down.

The two men looked each other over. Bram spoke first. "Are we related?"

"That's one of the things I'm trying to figure out. Let me explain."

"Believe me, I would appreciate an explanation. I've been told by at least a dozen good citizens that two strangers have been in town asking questions about the Coltons."

"*Two* strangers?"

"The other guy isn't with you?"

"No, and I can't imagine who he might be."

Bram studied the frown on Rand Colton's face. "No idea at all?"

"Do you have a clue to his identity?"

"I didn't have any clues about either one of you. Your being a Colton and walking in like this is one very big surprise. Someone said you were driving a pale gray Lincoln, and I've been looking for it ever since."

"I've been staying in Oklahoma City and driving over here."

"To stay out of sight?"

"Sheriff, I don't have any reason to stay out sight. No, I've been staying in Oklahoma City for various reasons, one of which is simple enough. I like the place. Maybe I should start at the beginning. I live in Washington, D.C. My father's name is Joe and I have an Uncle Graham. Other than siblings and kids, Dad and Graham are my only living blood relatives. About four, five months back, Dad was going through some old boxes stored in his attic that had once belonged to *his* father, and he ran across some old letters from a Gloria Colton. No, that's not right. What he found were envelopes with Gloria's name in the return address corner. Her name and the name of this town, without, I might point out, a street address. Whatever had been mailed in the envelopes—letters, I'm assuming—were missing, either accidentally misplaced or deliberately destroyed by my grandfather.

"I'm a lawyer, and Dad asked me to look into it, for, uh, reasons of his own. I agreed, of course, and went to Oklahoma City and began searching records. To my surprise I kept bumping into the Colton name—obviously a prolific family. Births, deaths, marriages…everything's recorded in the capital. But I still don't know exactly who Gloria Colton is and what connection she has to the Oklahoma Coltons, or if your family and mine are related. I would have come here to see you the minute I hit town if I'd known the sheriff was a Colton, but I only recently stumbled upon that fact. That's about it. I checked records at this courthouse as well, but…"

"Did you burn it down, too? Or *try* to burn it down?"

Rand looked stunned. "Good Lord, no! I heard it was arson, but I'm not a criminal, Sheriff."

"Bram. My first name is Bram."

"Well, Bram, who's on your family tree that might be related to some ancestor on mine? Can we discuss it?"

Bram eyed him speculatively. Sheila was right. Rand Colton looked well-groomed and well-off. He was dressed casually, but he hadn't bought those slacks and shirt at a discount store. Still, what in hell was this all about? Gran hadn't told any of them about her past. Was there any way she could in her present condition? If this guy calling himself Rand Colton wasn't some kind of con artist, and there was something *to* tell, that is?

"Before I discuss anything with you about Colton family business, I'd like to do a little checking of my own. Any objections?"

"None whatsoever." Rand got up. "Do you want to call me or should I call you?"

Bram shoved a pad and pen across the desk. "Write down where you're staying in O.C., and the phone number, if you have it. I'll phone when I have something to say."

"Fair enough." Rand bent forward and wrote on the pad. "Thanks for seeing me, and I wish I'd known the law around here was headed up by a Colton. This would have been my first stop. I think it would have gotten us off on a better footing."

Bram rose, they shook hands again and Rand left.

Bram fell back into his chair, feeling all but stupefied. One more shock like that one and he'd be a gibbering idiot.

"Hell's bells," he mumbled.

Thomas and Alice dropped in, each carrying a gift of food. Jenna had come to genuinely like this uncle and aunt of Bram's, and she greeted them warmly.

After discussing Gloria for a few moments, Alice said softly, "You're here six days a week, Jenna, dear. Why don't you regard our visit as an opportunity to get away for a few hours? We'll stay with Mom while you're gone."

"That's very generous of you," Jenna murmured. "There is something I'd like to do, and it wouldn't take more than two hours, probably less."

"Wonderful. Just tell us if there's anything we should do for Mom while you're gone."

"Thank you, but there's nothing right now. She's had lunch and her scheduled medication, and I believe she's napping. Just sit with her quietly until she wakes up. I'm sure she will be pleased to see you."

"I wish I were sure of that," Thomas said.

Jenna sympathized with the man wholeheartedly. His mother was daily losing ground, his grandfather was already mourning her demise, and the whole tragic scenario had to be one very bitter pill for Thomas to swallow.

But Jenna suspected he *was* swallowing it, however painful. George WhiteBear, after all, had practically raised Thomas and Trevor. He had to have been a strong influence in the twins' development, and Jenna could hardly fault Thomas for respecting his grandfather's ways and beliefs when he'd grown up with them.

Still, a tale about a message from a coyote wasn't something Jenna could just accept and go on from there. Her logical mind worked on proved facts. Most of the time, anyway. She wasn't very logical about Bram, she knew, which could very well be the reason she suffered such bone-jarring ambivalence whenever she thought of him.

Anyhow, she accepted Alice and Thomas's kind offer and drove away from the Colton Ranch enjoying the warm and sunny end-of-June day. The Fourth of July was just around the corner, and Black Arrow always put on a parade, a carnival and after-dark fireworks. This year she probably wouldn't be attending any of the events because of her patient.

Tears suddenly stung Jenna's eyes as she wondered if she would still have Gloria for a patient on the Fourth.

"Damn," she whispered, and wished all the way into Black Arrow that she hadn't volunteered her services that day in the hospital when she'd overheard Dr. Hall talking about needing a full-time nurse for Gloria. Jenna had wanted to force something to happen between her and Bram, of course, and it had.

But it wasn't exactly what she'd had in mind, and now she was all confused about Comanche lore and worrying constantly about Gloria.

Bram might have dropped his guard for a few teasing remarks on the phone this morning, but he had reverted to his usual brusque self mighty fast, practically hanging up in her ear.

Jenna sighed. She must lie in the bed she'd made. The situation was nobody's fault but her own, and despising Bram for being himself wasn't an option. He was, after all, no different today than he'd ever been.

In Black Arrow she drove directly to her father's huge home, parked her car and entered the house with her key. "Martha?" she called.

The cook and housekeeper appeared. "Why, Jenna. How nice to see you. You've been busy with Mrs. Colton for how long now?"

"Maybe a little too long, Martha," Jenna said with a smile, then realized how her reply might have sounded. "I don't mean to imply that I have a problem with caring for Gloria Colton. It's something else. Anyhow, I had a couple of hours off and came here to pick up a few things."

"Well, it's your home."

Jenna wanted to say that it wouldn't be her home for long. She'd been watching the *Chronicle*'s classified section for apartments to rent, and eventually realized that there were always units available in and around Black Arrow. When she was ready to rent a place and move out of her father's house, she would have very little trouble finding something to her liking.

"I don't have much time. It was nice seeing you, Martha." Jenna hurried up the stairs and went to the bed and bath suite that had been hers since childhood. Everything was in place, just as she'd left it, and she gathered a few items of clothing and then some things from the bathroom. She was putting them in a small overnight case when her father walked in.

Startled, she merely said, "Oh! I...didn't expect you to be home."

"I didn't expect to see you, either. Martha told me you were here when I came in."

"I'm only going to be here for a minute, Dad. I came to pick up some things I need at the ranch." She saw her father's expression change from elated to furious.

"I had hoped you were through with that band of Indians!" Carl said with a sneer.

Jenna winced at his crudity, but held her head high. "Well, I'm not, and if you must talk about some very nice people in that arrogant, holier-than-thou manner, please do it somewhere else."

Carl looked as though she had physically struck him. "I can't believe you would say something like that to me, your own father."

"I'm not a child anymore. Dad, I haven't been a child for fifteen years! I have a mind of my own and everyone has a right to like whom they please."

"Well, that includes me, missy, and don't you forget it."

"I'm sure I won't," Jenna said, and lowered her eyes to the things in the little suitcase. "That about does it." She zipped the case shut.

"Is that big sheriff chasing you around his house yet? Maybe you've let him catch you, huh? Is that what all this rebellion is about? I knew a long time ago that your being friends with that Willow Colton would cause me trouble."

Jenna stared at her father with unconcealed pity. "I feel sorry for you, Dad." Gripping her suitcase, she walked from the room.

Carl followed her down the stairs. "You feel sorry for me? *I* feel sorry for *you*! What in hell's come over you? You're sure not the same girl you were before your mother died."

Jenna whirled around at the foot of the stairs. "I don't *claim* to be. And you don't feel sorry for me, you're con-

cerned strictly with yourself and how other people perceive
you. Do you actually believe that people would think less
of you if you mingled with Native Americans? Called
some of them friends? Dad, what makes you think you
have a spotless reputation around town? Throughout the
entire county, for that matter, or maybe the whole darned
state?''

"And what's that supposed to mean?" Carl snarled.

"I'm sure you know, or you would if you'd let yourself
face the truth." Jenna walked away and exited by the front
door, the same way she'd come in only minutes before.
She got in her car, drove away and then had to pull over
to dry her eyes. She had never talked so harshly to her
father before; especially painful to her was the cruel way
in which she had referred to his unscrupulous business
methods. Even if people did talk behind his back, she
shouldn't have hurt him like that.

Troubled all afternoon about Rand Colton's sketchy tale
of a possible blood tie between the Washington Coltons—
wasn't that what he'd said, that he was from Washington,
D.C.?—and the Oklahoma Coltons, Bram drove around
aimlessly after eating dinner at a downtown diner. He
knew he should still be on the job, looking for the missing
gun, working on finding Black Arrow's infamous arsonist
and also the person who had burgled the newspaper office—maybe the same guy, maybe not—but he couldn't
force himself to concentrate on anything but personal problems, which just seemed to keep stacking up.

The jolt delivered by Rand that morning was one for
the books, though. How could there be a whole other
branch of Coltons that no one in Oklahoma had ever mentioned? Did Uncle Thomas know anything about it? If
there were any truth to it Gran would know, but even when
she tried her hardest to speak—which wasn't often—Bram

found it nearly impossible to understand her. And if Gran *did* know about the Washington Coltons, why had she never talked about them?

Bram found himself slowly cruising the street that Will and Ellie lived on. He hadn't seen or talked to Will since right after Gran's stroke, and he suddenly felt a strong desire to communicate with the best friend he'd ever had. Bram pulled into the Mitchells' driveway and got out of his patrol car. Will's pickup was there and so was Ellie's compact. Everyone was home.

Bram rapped on the front door and Will opened it. "Hey, look who's here! Come on in. Ellie's putting the boys to bed. How about a beer?"

"I'm driving a patrol car, so thanks, but no. I'll have a cup of coffee, though, if there's some made."

"There's *always* coffee in this house. You know that." They went to the kitchen and Will filled two mugs with coffee and brought them to the table. They sat and sipped hot coffee and eyed each other. "What's wrong?" Will finally asked.

"So many things I wouldn't know where to start," Bram admitted.

"Well, I'm listening if you want to talk."

"I know." Will was the only person Bram knew that he could sit and drink coffee with and not feel pressured into talking even if he had nothing to say. At the same time Will was the one person to whom Bram could tell something and not worry that it would get around town with the speed of light.

He took the medallion from his shirt pocket and laid it on the table. "I found this on the floor of the old depot. Take a look at it."

Will reached for it, held it up and peered at it. "Is this engraving or whatever it is the head of a coyote?"

"Looks like it to me."

"And you found it?"

"At the old depot."

Will's eyes met Bram's. "Kind of spooky, if you ask me. I mean, considering your great-granddad's relationship with coyotes, it strikes me as pretty darned odd that you'd walk into the old depot and find something like this."

"It strikes me that way, too." Bram picked up the medallion again and frowned at it. Then he dropped it back in his shirt pocket and heaved a sigh. "I talked to a man today who thinks he and his kin might be related to me and mine. He's from Washington, D.C., and I'm assuming that's where his whole family lives, although they could be scattered to hell and gone for all I really know about them. To tell you the truth, Will, I was so rattled by this guy introducing himself as Rand Colton that I didn't ask him a lot of the questions I *should* have asked. But he said he has some old letters—no, envelopes—with Gran's name on them that once belonged to his grandfather, which was what got him digging up the past."

Will slowly shook his head. "Your life is never dull, I'll give you that, Bram. But a guy you never heard of claiming to be a relative seems darned strange to me. What does he want? I mean, in the end, what is he really after?"

"Good question." Bram became thoughtful for a long moment, then said, "It can't be money, Will. The Coltons around here have jobs, but no one's wealthy by any stretch of the imagination. Just from his car and clothes I'd have to say that Rand—if that's really his name—has more money than any one of us. Maybe more than all of us put together."

Ellie walked in. "Well, hi, Bram. I didn't hear you come in."

"I was about to leave, Ellie. I'm still on duty. Just stopped by to say hello."

"How's your grandmother doing?"

"Not very well, I'm afraid." Bram got to his feet and drank the last of his coffee. "Will, thanks for the coffee. Ellie, tell the boys I'll come by and see them when I get the chance."

"Try to bring Nellie with you," Ellie said with a laugh.

"I'll try. Bye, Ellie." When Will walked with him out to the patrol car, Bram asked, "Is she pregnant, Will?"

His friend's proud grin lit up his whole face. "Yes sir, she is."

Bram got into the vehicle. "I'll pray for a girl this time."

"Do that. Nothing would make Ellie happier. Of course, if it's another boy she'll welcome him, too."

"She's a wonderful mother and you're a lucky guy."

"Hey, you could be just as lucky if you'd give the poor lonesome gals of Comanche County half a chance."

Bram started the ignition and began backing out of the driveway. "Blow it out your ear, Mitchell," he called through the open window.

Chapter Eleven

It was going to be another long, lonely evening, Jenna thought while wandering Bram's big empty house. She had completed her nighttime ritual with Gloria, and the elderly woman was already sleeping. Jenna knew it would be hours before she herself felt sleepy, and she had her choice of watching TV or reading, neither of which seemed at all appealing. She was on edge and had been since exchanging those cross words with her father. Thomas and Alice had stayed only a short time after her return to the ranch, but there had been Gloria's needs to keep Jenna occupied. Now there was nothing to occupy either her hands or her mind, and while she restlessly roamed, resentments old and new gnawed at her.

Volunteering to come out here had been a huge mistake, she thought unhappily. Sleeping with Bram had been an even bigger mistake, even though her lack of good sense in that department had been caused by her deeply rooted feelings for him. Obviously he didn't suffer from the same weakness of mind and spirit that she did. When he thought of her at all—*if* he did—what went through his mind? Did he consider her cheap? Easy? Just another notch on the old bedpost?

At moments like this she could easily hate him. No one would ever convince her that he had lived the way he was living now before *she* moved in. He stayed away from his own home as much as he could because she was in it.

And yet she knew he didn't want her to leave. He had praised her on her care of Gloria more than once, and Jenna believed wholeheartedly that Bram Colton didn't hand out undeserved compliments to anyone.

"Oh, shoot," she said out loud, heaving a sigh. Why couldn't Bram come home and just be nice? Share a meal with her? Talk and laugh with her? She would never make demands he didn't want to fulfill…would she?

Jenna plopped down into a living room chair and cursed herself for falling in love with the wrong man. She had let him take advantage of her weakness for him, and even worse, would probably do it again if he were ever around long enough to make another pass.

Tears threatened, which only made her angrier than she already was. There were more fish in the sea than Bram Colton, and she was *not* going to spend the best years of her life crying over him.

Rising, she went to the kitchen and put on the teakettle. While waiting for the water to boil, she remembered the old books in Bram's closet. Were they still there, hidden under that blanket? She didn't feel comfortable accusing Bram of anything that even hinted at dishonesty—despite resenting him on a personal level—but why on earth would he have obviously valuable old record books from the courthouse concealed in his closet?

He must have a reason, she told herself, a perfectly ra-

tional reason, and she should never think otherwise. And
if that were the case then he wouldn't mind if she looked
through them. It might be a pleasant way to pass the evening.

With that seemingly logical decision in mind, Jenna
strode boldly to Bram's bedroom and went to his closet.
The blanketed bundle was still there, and she hesitated a
moment, wondering why. But then she told herself to stop
trying to analyze a man she would *never* understand. Bend-
ing down, she pulled the top book from under the blanket
and carried it to the kitchen. It was much heavier than
she'd expected.

Jenna placed it on the kitchen table, then hurried to the
stove to turn off the burner under the whistling teakettle.
After preparing a pot of tea, she sat at the table with a cup
and turned back the cover of the old book.

She loved the precise, formal penmanship. In places the
ink had faded badly, but most of the entries were legible.
Jenna turned page after page, reading some of the notations
that recorded important data about Black Arrow's early
inhabitants. Occasionally she ran across a name she recognized, which she found fascinating. She'd always known
that some of the families in the area had ancestors who
had pioneered in Oklahoma long before statehood.

She had almost finished drinking the pot of tea and had
reached the last section of the book when some script on
the yellowed pages suddenly leaped out at her. Excited by
her discovery, she read the dozens of entries recording the
transfer of federal land to people of Comanche blood. And
much to her delight, she found an entry for "WhiteBear,
Juab."

Juab must have been George WhiteBear's father, she
thought, and quickly scanned the final few pages for more
information on that rather famous land transfer. When she
reached the end, she pushed the book aside and hastened

to Bram's closet for another one. She toted it to the kitchen as well and eagerly opened it.

The land transfer recordings took up several pages of the second book, and Jenna looked them over in a perfectly innocent search for other familiar names. But nothing could have prepared her for one entry. The name was Elliot GrayEagle, and "Elliot" was spelled exactly the same way as her own last name.

She stared at that entry as though it should mean something, but of course, it couldn't possibly. There were no GrayEagles on her family tree. And besides, the name was reversed. If it had been GrayEagle Elliot, she might have cause to wonder, but...

With her heart pounding, Jenna sat back. She knew perfectly well that Elliot wasn't a common Comanche name. And yet...?

She began turning pages again, looking, reading, searching for another notation for Mr. GrayEagle. She was so accustomed to listening for any sound Gloria might make that she was able to do that and still concentrate on the book in front of her. Jenna was almost to the end of the second book when the GrayEagle named jumped off the page at her.

Only this time it was an entry that read: "Son, born to GrayEagle and Moselle Elliot."

"My God," Jenna whispered in shock. She had heard the name "Moselle" before—from her own father, in fact, a long time ago when he'd been boasting proudly of the Elliot family's contributions to Oklahoma's development.

Was it actually possible for him to be ignorant of the true nature of his own history? He had Indian blood, *Comanche* blood! So did she!

Well, that wasn't a given. A white man could have sired Moselle's children, but Jenna didn't think so. In fact, she was convinced that her dad, Carl Elliot, was a direct descendant of GrayEagle and Moselle Elliot.

And so was she.

Jenna felt weak and shaky. This was incendiary information and just might destroy her father if it became common gossip. Dare she even tell him about it? Dare she tell anyone what she'd unearthed in these old books?

Through the density of fog and confusion clouding her brain Jenna heard the front door open and close. Bram had come home! Startled out of her fearful preoccupation, she jumped up and tried to pick up both books at once. One fell to the floor with a horrendously loud bang, and Jenna scrambled to scoop it up again.

Bram walked in. He stopped and frowned at her. "What are you doing?"

Jenna turned three shades of red. "I...I—"

"Damn!" he said. "I forgot all about those books. But suppose you tell me how they got from my closet to the kitchen table? And where's the third one?"

"Don't you dare yell at me!"

"Then start talking!" He was tired and so saturated with problems of every description that there wasn't a drop of patience in his entire system. Not even for Jenna, who truly looked like the proverbial kid caught with her hand in the cookie jar. She also looked mad as hell, probably because she *had* been caught.

"I'm not one of the criminals in your jail, so don't treat me like one!"

"I never said you were a criminal. Hell's bells, don't put words in my mouth. The ones I come up with on my own are bad enough."

"I could come up with a few choice ones myself right about now," Jenna retorted, although she was so internally shaken at being caught like this that her only wish was for invisibility. But would she back down from this man's righteous fury? Never! "What I'd like to know is why you've been hiding in your closet important and probably valuable books that had to have come from the courthouse!"

"I brought them home for safekeeping!"

"Likely story!"

"Don't believe me. Right now I personally don't give a damn what you think." Bram stormed out.

Jenna sank back in her chair, totally drained by anger she had no right to feel. She'd snooped and gotten caught; it was as simple as that.

Bram was at the front door before he remembered the reason he'd come home this early. Veering to the right, he went to see if Gran was still awake. All things considered, the only person who could prove or disprove Rand Colton's theory of relativity, so to speak, was Gran. If it had happened—whatever *it* was—then she had lived it. There had to be a way to communicate with her, and he'd come home to the ranch with several ideas on how to go about it.

The master bedroom was shadowed, but Bram could see well enough because of the night-lights dimly illuminating the room and the adjoining bathroom. Gloria was clearly sleeping. He would have to put his theories to the test tomorrow.

Bram turned on his heel and again headed for the front door. He went outside, breathed in the pleasantly cool night air and felt something give within himself. He'd been wound too tightly lately and the bomb inside him had gone off with the wrong person. He felt like a dog for talking that way to Jenna. She didn't deserve his wrath for any reason, and her looking at those old books should not have lit his fuse the way it had.

Cursing his temper, which rarely surfaced, Bram walked down to the barns. Nellie was with him, as she always was when he was at the ranch, and her presence helped to calm his frazzled nerves. But even feeling less explosive didn't alleviate the severe remorse eating holes in his gut. Jenna would probably never forgive his rudeness tonight, and why should she?

He filled Nellie's food and water bowls, then checked the horses' water trough. A couple of them approached the fence and Bram petted the nose of one.

"Everything's gone to hell in a handbasket," he said to the pretty mare. "And tonight I just might have proved that I deserve every damn thing that's happened."

He turned and walked away, stood near the barns and looked up at the night sky. Instead of stars he saw clouds. It looked to him like the area was in for some rain.

Dropping his gaze to the house, he wondered if Jenna was packing to leave. It wouldn't surprise him. In fact, why in heaven's name would she stay?

But what would he do if she left? There were other nurses, there must be, but Jenna was so perfect with Gran.

She was also perfect for him, even if he couldn't admit his feelings to her. If only he could. If only he could go back in the house, take her in his arms, tell her how much he loved her and hold her throughout the night.

It was an impossible dream and totally unrealistic, but he *could* do one thing. He could apologize and hope to high heaven that she would believe in his sincerity and stay on.

Bram walked to the house, not hurrying, because he was honestly afraid of what he might find when he went in. All too soon and yet not soon enough, he had covered the ground from the barns to the house. He chose to enter by the back door, and he went in quietly.

The kitchen was dark, and he stepped beyond it and looked around. From where he stood the master bedroom looked the same, still dimly lit, but the living room lights were on. It appeared that was where he would find Jenna.

Inhaling an anxious breath, Bram went to the entrance to the living room and looked in. Jenna was sitting in a chair with a handful of soggy tissues and reddened eyes. When she saw him, a fresh flow of tears dribbled down her cheeks and she mopped them up with the tissues.

He'd made her cry. Feeling lower than pond scum, he slowly and hesitatingly walked toward her. Encouraged because she didn't say something like "Back off, jerk!" he knelt on the floor in front of her knees.

"I'm so sorry," he said huskily. "You can look at those old books anytime you want. The only reason I have them is because the insurance adjuster found them still intact in a metal cabinet in one of the burned rooms and suggested I give them to a local museum. He thought they might have some historical value. I brought them home that day and forgot all about them."

Jenna's heart skipped a beat. Historical value? A museum? Anyone examining the old books just might figure out the same thing she had tonight.

But that would take the onus off her. She wouldn't have to wonder and worry if she should tell her dad or anyone else about her discovery. If anyone *did* study the books and eventually put it all together, it would get around, make no mistake. Carl Elliot might know people in high places within the governing and business sectors of Oklahoma, as Bram had pointed out, but in Black Arrow he had very few friends. Actually, the yes-men who dogged his footsteps weren't friends, in Jenna's estimation. They were leeches, only hanging around for the occasional crumb her father threw them.

Biting her lower lip, she raised her teary eyes and gazed directly at Bram, who looked so downcast and sick at heart that her own heart reached out to him.

But he had hurt her terribly, and not just tonight. Knowing the reason behind his almost constant determination to stay away from her didn't lessen the pain it caused. And she kept letting it happen because she loved him. She was a pretty sad case, but so was he.

"Can you forgive me?" he asked in a shaky voice completely alien to the way he normally spoke.

She dabbed at her eyes again, not giving a whit if he saw her crying tonight. "I...don't know. You yelled at me for no reason at all."

"I yelled because I'm so on edge that I feel like I'm just barely hanging on with my fingertips. You don't know all that's been going on."

"I might, if you ever really talked to me."

Bram had long dedicated himself to avoiding a conversation like this one with Jenna. It was heading in a dangerous direction, and he knew that if he ever started spilling the truth of his feelings for her, he might never stop. He couldn't let it happen.

"Jenna," he said pleadingly, and laid his hands on her thighs. "Tell me you can forgive me."

Even knowing that he had completely ignored her last remark, she found that his big hands touching her totally turned the tables. It wasn't fair that she melted at the contact, but she didn't know how to combat that sort of power.

In the back of her mind were Moselle and GrayEagle Elliot and the fact of the Comanche blood that she was so certain flowed in her own veins. She would give almost anything to tell Bram all about it, but if he ever fell in love with her, she wanted him to love her for herself, not because she had suddenly discovered that a pint or so of Comanche blood mingled in her body with that of so many white ancestors.

No, she couldn't tell Bram about it any more than she

could tell her father. They were both so ridiculously prejudiced that it was a wonder she loved either one of them.

And yet she did, and if Bram would just once say something real and meaningful to her, and she could love him openly, her life would be truly complete.

"Why would you care if I forgave you or not?" she whispered, praying he would stop measuring their worth as human beings through the screen of racial prejudice.

"Why would I care?" he repeated with a frown. "Why *wouldn't* I care? I need you here, Jenna." He leaned forward and slid his hands up to her waist. "I need you," he whispered.

Her pulse rate quickened. She needed him, too. Without dissecting his simple message for hidden meanings, she shut her eyes and savored his nearness, his scent. In the next instant she felt his lips brush hers, linger on one corner of her mouth and then the other. It was a sensual kiss, and all of her vows to keep Bram at arm's length completely disintegrated.

She put her arms around his neck and parted her lips for his next kiss. He didn't disappoint her, and when their lips met this time the kiss turned hungry almost at once. They quickly became frenzied with desire and tried to undress each other.

But she was wearing slacks, he was still in uniform with all that leather stuff—including his gun—around his waist, and everything was a hindrance to lovemaking, even the badge on his shirt.

He got up, pulled her to her feet and said two words. "My bedroom."

She almost went. She was so close to going that she started to take a step. But then the reality of their relationship—or rather, their *non*relationship—struck full force, and she dug in her heels.

He looked at her questioningly. "No," she said. "We can't keep doing this."

If he said right now, "But I love you, Jenna," she knew that she would follow him anywhere, be it his bedroom or the moon. But he didn't say it, and her heart broke into a dozen pieces one more time.

"You're right," Bram said, and though he felt a lot more like punching himself than acting all noble about this rebuff, he told himself to be glad that one of them had a little sense. He obviously had none where Jenna was concerned, but did he have to keep proving it over and over again?

Disgusted with himself, he said, "I'm not through working yet today. I'll see you later." He walked from the room, and a second later Jenna heard the front door open and close.

"Sure you will," she said with a sob she absolutely could not hold back.

Bram had only one good thought during his drive back to town. At least Jenna hadn't packed her clothes after his rude and completely unreasonable outburst in the kitchen.

Bram hadn't had to go back to work at all, but he didn't have to rack his brain to find something to do to kill a few hours. He visited the homeless shelters and talked to anyone who didn't try to slink out of sight when they saw him walk in.

Even the ones who weren't afraid of the law claimed to know nothing about John Doe's death at the old depot, so Bram was making very little headway with the case.

He was about to give up and leave the second shelter when one of the volunteers who kept the place running motioned him over. The volunteer was a woman, around sixty, Bram figured, with a round, friendly face and short gray hair.

He followed her into a storage room, where she switched on a ceiling light and closed the door. "I couldn't help overhearing your conversation with those fellows out there," she said. "Have you ever run across a guy named Tobler? I think that's his last name, but I've heard him called Toby, too. He's short—around five-four, I'd guess, and sort of pudgy. A nasty sort with a big mouth. He comes here every so often and I doubt that anyone's glad to see him, 'cause most everyone avoids him, or tries to.

"Anyhow, he was here a few nights ago. I was on my knees behind that long buffet cleaning out some drawers when I heard Tobler's voice just on the other side of the counter. He was telling someone about a gun that he'd found and pawned. Would that have anything to do, do you think, with that poor fellow who died near the old depot?"

"It might. What's your name?"

"Lily. I'm here almost every day. Got nothing better to do, and most of the people who come in here are in genuine need of a helping hand."

"Well, it's folks like you that keep these shelters open, Lily. Would you happen to have any idea where I might find this Tobler or Toby or whatever his name is?"

"Not a clue. They come and go, Sheriff, and it's a rare day when I recognize any of them on the street."

"I understand. Toby said he pawned the gun? We've checked the pawnshops several times."

"Well, he probably lied about that. That's the kind he is."

"Do you know the name of the guy he was talking to?"

"No, and that was the one and only time I've ever seen him. We have lots of those, Sheriff. They're passing through on their way to only heaven-knows-where and stop in for a hot meal and sometimes a shower and a cot for the night. Then they're gone."

"But Tobler sticks around."

"Oh, he's hung around Black Arrow for at least a year. Between you and me, I think he's involved in the drug trade. I have no proof of that, you understand, but it's still my belief. I'm surprised you don't know him."

"Maybe he's smarter than he looks, Lily. Is there anything else you can tell me?"

"Not at the moment, but if I see or hear anything else about a gun…or if Tobler should happen to drop in…I'll give you a call."

"Thanks, I appreciate the information."

Bram left the shelter, at long last harboring a ray of hope about the old depot case. He drove directly to the station and processed an APB—all-points bulletin—with Tobler's name and description, and an order to bring him in for questioning so every deputy would be on the lookout for him.

Bram cruised the town's darker streets before going home again, checking alleyways and the places where some of Black Arrow's more disreputable residents hung out. Water sought its own level and so did criminals. Bram had no pity for lawbreakers, especially ones who trafficked in drugs or abused children. Those were the two deadliest sins as far as he was concerned and, sadly, they were the crimes that were the most common, even in a nice little town like Black Arrow.

Finally, of course, Bram had to go home. He was so tired that his eyes were threatening to close on him.

Driving between town and the ranch, Bram saw on the windshield the first raindrops of the storm he'd known was on its way. They slid down the glass and looked like tears to him. Like Jenna's tears.

A sorrow of such mammoth proportions struck him that he nearly drove off the road. He turned the wheel just in time and finally had to face what he'd been doing to himself. To avoid Jenna, the only woman he would ever love, he'd been working himself into an early grave—which would result in permanent avoidance, all right.

He clenched his jaw so tightly that his back teeth ached. He would *never* have Jenna, and he could count what blessings he did have from now till the day he died and still be miserable. Oh, he could make do. He'd still work, still raise horses, still attend family functions and still act as though he was glad to be alive and breathing Oklahoma air. And Jenna would eventually meet the right man, get married and have kids. If they ran into each other they would say hello and how are you and goodbye.

How would he bear it?

Grim-faced, he drove into his driveway, parked and went into the silent house. With barely a glance toward the master bedroom, where Jenna lay warm and silky and sleeping, he went to his own room, undressed and crawled between the sheets.

He had thought he would go out like a light. But he lay there listening to the rain on the roof and thinking of Jenna for a long, long time.

Chapter Twelve

It was early, the house was quiet, and Jenna woke up with one thought clear and vivid in her mind. *I've had enough!*

It was all about Bram, of course. She would do her job and give Gloria the best possible care and encouragement, but from this moment on Bram Colton was a big zero to her. If he dared to touch her again he was going to rue the impulse. Never mind that she always kissed him back; he had no right to kiss her in the first place. What did he think she was, a toy to play with when he was in the mood and then ignore until the next time his blood heated up?

Last night he had backed off the second she had told him no. At least he knew what the word meant, which was a point in his favor.

But in her estimation, any of his other good points had nothing at all to do with her. He didn't need her in his life, it was that simple, and it was time she relegated any and all romantic nonsense about Bram to the trash can, where it belonged.

Of course, if she told him what she'd discovered in the old courthouse books…

But then her dad would be hurt, and despite his many flaws, he was still her dad.

No matter how hard she tried to reconcile her hopes and affections with the realities of her life, she always ended up on the same old merry-go-round, Jenna thought disgustedly, and threw back the covers to get up.

It was close to ten before she finished with her patient's morning schedule. Gloria had been gently bathed, fed and medicated, and she was awake but resting. It was time for Jenna to tend to her own bodily needs; a little breakfast was in order.

She went to the kitchen, ran water into the teakettle and placed it on the stove. Then she heard a sound and froze. Someone was in the house!

After a long moment of spine-tingling fear, Jenna regained her wits. She was hearing the shower in the second bathroom, the one Bram used. Hadn't he gone to work before dawn this morning? He was *never* home at this time of day. Was he ill? Had something happened to keep him in bed this late?

Jenna's heart began pounding, and that infuriated her. Envisioning Bram naked in the shower was lunacy. Hadn't she just vowed to forget the man, to put him out of her thoughts forever?

"You fool, you fool," she whispered, and went over to the table, weakly sinking onto a chair. Fat lot of good any common sense she might actually possess did her, when all Bram had to do to remind her of his strong, hard body and exquisite lovemaking was to take a shower. She loved him and she might as well face facts: nothing was ever going to destroy that love, not her vows, not his emotional cruelty.

The teakettle whistled and she got up and made a pot

of tea. She eyed the coffeemaker and then sighed and made coffee for Bram. She was too darned softhearted, she knew. She should have let him make his own coffee.

But she'd never been anything but softhearted, and she wasn't apt to suddenly turn cold and hard at thirty, even if she would be a heck of a lot more capable of dealing with Bram if she did.

She was eating toast with her tea when Bram walked in. Jenna thought she might die on the spot; he was just too gorgeous in his crisp, fresh uniform, with his face all shiny and his hair still damp from his shower.

"Morning," he said without really looking at her.

"Morning," she replied. "That's fresh coffee. I just made it."

Bram turned and looked directly at her, realizing that she was drinking tea, yet had made him coffee.

"Thanks," he said, feeling guilty because of her kindness. This was how their mornings would be if they were married, he thought while pouring himself a cup of coffee. She would have her tea, but she would go out of her way to make his coffee. And then they would sit across the table from each other and talk about yesterday and the day ahead, eat breakfast together and…and—

Cut it out, you damn fool! Bram drank his coffee standing up, leaning against a counter.

"Aren't you going to eat anything?" Jenna asked.

"I never eat when I first get up."

"I…I've never known you to sleep so late. You're not ill, are you?"

"I'm not ill. I was just so knocked out when I went to bed that I didn't wake up at my usual time." He took another swallow, then added, "But sleeping in was all right this morning. I have to talk to Gran. Is she awake?"

"She was about ten, maybe fifteen minutes ago."

"I'll go and check on her." He topped off his cup and took it with him.

Jenna mourned her defenselessness after he'd gone. He didn't even know the power he had over her. Oh, he was probably relatively confident of his sexual appeal to women in general, which was all she was to him—a woman in general. It hurt like hell to acknowledge, let alone dwell on.

But how could she not know where she stood with Bram? Sure, he would make love to her. He'd probably go to bed with her every darned night she was here, if she let it happen. But sex—even incredibly good sex—wasn't love, and love was what she really wanted from him.

Jenna refilled her teacup, lifted it to her lips and wondered why Bram was going to attempt conversation with his grandmother. If Gloria had taken any steps to better her condition, she might be speaking with some clarity today. Instead, the few times she actually tried to say something, it came out so garbled that Jenna rarely comprehended even a syllable.

Bram had moved a chair close to the bed. He held his coffee cup and smiled at his grandmother. "Are you feeling any better, Gran?" She merely looked at him. "Gran, something funny is going on and I have to talk to you about it." Her expression never changed, and Bram took a breath, got rid of his cup and then closed his big hand around one of hers.

"Gran, did you ever know any Colton other than the one you married?" To his astonishment, Gloria's eyes widened and she moved her head on the pillow to signify "no." Bram got that message clearly and was elated that he had succeeded in gaining her full attention. Possibly arousing her curiosity, as well.

"Let me explain, Gran. A guy named Rand Colton came to my office and introduced himself. He and another man

I haven't yet located have both been asking questions all over town about the family. About you, Gran, in particular. According to Rand, there's a mystery in *his* family regarding some old envelopes, supposedly sent by you to Rand's grandfather. Gran, I know you never liked talking about the past. I recall getting curious at times and asking questions that you never quite answered. I respect your right to privacy, but this thing with a stranger named Colton has me spinning. Gran," Bram said gently, "I have to know if there's any truth to his story."

Gloria's mouth moved spasmodically. She was trying to talk! Bram leaned down and put his ear close to her lips. The sounds Gran made weren't words, he realized, but she was trying so hard to get something out that he didn't move away from her.

And finally, after numerous attempts, she said something he *did* understand. "Truth…find the truth." And then another few words came through. "For…you kids." She heaved an exhausted sigh and shut her eyes.

Bram slowly sat up and pondered what Gran had said. And she *had* spoken, she really had. But what "truth" was he supposed to unearth, and *what* was for "you kids"?

Another mystery, Bram thought with a deep frown. Well, he'd accomplished one thing, anyway. Gran didn't know Rand Colton, if that was really his name, and Bram wasn't going to waste any time "searching family trees" with the guy, as he'd suggested. Bram had too many other, much more serious things to concentrate on than that.

Although when he *did* have some time he would try to figure out what Gran had meant with the few words she'd struggled so hard to impart.

None of it made a drop of sense to Bram, and he doubted that he'd ever get to the bottom of it. Although if Rand Colton kept pestering him, and that other guy kept nosing into Colton family business, they were both apt to end up cooling their heels in the county jail. Besides, Rand's projection of complete shock when Bram had asked him if he'd tried to burn down the courthouse might only mean that the guy was a good actor.

Bram sat back and, with heartfelt sorrow, watched his grandmother sleep. Seemingly overnight she had changed from a strong, independent, active woman to a frail, help-less little thing. It hurt terribly to see her like this, and when he felt the powerful suction of unbridled grief pulling him down, he got up from the chair, took his cup and quietly left the room.

He returned to the kitchen, where Jenna was rinsing the few dishes she'd used and putting them in the dishwasher.

"Was she awake?" she asked.

"Yes." Bram waited until Jenna had finished at the sink, then rinsed his own cup.

"But you didn't get her to talk clearly enough to un-derstand what she said, did you?"

"I heard a few words."

Jenna looked at him. "You did? What did she say?"

"Something about finding the truth."

"Those exact words?"

"Yes."

"Bram, that's wonderful! I try every day to get her to at least attempt speech, and I get nowhere. How did you get her to at least try to talk?"

He didn't want to discuss it. It was probably all utter nonsense, anyway. "I don't know why she would talk to me and not to you. I have to go to work now. See you later." He was just beyond the kitchen doorway when the phone rang. Turning back, thinking the call was for him, he heard Jenna answer.

"Colton Ranch...oh, hello Dr. Hall," she said. "All right...Richard. Apparently this isn't a professional call." After another pause, she stated, "Oh, I can't. I'm sorry, but I really can't leave her at night. I know I've been refusing my Thursdays off, but I've developed a true bond with Gloria and I hate leaving her with any other nurse.''

Bram leaned against the wall next to the doorway and listened. Dr. Hall, that jerk, was trying to talk Jenna into leaving Gran with someone else and go out with him! Bram's hands curled into fists as jealousy nearly ate him alive. He could not stop himself from peering around the doorway to see what expression was on Jenna's face.

"Well, yes, after I leave here I suppose we could have dinner together," Jenna said, and accidentally turned just enough to see Bram watching her. And listening! "Richard, I have to say goodbye.'' She quickly put down the phone, and just as quickly Bram walked away.

She was angry enough to not let him get away with this, and she ran after him. He was in his bedroom, securing his leather belt with all its paraphernalia—including that big holster and gun—around his waist, and he glanced at her when she appeared in the doorway.

But instead of the fury that had brought her from the kitchen, which she'd planned to unload on Bram for eavesdropping on a personal conversation, she found herself apologizing and trying to explain Richard Hall's call. She made a mess of it, too, stumbling over her own words.

Finally Bram shrugged and said coolly, "You're entitled. Don't sweat it.''

Jenna was stunned and then angry again. "Are you as rude to everyone else as you are to me? I'm entitled to have friends? How generous of you to say so.''

"Well, you weren't getting very far with your explanation and so I thought I'd help you out.''

"You thought nothing of the kind! You saw another opportunity to make me miserable and you took it!''

"Jenna, that's not true.'' Bram finished with the buckle on his belt and then stood looking at her. Why were they constantly at each other's throats? "Damn it, I wouldn't hurt you for anything. Don't you know that?"

"And I would know that because…?" Doubt and disdain were clear on her face.

Bram clenched his jaw, rebelling at the ridicule he heard in her voice and saw in her expression. "It's either something you know or you don't. Obviously you don't."

"Obviously! And just remember this, you…you jerk! There are many, *many* things about me that *you* don't know!"

"The only things I don't know about you are things I don't *care* to know."

"Oh, really," she drawled sarcastically. "Your ego can't deal with reality, can it? To maintain your swelled head you have to believe you're the only man who turns on a woman who just happens to turn *you* on!"

"That's absurd. You're talking nonsense and I don't have time to waste. I have to go." Bram moved toward her. "Are you going to move on your own or do I have to move you?"

"You wouldn't dare!"

"Oh, for hell's sake," Bram muttered, and put his hands around her waist with the intention of lifting her off the floor and setting her down anywhere but in the doorway.

But it didn't turn out that way. Without even a glimmer of forethought, he pulled her up against him and began kissing her. "Jenna…Jenna," he said yearningly, hoarsely, between kisses that got hungrier by the second.

And fool that she was, she kissed him back…again. She leaned into him and kissed him with as much fervor as he was kissing her.

And then, just like that, he let go of her. Jenna reeled as he strode out of his room, anger clearly visible on her face and in the set of his shoulders.

It was too much for her to take. She had kissed him

back instead of saying something scathing to make him rue the day, and she'd been so sure she could deal with his next pass!

She couldn't just stand there and despise both of them as she was doing, she realized, and she took off running, pulling open the front door just as he was driving away.

"I hate you!" she yelled.

Bram heard her, and he drove to Black Arrow and the sheriff's station with the heartbreaking phrase *I hate you* repeating over and over in his head, along with enormous amounts of self-disgust. Why wouldn't Jenna hate him? He wasn't particularly fond of himself these days, and God knows he hadn't been treating Jenna in the way she deserved.

But he wanted her—his beautiful golden girl—and he couldn't have her! The pull and tug of that knowledge would make any man a little crazy.

Bram tortured himself with memories of making love with Jenna until he braked to a stop in his parking place at the station. With a pain in his stomach that felt like the start of an ulcer—he was going to have to begin his days with something other than strong black coffee, he acknowledged—he went inside.

"What's happening?" he asked the duty officer.

"Nothing much. Last night's reports are on your desk."

"Thanks." Bram went to his office, passing up the coffee machine, while longing for a cup. At his desk he read the reports, then sat back and pondered the few words Gran had managed to convey. Should he put an end to this whole Colton thing by phoning Rand and telling him "No deal"? And maybe adding, "Frankly, I'm not all that sold on your story and can't help considering the possibility of your being up to no good."

But perhaps he was putting the cart before the horse.

Should he make that sort of decision without further investigation? Maybe Great-granddad knew something of the past that he'd never talked about.

Abruptly Bram got to his feet. On his way out of the station he announced to everyone present, "Get me on the radio if you need me. There's something I have to do."

The usual parade of Coltons came and went all morning. They were not a happy or boisterous group. Some of them left the house weeping quietly, and Jenna empathized so strongly with their sorrow over Gran's condition that she shed a few tears herself.

But it was Willow who worried Jenna. Something besides her grandmother's bad health was bothering the young woman, Jenna sensed, and she wished Willow would talk to her about it.

When she took her leave, Jenna hugged her. "If you ever need someone to lean on, Willow, you know where to find me."

"I know, Jenna, and I've always valued your friendship. But some things…well, some things just can't be discussed with even the best of friends."

Those few words from her friend, an admission of sorts, made Jenna positive that Willow was feeling the weight of a problem she couldn't bring herself to share.

After Willow had gone, Jenna compared their situations. Chances were that Willow's "problem" was a man. Jenna's certainly was, and she couldn't talk about it to anyone, either. Willow was right. There were some secrets a woman couldn't reveal to anyone.

Bram parked in his great-granddad's driveway next to George WhiteBear's old pickup truck. As usual, George's three friendly mutts wriggled all over the place and put their wet noses against the legs of Bram's pants.

"Hey, knock it off," he told them, but in a fond way.

George stepped out onto his porch and Bram began walking toward him. "How are you, Granddad?" he called.

"I am well. How is my daughter?"

"Not so well, I'm afraid."

"Come in."

George sat in his favorite chair and Bram took another. "Soon you will be delivering bad news," George said in that somber way he had of speaking about serious matters.

"How soon?" Bram asked quietly as a stab of deep sorrow shot through his chest.

"Soon," George repeated.

Bram took a breath. "Granddad, there's something I have to ask you about."

"Go ahead."

"Have you ever known any person with the last name of Colton besides the man Gran married?"

"I never even knew him. He died shortly after their marriage. He was a white man, you know. Maybe he had weak blood. I felt bad for Gloria."

"Are you saying you never saw him at all?"

"I think that's what I said. Should I say it in different words?"

"No, I understood you. It just surprised me. So you've never met anyone named Colton?"

"I think you do need to hear some different words."

Bram held up his hand. "No...not necessary. I heard what you said just fine. It just seems so peculiar that Gran never brought her husband home to meet you."

"He died. How could she bring him?"

"Well, he didn't die two minutes after the ceremony, did he? Granddad, they were married long enough for Gran to conceive Dad and Uncle Thomas. Exactly how long were they married before he died? Do you know that?"

"You sound as though you might be thinking he did a little teepee creeping before the ceremony."

Bram almost laughed, but managed to stifle the impulse. "That's pretty immaterial at this late date, but I'm still amazed that Gran didn't bring him home to meet you. So how long was she away before returning home, pregnant and widowed?"

George became thoughtful for a few moments, then said, "Two, three months is a pretty good guess."

"I see. Then she was just barely pregnant…and newly widowed. Must have been hard on her."

"You play, you pay," George announced solemnly.

Bram nearly choked. "That's definitely not a Comanche saying, Granddad."

"I've learned a few things from my white brothers over the years."

Bram got to his feet. "I'm sure you have. I have to go, Granddad. See you later."

"Yes, you will."

Bram drove back to town, even more perplexed over the Rand Colton problem than he'd been during the drive to George's place. It was hard to believe that another bunch of Coltons—ostensibly residing in Washington, D.C.—suddenly gave a whit about a family of Coltons living in Oklahoma. There was something strange going on, and Rand probably knew what it was.

Bram would use that Oklahoma City phone number Rand had left him and ask a few questions. After all, he thought, nothing ventured, nothing gained.

But the second Bram walked into the station he was told, "Wagner and Hobart picked up Tobler. We put him in a holding cell until you got back."

Bram's outlook on life in general brightened considerably. "Did he say anything?"

"Yeah, he's really got a mouth on him. Called us every

name in the book and some I think he must have invented. He had a good-size stash on him, Bram, enough grass to make his charge a felony instead of a misdemeanor, if you decide to arrest him.''

''Bring him to the small interrogation room. We'll let him sweat in there for about thirty minutes while I run and grab something to eat. I haven't had a bite yet today.''

Four hours later Bram was still trying to get Tobler, the little creep, to talk. He had to wear the guy down, and if that meant repeating the same questions over and over until they gagged even him, Bram would do it.

''Tell me about the grass.'' ''Tell me about the gun.'' ''Where is it now?'' ''Did you pawn it, sell it, hide it or give it to someone else?''

Tobler's repeated responses were, ''I'm thirsty.'' ''I have to go to the john.'' ''You're full of crap.'' ''You're wasting your breath.'' ''I need a smoke.''

That last one always gladdened Bram's heart, because to that complaint he could respond, and he did, with great pleasure, ''This particular lockup happens to be a no-smoking facility. If I put you in a cell for three days or three months or three *years,* you still couldn't smoke.''

Tobler always sneered. ''You can't hold me for three years. I ain't stupid, you know.''

''Now there's where you're wrong. You just might be the most stupid dirtbag on the face of the earth. I could arrest you right now for the grass, but I've been hoping you'd wise up and help yourself by telling me about the gun. That makes you stupid, Tobler or Toby or whatever in hell your real name is.''

''It's Toby Tobler.''

''Your mama named you Toby when your last name was Tobler? Was she stupid, too?''

''Don't you dare call my mama stupid!''

''Tell me about the gun. Where is it now? Where'd you

get the grass? Is it possible you traded the gun for the grass?'' Bram sat back and stared across the small table at Toby Tobler. ''Maybe you've been doing some dealing of your own.''

''I ain't no dealer!''

It went on and on until Bram's back and head ached, at which point he left the room and let Lester take over. At ten that night Tobler cracked.

''All right!'' he yelled. ''I'll tell you everything. Just leave me the hell alone!''

Bram turned on a tape recorder. ''So, talk.''

Later, in his office, he listened to Tobler's recorded story. It was one for the books.

''I was at the old depot, trying to find a place to sleep. A couple of other guys were already on the floor, wrapped in blankets, so I was trying to be quiet. I heard a commotion outside and went to see what was going on. I hunkered down behind a pile of old bricks and I spied two guys. One of them was a little guy and the other was tall and stringy.''

Bram heard his own voice on the recorder. ''Did you or do you now know either or both of the men?''

''Just one of 'em. The stringbean. He's a…a dealer. Damn you, you're making me dig my own grave here.''

''What's his name and where does he hang?''

''I don't know his real name. Everyone calls him Joker, 'cause he's always saying something dumb that he thinks is funny. I don't know where he hangs. He's just always around when you need something. That's what the little guy was doing with him that night, bargaining for drugs. Said he needed them powerful bad.''

John Doe had been trying to buy drugs? Bram didn't like that picture at all.

Tobler's narration continued. ''The little guy took out a wad of bills and I got nervous for him. Joker ain't a guy you should be flashing money in front of, if you know what I mean. Anyhow, Joker acted all sympathetic and handed the little guy something. I figured he'd sold him some coke or meth, but then, just like that, he grabbed the guy's money and the little package he'd given him and took off running. I saw the guy go down on his knees and the next thing I knew he pulled out a gun and shot himself.

"I watched for a long time and then when it hit me that no one else had heard the pop of that little gun, I snuck out and ran over and picked it up. I checked the guy for a wallet or jewelry, but he didn't have anything in his pockets, not one thing. Then I heard a car and I took off. About then the guys sleeping in the old depot came running out, but I'm sure none of them saw me. I was long gone by the time they found the dead guy."

"So, where's the gun?"

"I traded it to Joker for the grass, just like you said."

"And when, exactly, did you do this?"

"A couple of nights ago. In the alley behind the Bucket o' Suds Saloon."

"Have you met Joker in that alley before?"

"A couple of times, but I don't think he sleeps there."

"And what makes you think that?"

"Nothing. I just don't think he sleeps in any alley."

"Because he makes big money dealing drugs?"

"Yeah, I guess so."

The recording went on for another thirty minutes, but Bram already knew what was on it by heart, and he was so worn out that he barely had the strength to switch it off. He actually had to force himself to stand up from his chair and walk out the door to the patrol car he'd been driving.

But exhausted or not, there was still a glow of satisfaction in his system that wouldn't be denied. He had accomplished a few things today at least; he had a witness to

John Doe's suicide and he also had a lead on Joker, a scourge on Black Arrow and a threat to every decent citizen.

The day had turned out to be productive, after all.

Chapter Thirteen

Before dawn the next morning Bram loaded the three courthouse books into the trunk of his prowl car. He planned to make some telephone calls later on to figure out who—or what institution—should have them. Maybe the old records should be in a museum, maybe they were worthless. But someone in charge of such things should be told they had survived the fire. He would take care of it today.

Jenna heard him leaving and experienced such a rush of emotional pain that she lay huddled under her blankets in abject misery long after the sound of his car had faded to nothing in the predawn darkness. Among the convoluted jumble of her thoughts one was totally clear: she never wanted to fall in love again. It hurt too much.

It started sprinkling before Bram got to Black Arrow, not a deluge but enough rain on the windshield that he had to turn on the wipers. He hoped it wasn't going to be a gray, gloomy day, because in spite of last night's success with Tobler, Bram felt down and dejected this morning. He didn't have to seek a reason for his low mood, not when even a few sprinkles of rain on the windshield seemed overwhelmingly sad.

But everything seemed sad and dreary this morning, he thought, even his job. Why in heaven's name had he ever wanted to be Comanche County's sheriff? He could have made a decent enough living from his horses.

Bram sighed. He'd needed something else, and for a while working hard as sheriff had done him a world of good. He'd been able to live and breathe without thinking of Jenna Elliot every minute of every hour. Now nothing, not even landing a small fish like Tobler, and the prospect of reeling in a bigger one, like Joker, could crowd the zillion images of Jenna from his brain. Right now she was in bed, all warm and silky-skinned, and if he had a million bucks he would happily throw it down a well if he could turn this car around, crawl in bed next to her and tell her that he had loved her for years.

"You're turning into a damn whiner," he said in disgust. "You can't have her! Get over it!"

But he knew that he wasn't going to get over Jenna, not ever. The rain fell harder and he turned up the wipers a notch. Like it or not, they were in for a gray, drizzly morning.

At the sheriff's station Bram wrapped the blanket more tightly around the three heavy books, then made a run for the front door of the building. Ignoring the teasing conjectures being tossed around about what the boss might be smuggling in under that blanket, he plopped the big books down on a table in his office.

Sergeant Lester Moore, apparently the day's duty officer, leaned against the frame of the door and watched while Bram removed the damp blanket and draped it over a chair to dry out.

"What've you got there?" Lester asked.

"Books from the courthouse, saved from the fire by a heavy metal cabinet. Maybe you know the person I should talk to about them. The insurance adjuster thought they might have historical value. They're about a hundred years old."

"Then they probably are valuable. But it's all local stuff in them, right?"

"I suppose so."

"Then I think we should keep them right here in Comanche County. I'd call Maddy Hempler over at the Western Oklahoma Museum, if I were you. You know Maddy, don't you?"

"I think we've met."

"Well, I can tell you that she'd have your hide if you gave those books to a state museum instead of to her. To WOM, I mean, though she definitely feels protective of the place. No one who worked there before her did as good a job as she does. Heck, today the museum is three times the size it was when Maddy took over a few years back."

"Sounds good enough for me. I'll call around what? Ten?"

"The museum should be open by then."

Bram sat at his desk. "Has the APB gone out on Joker?"

"Hours ago, before I got here this morning."

"To the state police, too?"

"Yes. It was faxed to every law enforcement agency in Oklahoma. How long are you going to hold Tobler?"

"For as long as the law allows. I'm going to talk to the prosecutor this morning." Bram began doodling on a yellow pad. "I need advice on our John Doe, too."

"I know." One of the deputies called Lester's name, and he said, "Talk to you later," and left Bram's doorway.

Bram dropped the pen, leaned back against his chair and stared at the ceiling. Despite a saturation campaign in the media, no one who knew John Doe had come forward. Either the poor guy had been completely alone in the world or he had lived somewhere else and no one around here knew him. Which meant he would have a lonely, solitary burial.

That struck Bram as just too sad, and he reached for the phone. He couldn't wait for the county prosecutor to get to his office, so he called the man's home.

Aubrey Kennecott didn't *like* being called at his home, which he let Bram know, but then he settled down and listened.

"Two things, Aubrey." Bram recited the particulars of Toby Tobler sitting in jail and possibly being an important witness when they caught up with Joker. "I could arrest him for possession," Bram said, "but right now he's a willing witness to Joker's drug trade and I'd just as soon keep him that way."

"And how long before you nail Joker?"

"Within days," Bram said in all confidence. "There's no reason to think that he might be aware we have Tobler, so I'm pretty certain it will be business as usual for him. We've got to get him off the streets, Aubrey. He's a fairly big dealer and a nightmare."

"You've known about him for a while?"

"Bits and pieces, nothing concrete. Tobler put it all together for us last night."

"Okay. You can hold Tobler for his own safety. Write it up as witness protection for the time being. Is that it? Can I go and finish shaving now?"

"Not quite yet. We have to do something with our John

Doe. I'd like to give him a decent send-off, but I need your release to do anything with him.''

"You're completely convinced it was a suicide?"

Bram hesitated. He hated even the word *suicide*, but how could he argue with scientific fact?

"Everything points in that direction, Aubrey. The medical examiner is positive and wrote it in his report, and then with Tobler's explanation of the incident...well, it all fits, and explains probably what took place."

"Okay. I'll phone the morgue and release the body. The county budget is very low for transient burials, you know."

"Yes, Aubrey, I do know," he said, figuring he'd cover any additional cost out of his own pocket. "I would appreciate your calling the coroner right away so I can move forward on this."

"The man could still be in bed!"

"Then wake him up. Thanks, Aubrey." Bram put down the phone and checked his watch. It was still before seven, but the director of Hanson's Funeral Home must be used to calls at all hours of the day and night.

At least that was what Bram told himself while dialing Darren Hanson's home phone number.

It took Bram almost thirty minutes to convince Darren to hold a funeral on such short notice, but Bram was adamant about burying John Doe today.

Bram's final call—for the time being—was to Will. "There's a funeral at three this afternoon. You don't know the deceased, nor do I. It's that poor little guy who offed himself at the old depot, Will. I pretty much know the story behind the story now, and even if he was a junkie I can't stand thinking of him being stuck in a hole without a few kind words and at least a couple of mourners. Anyhow,

I'd like you to attend the service with me. Can you do it?''

Will didn't hesitate a second. "Of course I can. I'll meet you at the cemetery at three.''

The minister recited the Lord's Prayer with feeling, then talked briefly about the hard paths some people had to tread in life. He spoke nicely of a man he'd never known, and after another prayer, indicated to Bram that the service was over. Bram thanked him and the minister departed.

Bram and Will stood alone then. Finally Will spoke. "Something like this makes a man realize his own good fortune, doesn't it?''

"Yes." Bram's eyes burned with unshed tears. The simple service had moved him. John Doe moved him. Gran's bad health tore holes in his gut, and Jenna...Jenna represented everything good that life had to offer. He felt like bawling and didn't dare do it. Not that Will would make fun of him for crying, but if he ever actually loosened the tight reins he kept on his emotions he might never *stop* crying.

"I really wonder about death sometimes. Don't you, Bram?''

"Yeah, I do. Probably everyone does.''

"Do you think you could ever do yourself in, like this poor guy?''

"No, but everyone's different. Who knows what a person might do in another man's shoes?''

"Right. It's an awful thought, though.''

"The worst. Well, I'd better get back to work. You, too.''

They started walking to their cars. "Will, thanks.''

"You know you can always count on me, Bram.''

They stopped next to Bram's vehicle and looked at each other. "And vice versa, Will.''

"You're a good man for doing this today, Bram. That's

why you're the best sheriff Black Arrow's ever had. You care about everyone, even this poor fella.''

"If no one cared, the world would be a sorry place, Will.''

Bram looked off across the cemetery. It was a pretty place with its many trees and flower beds, but the aesthetic beauty of this final resting place was the furthest thing from his mind. He had the strongest urge to tell Will about Jenna, and somehow felt this was the time to do it. It would put an end to Will's teasing remarks about him finding the right woman and getting married, but maybe that was okay, too.

"Will, I'd like to tell you something.''

"I'm listening.''

"I've been in love with Jenna Elliot for at least ten years. She's the reason I'm not married.''

Will looked puzzled. "You're in love with her and she's the reason you're not married? Bram, that doesn't make a whole lot of sense.''

"Yes, it does. She has no idea how I feel about her and she never will.''

"For crying out loud, why not? Oh, wait a minute. You've sensed that she doesn't care all that much for you, right? That's tough, man. I feel for you.''

"No, that's not it at all. Well, I guess it could be part of it, but, Will, she's white, and you know how her father looks down on Native Americans.''

Will stared at him. "Hold on a minute. You don't *really* give a damn about anything Carl Elliot might think, do you? I can't believe that, Bram. Good Lord, man, Jenna's opinion is the only one that matters.'' Will narrowed his eyes. "And she's living in your house. How can you be in love with a woman who happens to be in the same house with you every time you go home to bed and still get any sleep? Wait, I'm not saying that right. Let me—''

"Don't bother, Will. I've said it all to myself too many times to count."

"You're denying your feelings for a woman because she's white? Bram, I honestly believe I know you better than just about anyone else, and so help me God it never would have occurred to me that you might be ashamed of your Comanche heritage."

"I'm not, Will. But Jenna might be."

"Because of ol' Carl? Doesn't she have a mind of her own? I don't know her real well, but anytime I've been around her she always seemed like a real nice lady."

"She *is* a lady, Will. Like your Ellie."

"Damn it, Bram, don't do this to yourself. To hell with her dad's bigotry. You wouldn't be marrying Carl Elliot, you'd be marrying Jenna."

"And you don't think she'd resent me for the rest of her days for being the cause of her father turning his back on her?"

"Well, if he's that thickheaded, she's better off without him!"

"Will, he's her father! You're white, how could you possibly understand how I feel about this? I never should've told you."

"That's just about the worst thing you've ever said to me, Bram. I have to go back to work." Will walked to his pickup with his head down, and Bram watched him go with a heavy ache in his heart. Will *didn't* understand. How could he?

Just before Will drove away Bram ran after him. "Listen, I'm sorry, man. I didn't say that to hurt you."

"Maybe you said it to hurt yourself," Will said. "Maybe *you're* the one who thinks a man with Comanche blood isn't good enough for Jenna Elliot. Think about that, Bram."

Watching his friend's car leave the cemetery, Bram

spoke under his breath. "It's Carl Elliot who thinks that, Will, not me."

But long after Will had gone, his words hung in the air. Bram looked up at the pale sun trying to break through the clouds and only partially succeeding. Heavyhearted, he walked over to a stone bench, made sure it wasn't still wet from the morning's rainfall, and sat down. He turned his back on the two men who came along to fill in John Doe's grave, and thought about how short a lifetime really was.

And he pondered a man so in need of illegal drugs that he would use a gun on himself before going without them.

Bram wasn't a man who normally felt hatred for anything, certainly not for members of the human race, however low they might have fallen. But hatred welled for a drug dealer named Joker, and Bram sat there and swore an oath to arrest him and make sure he was brought to justice in a court of law.

Bram stayed on that bench until it began sprinkling again. When he got in his car he was surprised by the time. He must have sat in the cemetery for a couple of hours. Did he really have so much on his mind that he could spend two hours just thinking and not realize it?

He couldn't deny it. For one thing, in all of his life he had never felt so overrun by complex problems. Usually he had one or two things going on that required a little time, maybe some work, possibly even some worry. But then Gran got sick and Jenna moved in and the courthouse burned and Rand Colton showed up.

Now *nothing* went smoothly. In fact Bram had never driven a bumpier road than the one he'd been on lately.

Somber and serious during the trip back to the station, Bram stopped at a drive-through and bought some supper, which he took with him. Seated at his desk, he ate his fish fillets and coleslaw. He took a few calls while he ate, and after the second one he put down the phone and found himself looking directly at the three old books on the catch-all table against the far wall.

"Well, hell," he mumbled. He'd forgotten to call Maddy Hempler about them. Shaking his head, he grabbed the telephone book and looked up the number for the Western Oklahoma Museum.

He got a recording. "Thank you for calling the Western Oklahoma Museum. Our visiting hours are from—" Bram slammed down the phone. He decided that he was in no mood to talk to Maddy Hempler anyhow, and he put the telephone book back in his desk drawer.

Then he sat there and wished he could go home. Some deputies were leaving for the day, others were arriving to begin their shift. If Jenna weren't at the ranch he *would* go home.

Heaving a disgruntled sigh, Bram got up and walked around his office. Every deputy was on the lookout for Joker. Sooner or later that piece of slime would show his face, but until then it was a waiting game. Maybe it was the waiting that had him so on edge, Bram thought.

But he knew it was more than that. It was what Will had said today, and Bram loving a woman he couldn't have, and Gran steadily losing ground, and on and on and on.

Lester stuck his head in. "Roy called in sick. He sounded like hell on the phone. Must have caught a bad bug. Should I work his shift, too?"

Bram considered the situation. Roy Emerson had been night duty officer for several weeks now. Bram could assign the job to another deputy, but he wanted every available man on patrol looking for Joker. And Lester couldn't work all night and then again all day tomorrow.

"No, you go on home. I'll take Roy's shift."

"You sure?"

"I'm sure. See you tomorrow."

Bram wandered into the central area of the building. In one corner of the large room was the radio equipment the dispatchers used. These people had had police training every bit as strenuous as the deputies in the patrol cars. Bram felt fortunate—as should every resident of Comanche County—that the department had such efficient dispatchers. At any given moment those people knew where each and every man and woman on the force was, along with the vehicles they drove.

Bram thought of calling the ranch and telling Jenna that he wouldn't be home all night, but he changed his mind. She wouldn't be looking for him at any particular hour, given the irregular schedule he'd been keeping—actually, no schedule at all.

About an hour later, though, he tried to remember if he'd filled Nellie's food and water bowls that morning and couldn't. He'd brought those books out to the car, but had he gone down to the barns before that?

"You're really losing it," he muttered under his breath as he stood at the counter and dialed the ranch's number.

"Colton Ranch."

"Jenna, Bram. Have you seen Nellie today?"

"A couple of times. She never comes to the door without you."

"Well, I can't remember if I fed her this morning. I hate to ask, but I'm tied up here. Would you mind running down to the smallest barn and checking Nellie's food and water bowls? They're right inside the door to the right, and there's a big sack of dry food on the shelf just above them."

Jenna glanced to a window and saw that it was pitch-black outside. There were a few yard lights, but she wasn't at all accustomed to running around in the dark miles from neighbors and traffic, and her heart was all of a sudden nervous and leaping around in her chest. Or at least it felt that way.

She wasn't thrilled about this, but how could she refuse? Nellie shouldn't have to go hungry just because *she* was afraid.

"Sure," she said, faking a confidence she didn't feel at all. "I'd be glad to do it."

For some crazy reason Bram got all choked up. She was just so darned special, so giving, so considerate of everyone else.

"Thanks," he said huskily. "I really appreciate it."

"You're welcome."

"See you tomorrow."

"I doubt that, but it's a good sign-off. Good night."

Frowning, Bram slowly put down the phone.

Jenna put her phone down as well, then stood there and stared at the darkness beyond the windows.

"You goose," she said out loud. "There's nothing out there at night that isn't there during the day." She took a quick look at Gloria, then grabbed a light jacket because of the drizzling rain and went out the back door of the house.

The yard lights helped a lot more than she'd thought they would, which bolstered her courage, and she jogged down to the smallest barn. But even if everything else had been just great, she didn't like leaving Gloria alone in the house, so she hurriedly filled Nellie's food bowl. The little collie wriggled all around Jenna's legs before she began eating hungrily, and Jenna was glad that she had overcome the after-dark jitters to do this simple chore.

But Nellie's water bowl was also empty, and where did one get water down here? Jenna looked around the shadowy barn with its dark, spooky corners. There had to be a water faucet somewhere out here, but where? Bram should have told her, she thought resentfully.

When she realized that a water pipe ran along the inside of a wall, she followed it until it vanished *through* the wall. Obviously the spigot was outside.

"Well, for crying out loud!" she exclaimed, and forced herself to walk around the side of the barn, which included climbing between the wooden rails of a fence. But she did it, and in the feeble light that reached that particular area she managed to identify a water trough. She didn't waste time looking for a spigot, but merely dipped Nellie's bowl into the trough to fill it.

She was about to reverse directions when she heard the howling of a coyote. With chills traveling her spine, Jenna froze, but strangely, Nellie, who had followed her through the fence, paid the bloodcurdling howling absolutely no mind.

"Don't you hear it? What kind of watch dog are you?" Jenna's mobility returned with a rush and she nearly fell over her own feet getting through the fence and into the barn to set down the bowl of water. Outside again, on her way back to the house, she heard the howling split the night quiet one more time.

Jenna hit the back door running. Breathing hard, she listened acutely, but there was no more howling. Why on earth hadn't Nellie barked? Didn't dogs bark at everything? Hell's bells, that coyote had sounded close enough to touch!

The hours ticked by and Bram restlessly paced the rooms of the sheriff's station. By midnight there were barely any radio communications to listen to on this quiet, mostly uneventful night in Black Arrow, and Bram went into his office and sat at his desk. He doodled, he looked at old reports, he twisted paper clips and finally, beginning to feel sleepy, he got up and toted one of the courthouse books over to his desk, figuring it was something different to look at and just might prove interesting enough to keep him awake.

He turned back the cover and then slowly, one by one, the book's pages.

Three hours later he was more awake than he'd been at midnight and so torn up emotionally that he didn't know where to put himself. He made himself check the pertinent entries again and again because he couldn't believe his own conclusions.

Finally he sat back, feeling dazed. Carl Elliot had Comanche blood? Jenna had Comanche blood? Carl couldn't be aware of these records or he would have found a way to destroy them.

My God, was *he* the arsonist? He wouldn't have had to actually light the fire; he had more than enough money to buy anything he wanted, even the destruction of his own past.

Bram was badly shaken, and he left his office and got himself a cup of coffee, which he'd been avoiding because of the discomfort in his stomach. But he sipped that hot, strong brew and wondered unhappily what to do with the information he'd stumbled upon tonight. Did Jenna know about it? Should he *tell* Jenna? If everyone learned the truth of the Elliot family's ancestry, there would no longer be a reason for Bram to deny his love for Jenna.

But what if she didn't know, and what if learning about it hurt her in some way? Bram didn't give a damn if Carl got hurt in twenty different ways, but he would die before knowingly causing Jenna any grief. And yet wasn't he hurting her in some manner every day that she lived in his house?

Bram glared at the three old books that once again lay on the table in his office. "Damned things," he mumbled. Yes, it did his heart good to know that Carl Elliot wasn't snow-white, but then neither was Jenna.

Groaning, Bram put his head down on his arms on the desk. Why did these things keep happening to him? Damn it, life used to be good! Had he committed some unpardonable sin that required constant and possibly endless punishment?

Independence Day, the Fourth of July, dawned sunny and bright. The Coltons began arriving around ten that morning, and by noon the yard was ready for a picnic. The family had set up tables bearing red, white and blue cloths, the American Flag flew proudly from its high pole, and red, white and blue balloons had been attached to trees and bushes to float on a gentle breeze.

Jenna had been told a few days prior about the holiday celebration planned by the family, but someone had called it "simple," and to Jenna, this wasn't at all simple; it was lovely and appropriate, and stirred feelings of patriotism and love of family. It also stirred old memories, and Jenna thought of her mother often that morning. She also thought of her dad, but she couldn't recall that he had ever liked picnics or even Black Arrow's Fourth of July celebration. Jenna's mother, on the other hand, had loved the Fourth and called it her favorite holiday of the year.

The amount and variety of food brought by the Coltons was almost unbelievable. This picnic was going to be a feast. While the family members joked and laughed outside, each and every one of them became sober and serious when they came in to spend time with Gran. Jenna prayed the generosity of her family would lift Gloria's spirits, but only time would tell on that score.

In truth, Jenna was so unnerved by another matter that it was difficult to smile at these wonderful people and act as though nothing was wrong. Bram had gone to work early that morning as though it were any other day, and his cold disregard for the time and money spent by his family to make today a special holiday seemed unforgivable to Jenna. She thought it rather strange that no one commented on Bram's absence, but she didn't feel it was her place to bring it up, and so it was never discussed, not in her hearing, at any rate.

The men were setting up chairs and the women of the family were placing the food on the tables when Jenna saw Bram's SUV coming down the road. Her breath caught as she suffered a jolt of genuine anguish. She'd been upset because Bram wasn't there, and then when he showed up she was even *more* upset? *Good Lord,* she thought disgustedly. *Get a grip, for Pete's sake. Do you want all these nice people knowing how weak-minded you get around their Bram?*

The men gravitated toward the driveway, and when Bram had parked and gotten out, Jenna watched out of the corner of her eye—not wanting to appear all giddy and lovestruck, which she was no matter how hard she fought it—and saw several of them helping George WhiteBear from the vehicle. She should have known they wouldn't leave the patriarch of the family out of the day's festivities. In fact, she realized suddenly, the big chair they had carried from the house and placed at the head of one of the tables had been expressly planned for George WhiteBear.

Jenna's first meeting with the very old man had provided her very little information about the true nature of his relationship with his family. That day, in fact, she had thought Mr. WhiteBear to be a bit light in the upper story, calling her a golden fox the way he had, and then slipping into a state of mourning over the impending death of his daughter, which he had apparently been made aware of by a coyote. What's more, his great-grandsons—two of them anyway, Jared and Bram—had tried to convince her that the old man's ways were perfectly normal.

Well, maybe they were. What was normal for one person wasn't necessarily normal for another. At any rate, Jenna felt that she was seeing George WhiteBear for the first time today. He wore boots that had been shined, clean jeans and shirt, and his long gray hair had been tied back with a buckskin string. He looked Comanche and he looked dignified and proud, and it was obvious to Jenna that his family respected and loved him.

"Jenna, sit over here, next to me," Willow called.

"Thanks, Willow, but I'm going in. You all enjoy your-selves."

Objections came from every direction.

"You have to eat!"

"My goodness, we'll all take turns sitting with Gran."

"Come on, Jenna, sit down and eat with us."

Jenna smiled. "You're all very kind, but I'm going to go inside. Please don't worry about me." She hurried to the front door and went in.

Perplexed as to how he should handle this without giv-ing anything away to his quick-to-catch-on family, Bram ran his hand over his hair.

"Maybe I should fix a plate and bring it in to her," he said to the group in general. "What do you think?"

Aunt Alice spoke up. "Why, that's a very sweet sug-gestion, Bram, dear. Yes, I think it would be very thought-ful of you to do that. Here, let me help you." She began filling a large plate. "Get a cup of that fruit punch for her."

Bram heard a snicker and turned around to glare at his sister. "Don't get any foolish ideas. In fact, if you want to deliver that plate, instead of my doing it, be my guest."

Willow's eyes fairly danced with excitement. "Big brother, I wouldn't deliver that plate for you if you paid me."

"Well, I'm sure as hell not going to pay you."

"I know." Willow smiled sweetly.

Bram grabbed the plate of food and the cup of fruit punch and headed for the house. It was a balancing act to open the screen door, but he managed without anyone else's assistance and then strode into the house.

Jenna was in the bedroom with Gloria, and quickly went out to meet him when she heard him tromping around. The food in his hands surprised her. Pleased her, too, for he had actually done something nice for her in front of his family.

"Bram, you didn't have to do this."

"You're welcome." Without so much as a hint of a smile on his granitelike features, Bram set the plate and cup on a table and all but ran for the door.

"And you're never going to be anything but rude, even while doing something nice for a person, are you?" She hadn't yelled, but she'd spoken loudly enough that he could have heard her.

This time she hoped he had, the jerk!

Chapter Fourteen

A week later Bram received a letter from Rand Colton.

Sheriff,

Since you haven't used the number I left for you, I can only assume that you do not wish to join my investigation of possible ties between your family and mine. It is your right, of course, as it is mine to proceed with all manner of research on my own. I feel it's only fair to inform you that I will be visiting Black Arrow and Comanche County again, possibly quite often.

Perhaps it's not my place to advise you on any subject, but I cannot ignore something you said the day we met. You said you were told of two men asking questions about your family. Bram, this is alarming to me and perhaps should also alarm you. Or at least alert you to the fact that I know nothing about this other man except that he could have been hired by a rather unscrupulous member of my family, in which case he is not to be trusted.

At the bottom of this letter is a list of addresses and telephone numbers where I can be reached, should you change your mind and wish to speak to me.

Rand Colton

Bram read the letter twice, then folded it, returned it to its envelope and put it in the bottom-right drawer of his desk. Maybe he would use one of those phone numbers one of these days, but researching the past simply wasn't as urgent as everything else going on right now. As far as that warning about the second man snooping into Colton family business went, Bram hadn't heard him mentioned by anyone for some time. Maybe he'd given up, or discovered the Coltons had nothing to hide, and left town. Bram hoped so. Actually, any time he had to spend on personal matters would be used to figure out the meaning behind Gran's plea for him to "find the truth." Right now, though, his calendar was full.

For instance, Joker had been spotted two different times during a dark night, but he had managed to elude the deputies each time. Regardless, those incidents proved the drug-dealing snake was still in Black Arrow, which kept Bram hopeful of eventually nailing his butt to a prison wall.

He was thinking about that very thing when his phone rang. "Bram, Aubrey Kennecott's on line two for you."

"Thanks." Bram punched the right button. "Aubrey?"

"Let me get straight to the point. You either charge Tobler today or you let him go. Understand?"

"If I let him go and he leaves town, you won't have a witness when we arrest Joker."

"Then charge him!"

"So he can get out on bail?"

"I don't write the laws, Bram. Just do what you have to. Goodbye."

Seething, Bram put down the phone. He didn't have Joker, and Tobler was probably going to walk, too. What in hell else could go wrong?

In a lousy mood, Bram got up and walked out of the building to his SUV. Maybe a drive would clear his head.

Jenna answered the phone at the Colton Ranch and heard a woman's voice asking, "Is Bram there?"

"No, he isn't. I could take a message, if you'd like."

"I don't have time for messages. He's not at the sheriff's station, either. Would you have any idea where I might find him?"

"None at all. Who is this?"

"Annie McCrary. I'm George's neighbor. George WhiteBear, Bram's great-grandfather. Who are you?"

"Jenna Elliot, Gloria Colton's nurse. Is this an emergency, Annie? Should you be calling 9-1-1? Is George ill or injured?"

"No, he's not sick and he isn't bleeding anywhere I can see. That's not the problem. I just came from his place— one of my usual weekly drop-in visits—and he's getting ready to drive to town."

"I don't think I see the problem."

"He hasn't driven in…in ten or twenty years! He doesn't have a license and he'll probably cause fifteen wrecks between his place and Black Arrow! Believe me, Ms. Elliot, there *is* a problem."

"Oh, my goodness! Why is he coming to town?"

"To see Bram. He said that he has to talk to Bram, that it's a matter of life and death."

"Maybe…maybe you could drive him. Would that be too much of an imposition?"

"Not at all, except I threw my back out a few days ago and just driving the short distance between George's place and mine nearly finished me off. If I drove all the way to Black Arrow I'd probably end up in the hospital. Oh, Lord, what'll I do? Do you have a car? Maybe you could come out here and get him. When he makes up his mind to something, there's no changing it."

"I would do it in a heartbeat, but I really can't leave Gloria alone."

"No, of course you can't. Oh, hell, I'll do it. But where will I take him once we're in town?"

"I'll try to find Bram for you. Call me again when you get to town. I wish I could do more."

"Well, I guess I've survived worse. Okay, you hunt down Bram and I'll get the old guy to Black Arrow."

Jenna suddenly had a better idea, or so it seemed. "Annie, bring him here, if he'll let you. You can always use the argument that Bram will be home eventually."

"Good plan. I'll try it. But you keep trying to find Bram, okay?"

"Yes, all right. Do you know how to get here?"

"Oh, yes. See you later."

After saying goodbye, Jenna sat with the phone book and began dialing Colton numbers. No one had seen Bram that morning; no one had any idea of where he might be. "His job takes him all over the county, Jenna. He could be anywhere. But why are you looking for him? Is Gran worse?"

Jenna quickly reassured whomever she was speaking with and then cut the call short so she could make the next one.

An hour later she had talked to every Colton she'd been able to reach. She'd called the police station, but Bram hadn't called in today. Feeling defeated and frustrated, she checked on Gloria, then sat near a living room window to watch for Annie McCrary and George WhiteBear.

They finally arrived, and Jenna went outside and helped Annie assist George from the cab of her truck.

"I haven't found him," she said in an undertone to Annie. "No one knows where he might be."

"Where's Bram?" George WhiteBear asked.

"He'll be here," Jenna said with a smile for the old gentleman. "Please come inside."

George went in, but he wasn't happy about Bram's absence. "I need to talk to him now. I have to warn him. My daughter's ill, but it's not her we should all be worried about. It's Bram. He's in grave danger and I have to tell him to watch out for the laughing man in black."

Bram's meandering drive took him into a neighborhood that seldom required police protection. There were numerous upscale homes and gated condominium communities, some that Bram had heard had sold for up to five million dollars. In fact, Carl Elliot lived in this area, about two streets over from the one he was on. Thinking of Carl brought Jenna to Bram's mind, which made his gut ache. Fumbling some antacids from a package, he chewed and swallowed them with a drink of water from the bottle he had with him.

What was he going to do about Jenna? Tell her the truth of her heritage and let her handle it with her dad, or tell her nothing and just stay the hell away from her and something that was really none of his business? What a lousy damned dilemma.

Driving past an elegantly landscaped area around one of the entrance gates leading into a very posh condominium project, Bram happened to glance at the complex. Everything was lushly beautiful—the architecture, the trees, the shrubbery.

And just like that, within the blink of an eye, Bram spotted a tall, unusually thin man in a black jogging suit running past the entranceway, inside the high fence. Bram pulled his SUV over to the curb and looked back at the gate. That man fit to a tee the description that Tobler had given on Joker, minus the fancy jogging suit, of course. Bram's heart pounded in his chest as instinctive questions and answers bombarded him.

Was the reason they hadn't made any real headway in finding Joker because they had been looking in the wrong parts of town? That theory made sense. Joker could be dealing drugs in the dark of night, dressed in old clothes to blend in with the street folk, and after finishing his dirty work he hightailed it back to his million-dollar condo, where he played proper citizen to the neighbors.

"What incredible luck," Bram said under his breath. He was convinced he'd just seen Joker, but he couldn't go barging through that gate without some proof.

This called for a stakeout. Feeling higher than a kite, Bram returned to the station to set the wheels of justice in motion.

Jenna didn't know whether to laugh, cry or simply collapse and hope for recovery somewhere down the road. This was insane, wasn't it? An old man's prediction of doom based on communication with coyotes?

And yet some part of her believed, and something else within her wept without tears. In all of her life she had never felt this kind of ripping pain.

In the kitchen she served tea and offered food to Annie McCrary, who looked as pale as Jenna felt. George WhiteBear had parked himself next to his daughter's bed and there he sat.

"Do you believe him?" Annie whispered.

Jenna was afraid to say yes, afraid to say no. The Coltons were intelligent people and they believed George WhiteBear's predictions.

"I...I'm not sure. There is one thing that's very confusing, though. He first thought it was Gloria who was going to die soon, and now it's Bram. How could that happen?"

"Jenna, *I* don't talk to coyotes and I doubt if you do, so how on earth would either of us even dare to hazard a guess about that?"

A chill suddenly traveled Jenna's spine. "I...heard a coyote the other night. He sounded close enough to touch, but I never saw him. I was outside...it was dark, very dark...and I was feeding Nellie. It was a bloodcurdling sound, but the really crazy thing about it was that Nellie didn't react at all. It was as though she couldn't hear it."

"Goodness, that gave me goose bumps." Annie rubbed her arms. "Listen, I have to run. Thanks for the tea. I'm in the phone book. Call if you ever need anything, okay?"

"Yes, thanks, I will."

After Annie had gone, Jenna peered down the hall into the master bedroom. George WhiteBear hadn't moved an inch. Jenna realized then that he was chanting or singing something in a rhythm that was unfamiliar to her ears.

He was singing softly in the Comanche language. With tears all but drowning her, Jenna ran to the bedroom no one used, the one with the second twin bed, and threw herself upon it. She loved Bram and she even loved his family, but would she ever truly understand them?

Bram walked into the station and immediately checked the duty roster. Locating the two names he had hoped to see on the chart, he put it down and strode over to the radio dispatcher.

"Marilu, get Hayes and Lowell on the horn and tell them I need 'em here. As soon as they can get here."

"Will do. Did you check your message box?" Marilu asked before sending out a call over the radio.

"Not yet. Why? Did something important come in?"

"Sounded important to me." She spoke into her headphone. "Sergeant Hayes, Sheriff Colton wants to see you and your partner on the double."

"We're ten minutes away." Tommy Hayes responded.

"Thanks, Marilu." Bram walked over to the message and mailbox on the wall and emptied the one with his name on it. He had four messages, one from Willow, one from Jared and two from Jenna.

Two from Jenna! *My God, something happened to Gran!* Rushing back to Marilu, he asked, "Did Jenna Elliot say anything about my grandmother?"

"No, but she did mention your great-grandfather. That was during her second call."

Relief that Gran was all right mingled with Bram's sudden worry about his great-grandfather. "What, exactly, did she say about him?"

"Something about a warning. And I think she used the word *urgent.* That's about all I remember. I was pretty busy when she called that second time."

"But he's not sick or injured."

"She didn't say anything about that."

"Then he's fine and scaring the hell out of her with another prediction," Bram said under his breath.

"Pardon?"

"Nothing, Marilu." Bram went to his office and shut the door. He didn't have time to call Willow, Jared *or* Jenna, nor did he really want to, even though it would be interesting to hear how his great-grandfather managed to frighten Jenna via long distance when he didn't have a phone.

There was a logical answer to that little riddle, Bram believed, but he couldn't let himself be drawn into family problems today.

Tense enough to shatter, Jenna fidgeted all morning. She worked around George WhiteBear when Gloria needed something, and at noon she offered the elderly man some lunch, which he refused. The moment she left the bedroom she heard that soft singsong chanting again.

She was so glad to see Willow's car arriving that afternoon that she nearly wept.

"Have you talked to Bram?" Jenna asked the second Willow entered the house.

"No, have you?"

"No, and I called twice."

"He must not have received our messages," Willow said. "He's probably not at the station." She started toward Gloria's room, then stopped and looked at Jenna. "Granddad is still here?"

Jenna nodded weakly. "Annie only stayed a short while. He wouldn't go with her."

Willow said quietly, "I should have called before coming. Jenna, I'm not going to stay. I left the feed store shorthanded to drive out here to see Gran. I really don't want to hear any more gloom and doom predictions from Granddad, so I'm going to take the coward's way out and just leave."

Jenna walked Willow to the door and stepped out onto the porch with her.

"Jenna, this all has to be really difficult for you. You weren't raised with our traditions, and it wouldn't surprise me if you thought we were all a bit loony." Willow looked off across the yard. "And you know something? Maybe we are."

"No more so than anyone else. We all have quirks that others don't quite get."

"That's true. Listen, at some point of the day, probably early evening, Granddad will want to go home. It's the way he is—it always happens. If no one else is here at the time, call me and I'll make sure someone picks him up."

Jenna squeezed her friend's hand. "Thank you. Willow, do you think I should try to get hold of Bram one more time?"

"Granddad really has you worried, doesn't he?"

"I...can't help worrying. Willow, I heard a coyote the other night, and Nellie was with me and didn't hear it. That means something, doesn't it?"

"Oh, Jenna." Willow threw her arms around her. "I can't explain something like that, and I really don't recommend that you ask Granddad for answers, because you'll hear much more about Comanche lore and tradition and guardian spirits than you ever wanted to know."

"But maybe I should know," Jenna said huskily. *I have Comanche blood, too, Willow, only I just recently found out about it,* she thought but kept it to herself.

"Jen, we grew up with it, Bram, Ashe, Jared, Logan and me. And our cousins, too, of course, and it doesn't always make sense to us. Think how confusing it could be for you." Willow stepped back and sighed. "Do what you want, but just remember that I warned you. See you later."

Wishing with all her heart that Bram would call, Jenna went back inside. Willow was right about the confusion, Jenna thought as she looked down the hall to the master bedroom. She couldn't *be* more confused, could she?

And to think it all started because she had leaped at an opportunity to spend time with Bram. What an innocent she'd been not even two months ago.

Just as Willow had forewarned, George WhiteBear came out of Gloria's room and announced that he wanted to go home. It was dinnertime, and Jenna tried to talk him into eating with her. Again he refused, and she said, "But you haven't eaten all day."

"I will eat when I get home."

Jenna gave up. "I'll find you a ride." She picked up the phone and called Willow. "He wants to go."

"I already talked to Logan and he said he would pick him up when you called. He'll be there in about twenty minutes."

"Thanks, Willow." Jenna put down the phone and turned her head to talk to Mr. WhiteBear, but he wasn't there. She wandered from the kitchen and looked into the other rooms, and finally she spotted him sitting outside near a huge old tree. She went out and called from the porch, "Logan is on his way, Mr. WhiteBear."

George nodded, then motioned her over. Jenna hesitated, for, like Willow, she didn't want to hear any more dire predictions, especially if they were about Bram. But she couldn't just ignore the old man's summons, and she finally left the porch and walked over to him.

"Is there something you'd like?" she asked gently. "Some more water, perhaps? Or tea? I could make you some tea to drink while you're waiting."

"I wish to say something," George said. "I saw the golden fox, and soon after, I met you. The meaning became clear, and now it's blurred again. My great-grandson is facing a mortal enemy and you must find a way to warn him. I have tried and failed. As his soul mate, you must do what I could not."

Stunned, Jenna sank to the grass next to George's chair. "You actually see me as Bram's soul mate?"

"Must I explain something you should know in your heart?"

Tears welled in Jenna's eyes. "No," she whispered. "I do know it in my heart. I've known it for a very long time."

"Bram knows it, too."

"He does?"

"You and he don't talk about it?"

"We don't talk about much of anything."

"You must talk to him very soon. You must warn him."

Jenna heard something and got up. "That's the phone." She ran for the house, praying it was Bram calling.

It wasn't. It was Annie. "Is he ready to be driven home yet?"

"Yes, Annie, but Logan should be here any minute. Thanks for the offer, though."

Jenna didn't go back outside. Instead she sat on the sofa, turned in such a way that she could see out of the window. She had much to think about and was deep in thought when Logan arrived. He was the spitting image of his older brother and *her* soul mate, Bram. But Logan was much more easygoing.

She jumped up and called, "Logan, could I speak to you for just a moment before you leave again?"

He walked to the house and went in. "Do you have any ideas about how I might locate Bram?" Jenna asked. "Your great-grandfather told me that I'm the one who has to warn Bram about the danger he's in."

"Oh, Jenna, Bram's in danger every time he gets in that patrol car or tries to arrest some spaced-out druggie."

Jenna nearly gasped at Logan's response. She was just too emotional where Bram was concerned.

"So I should disregard George's prediction, or premonition, or whatever it is?"

"I'm disregarding it, Jenna. The whole family is. If we got all worked up every time Granddad gave us his interpretation of signs and omens, we'd be chasing our tails half the time."

Jenna dropped her gaze. Was the coyote cry she'd heard

a sign? An omen? Why would a spirit coyote visit her and not Logan? Or Willow? Or Jared?

"All right," she said quietly. "That's all I had to say. Take him home. He wouldn't eat anything I offered. He said he would eat when he got home."

"Jenna, he ate with us on the Fourth, and enjoyed it, too. He's just in one of his moods today."

"He…he's worried."

"Maybe, but don't let it get you down, okay? Talk to you later." Logan left the porch and hurried over to the old man. "Ready to go, Granddad?"

"I've *been* ready for an hour."

Logan sent Jenna a grin and a shrug, as if to say, "See? He's just in a bad mood."

Jenna wasn't completely convinced, but had no idea what to do about it. She kept getting mixed messages from the Coltons. It was as if they sorted and sifted through George's warnings and only dealt with those they *could* deal with. And yet Jenna had heard several members of the family profess belief in the elderly man's supposed words of wisdom.

It was far, far beyond her ken, she thought sadly, and waved off Logan and George, then went inside the house and shut the door.

At midnight, Bram was lurking in some dense bushes watching one entrance into the high-toned condo project, while Tommy Hayes was watching a second entrance and Robb Lowell was parked down the street just waiting for something to happen. The three men stayed in contact with high-powered two-way radios, but only used them when something had to be said.

"There's a black SUV coming out," Bram said quietly into his handheld radio. He peered through the dense leaves of the mulberry bush he was crouched behind as the vehicle stopped for the gate to open and then shot forward. It happened fast, but Bram saw enough to alert his men. "It's him! Robb, pick up Tommy fast and get on his tail. I won't be far behind." He ran for his own SUV, which he had backed into the driveway of a vacant house with a For Sale sign on its front lawn.

He jumped into the driver's seat and started the engine, then put a heavy foot on the gas pedal. The SUV jumped forward and Bram searched the street ahead for Robb's taillights. They had marked the left taillight of Robb's rig with a piece of black electrician's tape, making it easy to identify. But first Bram had to catch up with his deputies.

He drove like a bat out of hell and thanked heaven that it was late and the roads, at least in this part of town, were mostly devoid of traffic. And then, up ahead, he spotted the crippled taillight. Relaxing a bit, he slowed his speed and drove less like a maniac.

But his heart was beating wildly. They had a damn good chance of nabbing Joker tonight. But they had to do this right and make no mistakes. He couldn't see the black SUV that Joker was driving, but he didn't doubt that Robb and Tommy had it in their sights. And he had them in *his* sights.

So, where was that piece of slime heading? It wasn't long before Bram *knew* where they were all going—to the alley behind the Bucket o' Suds Saloon. Tobler had steered them right.

But that alley could be their undoing. Bram pushed the talk button on his radio. "Don't follow him in. Approach on foot from Abbott Street. I'll take the Green Street entrance. Be careful."

He made a left turn, a right and then sped up Green Street. He parked a safe distance from the alley entrance, turned off the motor and listened. Music drifted on the night air, and an occasional voice and burst of raucous laughter. When he felt it was time, Bram got out and walked toward the alleyway. He took his gun with him.

Suddenly there was shouting and gunshots. Bram ran to the building next to the alley and peered around it. There wasn't a soul to be seen.

Sweating, sick-to-his-stomach concerned about Tommy's and Robb's safety, he took another look. Still nothing moved.

But someone had fired a gun, maybe more than one person. He couldn't risk one or both of his deputies bleeding to death in that dirty alley while he remained safely concealed behind a brick building.

He stepped into the alley and began making his way down it, cautiously moving from garbage can to doorway to anything else that offered protection. He stepped from a doorway and someone yelled, "No, Bram, stay there!"

But it was too late. Two shots rang out. One bullet grazed his left arm. The other one hit him full in the chest. He went down like a sack of potatoes.

In her little bed at the Colton Ranch, Jenna, engulfed in fear, awoke with a start and grabbed at her chest. She tried to remember the dream that had caused such a shocked sensation, and couldn't.

But she knew it had been about Bram and it hadn't been just a dream; it had been a nightmare.

"Well, you're one lucky SOB, Sheriff," the ER doctor said for perhaps the fourth time since Bram had regained consciousness. "That strange little metal thing in your shirt pocket saved your life tonight. Oh, sure, you've your arm to heal and a bruise on your chest that'll probably hurt like hell for a couple of days, but what's that compared to certain death, right?"

"Right," Bram murmured. He was groggy from pain medication. Robb and Tommy were pale but beaming because they'd gotten Joker. They had shot him when he shot Bram. They'd had no choice.

"Where's the…medallion?" Bram asked.

"Right here." Someone put it in his right hand. "It was probably flat as a silver dollar before tonight, but it's not flat now."

Bram moved it between his thumb and fingers and felt the curved shape. "No, it's not flat now," he said. "Tommy, did you call Willow? Be sure not to call Jenna. Call Willow."

"It's all taken care of, Bram. Just relax, man."

"Who's driving me home?"

"They think you should stay here tonight…or what's left of tonight."

"No way. Someone's gotta drive me home."

"Okay, okay. I'll do it. You know, Bram, if Joker had used a bigger gun than that .22 when he shot you, that medallion might not have stopped the bullet."

"It would have, Tommy. It was in the cards."

"Bram, are you ready to hear what Joker said before he died?" Tommy asked.

"I didn't know he said anything."

"How could you? You were out cold. Anyhow, the John Doe you buried was Joker's supplier. Joker knew him only as Feeny, and he showed up about once a month to deliver his wares. Joker said that the gun was Feeny's and that he tried to haggle on a price that had already been agreed upon, and when Joker wouldn't pay more for the goods, Feeny pulled the gun. Enter our pal Tobler. He grabbed Feeny from behind, and Joker took the gun from his hand. They both killed Feeny, Bram. He was a little guy and they easily shoved the gun back in his hand and put it to his head, which explains the powder burns. Then they emptied Feeny's pockets, took his bag of drugs, snatched his car keys and the gun and took off. They got rid of

Feeny's car, apparently, but Joker took his final breath before he could tell us where.''

Bram felt numb. In mind, in spirit, in body he felt numb and stupid and bitter. He'd paid for the burial of a criminal because he'd believed him to be a better person than he was.

"Charge Tobler with murder one," he said dully. "And get me the hell out of here."

Chapter Fifteen

Jenna couldn't go back to sleep. After a while she quit trying and got up. Moving quietly so she wouldn't disturb Gloria, she put on a robe and slippers, then left the bedroom and went to the kitchen, where she made tea.

It was late. The nightmare had awakened her at exactly 12:48 a.m.; she should have slept for at least another four hours. Five would have been better.

But she knew that she could lie in that bed for three days and not fall asleep again. Something had happened at 12:48 a.m., and until she was told what it was she would not be able to shut her eyes.

She sat at the kitchen table and sipped hot tea, experiencing a strange calmness that kept her hands steady and her eyes dry. When the phone rang an hour later, she wasn't at all surprised. She'd been waiting for the other shoe to drop, so to speak, and apparently this was it.

Jenna picked up the phone, clutched it tightly in her hand and said, "Yes?"

"Jenna, it's Willow."

"Is he alive?"

"Bram? Jenna, he's fine. He was shot but he's fine. How did you know I was calling about Bram?"

"I just knew, that's all. Is he in the hospital?"

"He's on his way home. Two deputies are driving him. I'm sorry I woke you, but I thought you should know before they got there."

"I was awake before the phone rang. He wasn't badly hurt, then?"

"It could have been bad, but... Jenna, I'll let him tell you what happened. I've been at this hospital long enough. I'm beat and I'm going home. Talk to you soon."

"Thanks for calling, Willow. Goodbye."

Jenna resumed her chair at the table. A tear slipped from the corner of her eye and she wiped it away. She didn't know where it had come from, because she didn't feel at all like crying. There was an unusual resolve keeping her strong, and while she didn't completely comprehend its source or cause, she knew that she had changed drastically.

Twenty minutes later she heard a car. Rising, she went to the front door and opened it. She watched while two men helped Bram from a vehicle and then walked him to the house. His shirt was partially unbuttoned and one sleeve was missing. His left arm was bandaged and his hair was sticking out every which way.

Jenna stepped back when the trio came in. Bram gave her a glassy-eyed look. "It's not as bad as it looks," he mumbled.

"I know," she said. "His bedroom is to the right," she told the two men. "Just follow me." She led them to the bedroom Bram was using, switched on lights and turned down the bed. "Undress him," she said. "You men know I'm a nurse, so don't expect me to blush and giggle at the sight of a man's underwear."

Tommy and Robb chuckled. "Bram said you were a pistol."

"He did, did he? Well, he should know."

Both deputies grinned. "Sounds serious, Bram," Tommy said. "You been keeping something from us?"

"I'm sure he has," Jenna said. "Sit him on the bed and pull off his boots."

Even in his partially drugged state Bram sensed something different about Jenna. "What's...going on?" he asked.

Robb thought he was talking to him and Tommy and answered. "We're putting you to bed, man."

Bram's eyes rose to Jenna's face and she flashed him a quick smile. It was there and gone so fast that Bram squinted and wondered if he might have been seeing things.

His shirt went and then his pants and socks, and when he was down to his shorts Tommy and Robb gently laid him back. Jenna pulled the covers up to his waist and stopped to study the bruise on his chest for several seconds. That was an injury with a story, she was positive.

"Jenna, I've got two bottles of pills here. One is an antibiotic and the other one's for pain. I've also got a bunch of papers and written instructions. You're supposed to watch his arm for excessive bleeding and change the bandage after about twenty-four hours." Tommy rambled on for several more minutes, reciting the ER doctor's instructions, and Jenna listened politely.

But she knew how to care for a flesh wound and a bruised chest. She walked the men to the door and asked them to wait a minute before they left.

"I need to know something. Who shot Bram?"

"A jerk named Joker," Tommy replied.

The laughing man. "And how was he dressed? What was he wearing?"

"I don't know. Something black—an old jogging suit, I think it was."

"Thank you. Those were my only questions." *Watch out for a laughing man in black.* George WhiteBear had been right again.

After Tommy and Robb said good-night, Jenna hurried back to Bram. As she'd figured would be the case, his eyes were closed. Along with normal weariness, whatever opiates the ER staff had administered to him would probably keep him knocked out for hours.

She sat on the edge of the bed and leaned forward to just look at him. He'd been shot but he was alive. That was all that mattered. She studied his face and fell even more deeply in love, and then she dropped her gaze to the purpling bruise on his chest and knew what had jettisoned her out of a sound sleep. It had been a nightmare, all right, but not in the normal sense. She'd felt the impact of whatever had made that bruise, as surely as though the projectile had struck her. Some very strange forces were at work tonight; rather, strange forces had been all around her since the day she walked into this house.

Jenna sat with Bram for another hour, then, finally feeling heavy-eyed, she returned to her own bed and instantly fell asleep.

She awoke again at seven and hurriedly got up to check on Gloria. To Jenna's everlasting surprise, the elderly woman reached for Jenna's hand. She had never shown any sign of affection for her nurse before and the gesture touched Jenna deeply.

"You're feeling better, aren't you?" Jenna asked gently, with a warm smile. "I'm so glad. I'll get dressed and give you your morning bath. I won't be long." She rushed through her own ablutions, and when she was dressed and ready for the day, she slipped away and went to Bram's room. He was still sleeping. She checked the bandage on his arm for blood and saw that it was only slightly tinged. He was fine. She left to tend to Gloria's needs.

Every time Gloria napped that day Jenna sat in Bram's room and watched him sleep. She felt not a dram of confusion anymore and knew exactly what she was going to do when he awoke and could talk. Her girlish reluctance to speak her mind with Bram had vanished completely. That, too, gladdened her, and she decided it was a very good day all around.

It was late afternoon—dinnertime, actually—when Bram finally woke up. He opened his eyes, realized he was in his own bedroom in his own home and breathed a silent prayer of thanks. His left arm was sore, as was that one section of his chest, but otherwise he felt good. Except for a few things like hunger, thirst and a need to use the bathroom, that is.

He pushed back the covers and swung his feet to the floor. He felt dizzy, but only for a second or two. Using the nightstand for support, he got to his feet, and after waiting another few seconds for his head to stop swimming, he walked from the bedroom and into the bathroom.

Jenna was trying to coax Gloria to eat more than two bites of dinner. Whatever good mood Gloria had awakened in that morning had gradually dissipated throughout the day, which Jenna didn't understand. This morning Gloria's happiness level had spiked and then fallen. Why? What had caused the spike in the first place, and why hadn't it lasted?

Jenna jerked her head up as sounds from the other side of the house reached her ears. Bram must be up. She should go to him. But Gloria was suddenly trying to speak, something she had never really done with Jenna before. Even if Bram did need her, Jenna felt a more serious responsibility right where she was. She *had* to listen to Gloria's garbled words and try to comprehend their meaning.

And then, almost as clearly as she spoke herself, Jenna heard, "Don't fret, child. I've had a good life."

Jenna's mouth dropped open. In the next breath she cried, "No, it's not you! Your father—George White-Bear—was talking about Bram, and he's fine!"

Gloria merely turned her head and closed her eyes. Breathing hard and fearfully, Jenna took her patient's wrist and felt for a pulse. She found it to be strong and steady, and Jenna released her enormous load of tension along with a huge expulsion of air.

She gathered her wits, set Gloria's tray on the dresser, then ran through the house to Bram's room. It was empty.

Of course, she thought. He's in the bathroom. She went to the door and knocked. "Are you all right?"

"Yes, and I'm starved. Think you could get me a bowl of soup or something? And some water?"

Jenna heaved a sigh of relief. He sounded great. "I'll bring you a tray. Please go back to bed when you're through in there."

"I will."

Jenna hurried to the kitchen, heated soup, made a sandwich, decided he shouldn't have coffee, and filled a glass with orange juice instead. She added a bottle of chilled water to the tray and carried it to the bedroom. Bram was in bed, but he was sitting up, supported by pillows.

"Thanks," he said quietly when she placed the bed tray across his lap. The first thing he reached for was the bottle of water, and he took a big drink.

Jenna went to the room's one chair and sat on it. She watched him and he finally looked back. "I can feed myself," he said. "You don't have to hover over me."

"I'll hover if I want to hover."

"Feeling sassy this morning?"

"This morning? It happens to be almost six in the afternoon. You slept all day. You might as well go ahead and eat. I'm not leaving.''

Bram frowned. There was something in her voice he'd not heard before. It wasn't anger or resentment, but it reminded him of the way she sounded during arguments.

''I'm in no mood for another fight,'' he said gruffly, and picked up his soupspoon.

''Neither am I.''

''Then how come you're staring at me like that?''

''Are you telling me that you can't tell the difference between an angry expression and one that's all fuzzy and lovesick?''

Bram's jaw dropped. ''Jenna...'' *She's in love with me...I'm in love with her. Tell her! Tell her what's in those old books.*

Jenna kept her gaze locked with his. Something wonderful was in the air. She felt it and believed he did, too. *Tell him what you discovered about Elliot family history. Tell him about your Comanche blood.* Her heart began pounding. Should she tell him? If he knew the truth, would he finally drop that abominable guard he had always clung to around her, as though his very life depended on his being tough and unbreakable?

''I really think you should eat that soup before it cools down. And I made you a really good sandwich. I'm happy to wait until after you eat to tell you how much I love you, and for how long.''

Bram nearly choked. ''And you expect me to eat after that?''

''I expect you to eat every bite.''

''While you watch. Jenna, what you were just talking about is not going to happen.''

''Bram, my love, it *is* going to happen. Now eat so we can get to it. I'll just sit here quietly. I won't say a word, I promise.''

He gave up. She wasn't going to leave him alone and he was still famished, regardless of the shock she'd delivered so nonchalantly. And determinedly. Yes, that was what he'd been hearing in her voice—determination.

"So," she said. "How's that arm feeling?"

"I thought you weren't going to say a word."

"That was a professional question. I'm your nurse, you know."

"Fine! My arm is fine, too!"

"No pain?"

"It's a little sore, but that's all."

"And the bruise on your chest?"

"It's fine, too."

She was silent for a moment, then asked softly, "How did you get it, Bram? You were shot, but that's not a bullet wound."

He finished the last of his soup and looked at her. "Yes, it is." He spoke in a tone of voice that raised goose bumps on Jenna's arms. "I had something in my shirt pocket that stopped the bullet."

"What was it?"

Bram looked around the bed. "I had it…I'm sure I had it when the guys brought me home. It has to be here somewhere."

"Let me take away the tray. Maybe it's under it." Jenna went over to the bed and moved the tray to a dresser. "Do you see it now?"

"No. Jenna, I have to find it. It's somewhere in the bed, it has to be."

The odd note of panic in his voice startled Jenna. Bram Colton didn't panic. Other people panicked, but not him.

"You get up and I'll go through the bedding," she said.

"Yes…thanks." He got up on his own and stood by while she shook out the bedding, every single piece of it.

"It's not there," he said in disbelief. "I have to call Tommy and Robb. Maybe they have it."

"But you said you were sure you had it when they brought you home last night."

"I was pretty woozy. Maybe I only thought I had it."

"I'll bring you the cordless phone."

Jenna rushed away while Bram crawled back into bed. When she returned with the phone he said, "Never mind. I don't have to call anyone. It's gone."

"Are you saying it simply disappeared?"

"Probably in the same incredible way it appeared."

"But…but that's not possible."

He looked at her. "Isn't it?" He broke eye contact and sighed, then started talking. Jenna perched on the edge of his bed and took in every word. "John Doe was really a big-time drug dealer named Feeny who supplied the local dealers. I felt sorry for him because no one claimed his body, and I believed he committed suicide and called him a poor little guy, because he wasn't very big. I paid for a decent funeral for him because I was stupid and believed that jerk Tobler, who all the while was one of Feeny's killers, laughing at me from his cell in my own jail.

"Anyhow, the night Feeny was murdered I found the medallion. Other men had searched the same rooms of the old depot and never saw it. *I* found it, and after I determined it wasn't evidence I started carrying it in my shirt pocket. You see, it had the head of a coyote on it, and I thought it odd that I was the one who spotted it."

"It *was* odd, Bram." She took his right hand and held it. "But it didn't disappear in the night. You'll never convince me of that, even if I have started believing in messages from coyotes and golden foxes and…" She stopped, then continued in a rush. "If you would have returned my calls yesterday you might not have been shot! Your great-grandfather—"

"Willow told me all about it last night at the hospital." Bram narrowed his eyes on Jenna. "So you've become a believer of Comanche omens and portents." *That's because you're part Comanche yourself, love of my life.*

But he knew now that he was never going to tell her what he'd unearthed in those old books. Carl Elliot would wriggle away from the truth if someone hit him over the head with it, so really, nothing at all had changed.

"Bram, I heard a coyote myself. Nellie was with me and heard nothing. It was the night you called and asked me to feed her. Anyhow, it sounded close enough to touch, and I...I don't think it was...uh, real."

"Oh, Jenna." Sighing, Bram put his hand on the back of her neck and drew her toward him. "It was real, Jenna. You're not hearing things that aren't real. You're just spooked by being around the Coltons for so long."

She looked directly into his eyes. "I said I'm in love with you and I am, Bram. Can't you say the same to me?"

He put his chin on the top of her head and shut his eyes. "I wish I could," he said softly. "I can say I want you, but please don't make me talk about love. Is wanting you enough?"

Tears welled, but she blinked them back. "Maybe it's enough for tonight. May I sleep with you?"

"I'm a fool, sweetheart, but not stupid enough to say no to that question."

"You're neither stupid nor a fool." Jenna eluded his chin, leaned closer and pressed her lips to his. "I'll check on Gloria and get into a nightgown. Be back in a minute."

Gloria was sleeping, and Jenna quickly shed her clothes and donned a lightweight robe rather than the nightgown she'd mentioned to Bram. All the while her heart pounded with anticipation. Bram might not have yet reached the point of being able to talk about loving her, but she was sure he would, and she was deliriously happy that she had found the gumption to confess her feelings.

She returned to his room, his bed and his arms. Rather, to his one arm. She was careful not to bump his bandaged left arm, and tried to avoid that purple bruise on his chest, as well.

But once they were both naked and kissing wildly, nothing else seemed to matter, and it wasn't long before their lovemaking reached a fevered pitch that blocked out the rest of the world.

"Jenna...Jenna," Bram kept saying in that hoarse way he had of speaking during lovemaking.

"At least you know my name, darling," she replied seductively.

"I know who I'm making love to, don't ever doubt it," he growled.

"I couldn't possibly," she whispered, and raised her legs to encircle his hips, drawing him deeper inside her. "Not when we're locked together like this."

"It's heaven, pure heaven." He began moving faster, taking her with him on that final joyous ride.

They cried out together and held each other while their breathing slowed to normal. And then, suddenly, frighteningly, they heard it, a sound in the night that each had heard before—the cry of a coyote.

Bram froze and mumbled, "My God." In the next second he rolled from the bed. Pulling a blanket around himself, he got to his feet and left the room as fast as he could go. No longer was he pain-free, and he'd obviously been a little too careless during lovemaking. His arm hurt like hell and so did his chest.

But he wasn't thinking of himself, and the second he saw Gran he knew that she had passed away. Dropping to his knees near to the bed, he hid his face in the blankets next to her and wept.

Jenna rushed in. She had grabbed her robe and pulled it on while following Bram. Tears began flowing down her cheeks, and she went to Bram and laid her hand on his shoulder.

He shocked the breath out of her by pulling away from her touch and saying bitterly, "I never even saw her today, and I could have. Instead of spending time with her this evening I welcomed you into my bed."

Wounded heart and soul, Jenna backed away from him. He never noticed, nor did he notice her leaving a short time later, fully dressed and carrying a suitcase.

She cried all the way to Black Arrow. She had never had a chance of winning him over. Why had she been so positive about that all day?

"Fool...*fool!*" she said, and sobbed even harder.

Jenna didn't call anyone at the hospital or anywhere else, nor did she take any calls. She stayed in her room in her father's house and barely talked to him when he attempted conversation through the locked door. She had never been this unhappy before, and she knew she was dangerously close to an emotional breakdown. But she didn't have the will or the desire to pull herself out of the bottomless pit of despair in which she floundered.

But then Martha rapped softly and said, "Jenna, darlin', Mrs. Colton's funeral is going to be held tomorrow at two. I just thought you might want to know."

Jenna turned over on the bed and stared at the ceiling. "To hell with what anyone thinks," she said out loud. She was going to that funeral, and if Bram dared to even glance at her crossways she would send him a look he would never forget. He'd get the message, the wretch; he'd get it loud and clear.

And the next day she put on her nicest black dress, dark hosiery and black high-heeled pumps. She started to put her hair up, then decided to wear it down. After all, wasn't she the golden fox? she asked herself cynically. A golden fox should flaunt her mane, shouldn't she?

She drove to the cemetery, parked behind a long line of cars and approached the crowd around the flower-bedecked grave site on foot. She met no one's eyes, not even Willow's, and she stood away from the family. The service was almost over before she saw her father. He was standing inconspicuously behind a huddle of mourners, and when Jenna spotted him she could hardly believe her eyes. What on earth was he doing here? He hated the Coltons, although he'd probably thought them to be no worse than the area's other Comanche families before she'd moved into Bram's house to care for Gloria.

But now that she no longer lived there, perhaps her father had forgiven the Coltons for breathing and her for trying to keep one of them alive. It was a bitter thought, and Jenna felt ashamed of herself for thinking something so awful. She dabbed at the corners of her eyes with a dainty white handkerchief just as the minister completed his final prayer.

People began going over to the Coltons to offer condolences, and Jenna turned to leave. She would contact Willow some other day, and perhaps Thomas and Alice and Jared and...

She loved them all, and she wasn't going to slink away like some thief when her only crime had been to fall in love with Bram! She didn't have to talk to him, didn't even have to look at him, but the rest of the Coltons deserved her sympathy. She turned around and had started walking toward them when she saw her father suddenly push ahead of some people and stop in front of Bram.

"What'd you do my daughter?" he snarled. "She won't eat, she won't talk, she's barely alive and I know you did something to her. Be a man, if you can, and tell me what it was.''

Jenna nearly fainted. Every eye was on her dad, every ear tuned to hear his unjust accusations.

Bram hadn't seen Jenna arrive nor did he look for her now. He had gone through hell during the last few days. Considering the mess he'd made of the John Doe case and his sorrow over that, over Gran's death and over Jenna, plus a dozen or so other problems, such as what had happened to the coyote medallion, and how come both he and Jenna had heard the coyote's cry the night Gran died, he was in no mood to put up with Carl Elliot's insults.

''Get out of my face,'' Bram said menacingly.

''Or you'll what? Have me arrested?'' Carl taunted. ''Like you arrested that Feeny fellow for bringing drugs into Black Arrow by the truckload? Be a man,'' he repeated snidely, ''and tell me what you did to make my little girl cry all the time.''

Bram had heard enough. Something snapped in him. He didn't care if Carl Elliot was white, Comanche or Chinese, and he didn't care if the whole damn town heard what he had to say.

''Nothing would make me happier,'' Bram said with an icy glare at Jenna's dad. ''I fell in love with your little girl, only she isn't a little girl, is she? She's a woman through and through. I will love her till the day I die, and I would marry her tomorrow, if she'd have me.''

A tornado could not have moved faster or with more force than Jenna did. She got through that crowd like a hot knife cuts through butter, and she nearly knocked her dad down when she threw herself at Bram.

''She'll have you! She'll have you!'' she cried.

Bram held her close to his heart and whispered, ''I love you, Jenna.''

''I love you, Bram. You *know* I love you.''

He tipped her chin, gazed deeply into her eyes and said it again, clearly and loud enough for everyone to hear. "I love you, Jenna. I've loved you for years."

The Coltons, weeping and sad only moments ago, were suddenly laughing in spite of their wet and teary faces.

Bram saw Carl Elliot turn and walk away with his head down. That man is no Comanche, Bram thought, but he *is* Jenna's dad.

"Go after him, sweetheart. No matter what he did in the past or does in the future, he's still your dad."

Jenna took a look behind her and saw the forlorn slant of her father's shoulders. Giving her beloved a soft smile of utter adoration, she left his embrace and ran after her father.

"Dad! Wait a minute!"

Carl stopped walking and waited for her. "You're going to marry an Indian," he said sadly.

"And I couldn't be more proud of it. Dad, please listen to me. You'll always be welcome in my life and my home, but it's going to be Bram's home, as well, and you're always going to have to remember that." She saw tears in his eyes. "Why are you crying, Daddy?"

"Because I love you." He turned and walked away, and Jenna watched for a moment, then turned and looked at Bram. His family was taking turns hugging and congratulating him, and Jenna had never seen a more moving sight. She walked toward the Coltons, her own family soon, and heard Bram saying, "I've loved her for so long and foolishly almost lost her. It won't happen again."

She smiled and Bram smiled back at her—a beautiful smile, such as she had never seen before—and just then George WhiteBear approached his great-grandson. "You won the golden fox. She will give you many sons."

Jenna started laughing and tried to conceal it with her hand. After all, this was still a funeral, hardly an event for uncontrollable mirth. But "many sons"? And then her laughter stopped as quickly as it began, for with all the proof of his psychic powers that she'd encountered first-hand, how could she possibly laugh at anything George WhiteBear said?

She was mulling over the high probability of becoming a mother to "many sons" when George looked around at his family and said quite clearly, "Willows are meant to blossom and will bloom during the brightest midnight."

Jenna's eyes darted around, searching the crowd and finally finding Willow. From the look on Willow's pretty face, the poor girl must have realized George's message had been aimed at her, but didn't know if it was good or bad news.

Bram came over to Jenna and put his good arm around her. "I think it's Willow's turn," he said in her ear with a small chuckle. Jenna turned up her face and Bram kissed her. "Let's go home, sweetheart," he said softly. "We have an awful lot of talking to do."

"Among other things," Jenna murmured, bringing a twinkle to her lover's romantic dark eyes.

They walked away, arm in arm.

* * * * *

*Be sure to come back next month
for Willow Colton's story in:*

WILLOW IN BLOOM

*by Victoria Pade
(SE1490, 09/02)*

MONTANA MAVERICKS

One of Silhouette Special Edition's most popular
series returns with three sensational stories filled
with love, small-town gossip, reunited lovers, a little
murder, hot nights and the best in romance:

HER MONTANA MAN
by Laurie Paige
(ISBN#: 0-373-24483-5)
Available August 2002

BIG SKY COWBOY
by Jennifer Mikels
(ISBN#: 0-373-24491-6)
Available September 2002

MONTANA LAWMAN
by Allison Leigh
(ISBN#: 0-373-24497-5)
Available October 2002

*True love is the only way to beat the heat
in Rumor, Montana....*

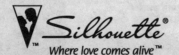

Silhouette®

Where love comes alive™